Dor Slinkard is an unstoppable storyteller. Be it through writing or voice, her stories will enthral. Inspired by life, especially as a jillaroo in outback Australia and later as a race horse trainer, her imagination thrives. In her lasting marriage to Wade, a jackaroo now horse trainer, they have produced two children and they, in turn, five grandchildren.

For the Love of Freedom is the second book in the trilogy.

Acknowledgements

To my husband, and all other proof readers, including a special mention to Sandy Gray and Julie Sparks, who have been supporters and constructive critics from the beginning, I thank you.

To my ever-patient mentor, critic and major editor Denise Doraisamy and my editor Margaret Mooney a further thanks.

And to Danny Mayson-Kinder for her brilliant photography, in both *For the Love of Patrick*, and now *For the Love of Freedom* I thank you.

To the beautiful, 'cover girl' Sascha Daisley, my thanks.

And to all the brave resistance fighters, particularly in the Second World War, I thank you with all my heart.

***For the Love of* Trilogy**

Book 1 – For the Love of Patrick
Book 2 – For the Love of Freedom
Book 3 – For the Love of Justice

Dor Slinkard

FOR THE LOVE OF FREEDOM

ISBN 9780648539100 (Paperback)
ISBN 9780648539124 (E-Book)

First Published (2019)

Chapter 1

South Australia: 1936

The Grand Adelaide Town Hall was the venue for young Millie Darcy's inaugural opera performance. The lush velvet curtain had risen for the fifth time when once again she embraced the overwhelming applause; her ample breasts heaving with excitement. I laughed, as I'd warned Millie that her neck line was cut far too low and she stood the chance of exposing her boobs to the audience – she almost did. From that performance on she catapulted to national stardom. The Australian public adored their new opera prima donna, as did nearly every young man she had the pleasure of meeting. Yes, Millie loved to be loved. Grandad Jonathon, I'm sure was a little more than pleased when his daughter left Adelaide to attend the conservatorium of music in London. Millie had just won herself a scholarship to further her singing career in Europe.

And so, it was after that magical night, that grandad Jonathon travelled to London to inspect and purchase an apartment where we three Darcy girls would eventually live together. Not long after he returned home, Marjorie, his wife, travelled to London with Millie. She stayed for three months until she was satisfied a suitable chaperone had been hired to care for Millie. Six months later, Millie's sister, Colleen, came across to London then twelve months after that came me, Sally Darcy, their niece (our age, not far apart). That was the beginning of the Darcy girls' reputation in London.

It was some four weeks after my arrival in London, that I found myself congratulating Millie on her successful singing career and Colleen on her promotion to trainee matron. Not too long after this, I found myself in the middle of an argument between Millie and Colleen. It seemed Millie was in trouble.

"You have to help me, Colleen. I cannot possibly continue my opera career with a child at foot! You *must* help me." And then Millie cried copious tears followed by great racking sobs.

Colleen was angry and disgusted, not with what her sister had done to get pregnant, but the fact she had taken no precautions. Millie continued to beg.

"Please, Colleen. I promise in future I will take care. Please just this once help me. It won't happen again. Please, Colleen."

As usual, Millie had her way and within a few weeks she was back to her old self: charming, talented, sexy and let me not forget, over-confident. She settled down with just one man after that. He was a rather dapper young chap named Chad Renwick. He adored the ground Millie walked on, which suited her. She used him as her slave, her lover and her business manager – unashamedly.

Millie's live-in nanny, cum chaperone, hired by Marjorie, was Miss Amy Applegate. A middle-aged spinster, who sometimes found it difficult keeping up with Millie's busy lifestyle. However, she did manage, as the pay was good and the apartment delightful. Miss Applegate had her own room which overlooked the Royal Parklands. Never had she experienced such luxury and informality. Her prior engagements were with the children of the aristocracy. This meant she'd had more than her fair share of late nights attending to crying babies and sick children. It had almost worn her out. So when this position was advertised, she jumped at the chance. Little did she know this job, in some ways, would be more draining, especially with Millie demanding Miss Applegate's constant attention to monitor her appearance. Added to this, Miss Applegate was delegated to dismissing the many male admirers who'd come knocking on the door for Millie at all hours.

"How do I look Granny Smith (our nickname for Miss Applegate)?" We'd hear Millie ask this often. Granny Smith's answer was always the same.

"Miss Millie, you look beautiful, you are beautiful, and you always will be."

At first Miss Applegate graciously protested at being called Granny Smith. Thankfully her rebuff was soon quashed when Colleen arrived in London and explained to her that Millie was simply likening her to the Granny Smith apples that were famous green apples from Australia. It was a compliment, a play on words with her name Applegate.

"Well, if I'm likened to something famous, then I suppose it's not so demeaning after all," she said with a justified smile.

We all liked Miss Applegate enormously. She became our friend and confidant. Not that she ever found out about Millie's abortion – heavens no!

We had fun playing with Granny Smith's stern appearance, until she changed to resemble a softer more attractive woman. Her light brown hair we gathered around her face and her tightly pulled bun was banned forever. We introduced her to different shades of lipstick and eye shadow. In the middle of our fun I asked:

"Do you really need to wear glasses Miss Applegate?"

"Well no, I suppose not. But I do need them to read."

The next day I purchased a fine gold chain which held her glasses around her neck. She loved it. Millie also took her shopping and bought her a wardrobe of ultra-modern fashions. Her pleasure in modelling her new purchases before us was heart-warming. We promptly took photos and sent them home to Marjorie. Her reply was that she didn't believe it was the same Miss Applegate and hoped we weren't leading her astray. We had to remember Miss Applegate was there to look after us, not the other way around.

I think this worried Marjorie, as two months later, she arrived in England for an inspection tour. Of course, it was not entirely just to see if we were being looked after. There was always somewhere in Europe where Marjorie was able to go and admire Millie's performances. On this particular visit, Millie was performing in Switzerland. It was summer at the time and the days melded slowly into night giving only a few enough hours of darkness. Marjorie returned to London two weeks later, admitting she was 'exhausted after not being able to acclimatize to the long daylight hours', not that it wasn't similar in England, but that was Marjorie's excuse. Millie returned to London two months later, when her performing contract ended.

Sadly, our wonderful interlude, free from Millie, ended then too. Colleen and I had thought it glorious having Marjorie all to ourselves without the over bearing selfish presence of Millie. Although I shouldn't be too hard on Millie, after all she is a beautiful loving person. She will always cry if you are sad, be a friend when you need a friend and she will forever have you looking at your best. I preferred to lounge around in baggy trousers and read a novel in my time off, but not when Millie was home. She'd have me dressed to the nines and off to the Ritz hotel for afternoon tea. I did love going there though. I would imagine my parents sitting together on their first date here and I would insist on the same table they shared by the window, so I could reflect. Millie would disagree most times, arguing there would be no room for admires to come join us, as it was strictly a table for two.

After an afternoon at the Ritz, there was usually a cocktail party to attend, so we'd hurry home to dress for the occasion.

"Sexy, dear, sexy. That's what cocktail parties are all about." Millie would say and so I would follow her orders and dress myself in some low cut, figure-hugging dress, usually black, and toddle off in the highest of high heels.

"I'd rather be in moleskins and riding boots, Millie," I said.

9

"Oh nonsense, Sally. How are we ever going to find you a husband if you don't dress to kill?"

One evening, Millie took a very long moment to study my appearance and then shocked me with what she said.

"You know, Sally, if the truth be told, you're more beautiful than me. Men just adore you; that long blonde hair, olive skin and your blue come-to-bed eyes. Every man I know says you have the most amazing eyes they have ever seen."

I just laughed. It didn't bother me what men said. I had my own agenda and had no intention of finding a husband. A lover, yes. I wasn't backward in enjoying the pleasures of the flesh, but it never took precedence over my work or my other interests.

*

In the few months we were separated from Millie, Marjorie, Colleen and I hired a car and drove around Ireland staying in bed and breakfasts. One fine day while driving through County Clare on our way to Bunratty Castle, I felt a shudder through my arm and then a bump-bump, coming from the front wheel on the car.

"Oh no," I said, "What a bloody rotten place to get a flat tyre. Right in the middle of Bunratty bridge!"

I wasn't too worried, as I had some idea how to change it. Luckily, Millie wasn't around, so I'd chosen to wear my baggy pants, a light blue men's shirt and my hair was pulled up under a tweed cap. I was having trouble with the wrench as it kept slipping off the wheel nut and I cursed aloud (I was a terrible curser).

"It would have helped if they gave us the right fuckin' sized wrench!" I said to Colleen.

I heard someone laugh and then a deep Irish voice said:

"Here, give it to me laddie. I'll have a go."

I'd been so intent on removing the wheel that I hadn't heard the shepherd, who with the help of his border collie, had moved his sheep up quietly behind us. I turned around and fell in love. Not really, but he was tall dark and handsome. He had a beautiful smile and that unmistakable Irish humour, shining from his sapphire-blue eyes.

"Oh, I'm sorry, Miss. I taught yer was a boy."

My mouth dropped open I'm sure. I handed him the wrench and he smiled with a mixture of surprise and, was it attraction, or was it because I was a woman dressed as a man? Within a few minutes he'd changed the tyre. I said thank you after freeing my hair from under the cap while he was working. I took his hand in mine and an electric current ran up my arm, he felt it too. We both slightly flinched, then laughed.

I drove the rest of the way in silence, until we reached a quaint little inn named Durty Nelly's. After my meeting with the tall handsome stranger, I felt something in me had shifted – morphed even. I'd lost all sense of where I was and who I was with. Only his face and his voice lingered in my mind. Marjorie kept snapping her fingers to wake me from my revere.

We entered Durty Nelly's Tavern and enjoyed a delicious meal of bangers and mash, then washed it down with two lagers. Before we left the tavern, the licensee gave us a map of all the best bed and breakfasts around town. He highly recommended a delightful cottage tucked away, about two miles out. After we agreed to take his advice, he dutifully rang the owner who said she would prepare for our arrival. He looked our way to confirm the time we'd be there.

"Six o'clock," I said. He then quoted the time into the receiver.

We spent the rest of the day admiring one of the most enchanted and historic villages in Ireland. Ghosts from the past seemed to brush past every so often and I'd quiver with the sensation. With our long drive to Bunratty and then walking over so many cobble stones in the village streets, weariness soon overcame us, and we were forced to find our bed and breakfast.

The narrow driveway leading to our refuge was almost overgrown with many varieties of fine leafed trees. A row of yellow daffodils shaded under their canopies seemed to wave a bright welcome. It gave me a feeling of being in an enchanted forest. Once in full view, the white-washed cottage with its grey thatched roof charmed us to the point where we stood still, just to admire the prettiness. Pots filled with purple pansies sat under every French window and a neat hedge of lavender bordered the path leading to the front door. Finally, we gathered our bags and took in the intoxicating perfume of the lavender while knocking on the door.

Our hostess welcomed us with a broad smile, especially when hearing our Aussie accents. She introduced herself and then hurried us into our rooms.

"Wash up now ladies, and I'll, get back inta' the kitchen. I'll be dishin' up some a me lamb chops and vegies for y' suppa and oh yes, some o' me homemade bread, served with butter that I've churned from me milking cow's efforts taday." She gave a giggle and left.

Over our delicious dinner, we found a lot to talk about with Miss O'Mara. Later, when in her sitting room, she wanted to know everything there was to know about Australia. We were amused with the fact that none of us had the opportunity to ask her anything about her hometown or life. After relaxing in our feather cushioned arm chairs for some time, we had reason to yawn. I bade her goodnight and proffered our thanks for her superb hospitality.

I think from memory, the feather mattress I slept on that night, floated me into one of the soundest sleeps I'd had in many years.

After I rose, I opened the window and there it was; a magic morning. The silken mist floated over the green hills and glens, while the sun sent warm rays onto my face. I breathed in the freshness and pulled my favourite cream woollen jumper over my head. Once outside, I leant against the stone wall of the cottage, gazing wistfully at the scenery. I felt peaceful and happy with the thought that perhaps I'd found another home and maybe I'd found the man I would marry. I shrugged it off with a smile. I'd probably never see my, 'tyre changer' again, although fate is something my parents strongly believed in and so did I. After placing this new experience in the hands of fate, I went back inside to eat a hearty breakfast.

While sipping on my tea, I thought just how much our hostess reminded me of Colleen Thompson; she was Colleen's God mother and her name sake. Colleen Snr was a major part of our lives while growing up and was one of my grandmother Sally's saviours when she was a troubled young woman, a true angel was our Colleen.

Miss O'Mara was plump, slightly older than middle aged and her red, curly hair was mostly tied up in a bun. She had a fabulous disposition, nothing was too much trouble and she laughed at nearly everything. Yes, she could well have been related to Colleen Thompson. I began, by asking her to tell us about her family. I then explained that I needed to know because she was so like our Colleen Thompson. When I said this, she tilted her head to one side, creased her brow in thought and then asked:

"Well now, let me see, would her name have been Colleen Murphy, before Thompson?" I sat up surprised.

"You know of her then?" Her round ruddy face creased up in smiles.

"I'd be tinkin' so. I remember me Da tellin' me about a cousin of his goin' to Australia just after she got married. Her maiden name was Colleen O'Mara. She and her first husband, Freddy Murphy, did real well in those gold mines over dere, den 'e died."

Marjorie and Colleen were enthralled by this revelation and fired question after question at Miss O'Mara until she refused any more.

"Now ladies, I have to be doin' some work and y's have to be goin' to the Castle. We can talk all about dis amazin' coincidence dis evenin' when you return. Now y' best be on yer way."

Marjorie kissed her on the cheek.

"Thank you, Miss O'Mara. It's a shame we lost our Colleen a few years back. This is a wonderful surprise though. Who would have thought we'd be staying with one of our dear Colleens cousins? We'll see you later and talk some more."

Before we left, Marjorie sighed deeply and repeated her favourite saying:

"It's a small world. Yes indeed, a very small world."

*

As we walked into the village admiring the rugged beauty of Ireland, the scenery took my thoughts back home to Australia. I found myself longing for the open paddocks, carpeted with sun dried rye grass and the Adelaide hills; a back- drop so often softened by a pastel blue horizon. I imagined the odd Kangaroo stopping inquisitively and cattle amongst emus dotting the landscape; that's when my heart ached to return home. I thought the green land of Ireland, with its dry-stone walls, gave the same sense of struggle against the elements as Australia did. No wonder the Irish settlers who came to Australia never gave up during the long droughts and floods. They were tough and resilient. In contrast, I found England blessed with just the right mixture of nature's gifts, to sustain a plentiful supply of food amidst easy surrounds. I felt England leant towards an almost gentrified type of living, never having to struggle with droughts and bush fires, hurricanes and the likes. Probably just nostalgic thinking and oversimplification from a homesick traveller, but it was how it appeared to me.

The two-mile walk from the boarding house to the castle was leisurely. We found peace in each other's company and the reminiscing of our childhood caused me to become melancholy. It was moments like these that I wanted to book my passage home. But only six months of study remained before I passed my journalist's degree, hopefully with honours. I'd stick it out till then and after that be on the first ship home.

Bunratty Castle, built of grey stone, stood four stories high with towers on each corner. Probably not as impressive as some I'd seen in England, certainly not as large, although it did have a welcoming feel to it. However, it was in a sad state of disrepair. I stood studying the architecture, thinking how sad it was that somebody could not come along with the interest and money to bring it back to its original grandeur. I was miles away, when from behind me came the same Irish voice that caught me unawares the day before.

13

"We meet again."

I turned and felt my heart jump in my chest. Once again, I realised my mouth had dropped open. Not a good look, so I closed it, then opened it and fought to speak.

"Yes, we meet again. We're walking today so there are no tyres to fix. We're waiting for the guide to show us the inside of the Castle." The twinkle in his eye highlighted his next words.

"That would be me."

Michael then turned to say good morning to Marjorie and Colleen. Next, he proceeded to show us the way. I found it hard to concentrate, especially when he stood close and pointed upwards at some piece of timber which needed repair. Or he'd gently touch me, so that I turned around to look in the right direction.

After an hour of having the heritage of the castle and the families who had previously lived in it explained to us in detail, and after climbing every stairway and opening doors to inspect rooms, we finally came back and settled in the kitchen. Here we were served tea and scones by a lovely young girl. Michael introduced her as his younger sister, Katherine. She appeared very shy and smiled meekly when placing the Devonshire tea down on the wooden table. When she left, Michael excused her shyness.

"She's been a bit strange ever since our parents died. Katherine thinks they're still alive and still living in the castle, along with all our dead relatives. It's a shame because she won't talk to anyone in the village any more. She says it's because they don't believe her when she tells 'em that Ma and Da are still here, living in the Castle. She just goes to school and runs straight home. I hear her talking to our Ma and Da, laughing and telling them all about the gossip she's heard in the village. I don't know what I'm gonna do with her, although mind you, she does like visitors coming here like yerselves."

I looked for a hint that he may have also liked me coming – there was none. We thanked Michael for his time and paid Katherine the money for the tour and the Devonshire tea.

This was one man I'd have to forget. Apparently, the attraction was one sided, although Colleen surprised me with her comment as we walked into the village.

"I think Michael likes you, Sally."

I was shocked. I couldn't see it. He'd paid no attention to me other than guide me physically when I was not being attentive.

"Oh, don't be silly, Colleen," I said with a hint of disdain. That made it sound like I didn't want him to fancy me, when in fact I did.

She retaliated straight away.

"He's shy, Sally. He'll contact you before we leave tomorrow. You mark my words."

She then looked away into the distance and I heard her say to Marjorie quietly.

"I'm a little jealous really."

I chose not to comment, pretended not to hear.

We decided to have a light lunch in Durty Nelly's again, as the food yesterday was delicious. When I opened the Tavern door to leave, there was Michael, he smiled directly at me.

"I thought I might find you here Sally." That was the first time he'd spoken my name, it sounded almost poetic. "I figured it being such a lovely day, you might like ta be moving the sheep with me."

He obviously realised he'd only asked me, so he quickly turned to Colleen and Marjorie and asked would they like to join us? Marjorie was the first to reply.

"No, no thank you, Michael. I've done enough walking today. The walk back to Rose Cottage will be far enough for me. But thank you anyway."

"I will also decline thank you, Michael. I want to finish Earnest Hemingway's latest novel," Colleen added, (I thought somewhat reluctantly).

"Yes, I would love to come," I said. My heart fluttered with the look he gave me.

I supposed it had been all business in the castle and maybe in front of his delicate sister he didn't want to show his feelings. We walked and talked only of my life and where I came from and why I was there. The only thing he'd told me about himself was that he lived in Bunratty house which sat in the grounds of the castle. He was an ancestor of the last family who owned the castle and so became the caretaker after his parents died. I felt as if there was something else he wanted to tell me, but he chose only to listen and ask me more questions.

We'd reached the paddock from where we were to move the sheep. We had to walk them another mile down the road from that point. His border collie dog Peggy obeyed his different whistles and hand commands. I was enthralled as I watched, although I knew I was capable of working kelpies similar to this. However, watching this Collie work with such precision was something else. It was truly amazing how this intelligent bitch moved those sheep so calmly and without a moment's concern or hesitation. I told him I'd like to buy a dog like Peggy and take her home to Australia. Michael smiled at this.

"I'll give you one of her pups to take home."

I had to stand still for a moment. I'd hoped he'd say, please don't go Sally, please stay here with me, but he didn't. Instead he said, after noticing my surprise:

"Why so surprised that I'd give you a pup to take home? Not waiting for my answer, he ordered, "Come on, we'd best keep up with Peggy."

I walked briskly behind him.

"Well yes, I am surprised, Michael. You don't even know me." Then he knocked me right off my perch.

"Yes, I do. Well I've seen you before. I was studying medicine at Cambridge University when my parents were killed in a car accident. On the day I was leaving Cambridge, I went to the main office to sign out and you walked in. You didn't see me, but I saw you. 'The face of an angel' I said to myself."

With his head lowered and the matter of fact way in which he'd said this, it seemed there was no hope for any romance between us. I stood still, only because I was dumbfounded by his statement. Then he turned back to me and ordered.

"Come on, Sally, we need to be opening the gate. Peggy can't be doing it on her own you know."

Suddenly, I felt like he was mad at me, like he blamed me for his predicament of having to leave University. I wanted to kiss him, sooth his anguish – not fight. I ran to catch up. When almost out of breath I impulsively said:

"Michael, can't we see each other, I mean ... can we meet occasionally?"

He smiled. "I know you think you might like to, Sally, but I think it may be just a momentary attraction." He shrugged his shoulders. "It'd be no good anyway. I'm tied to this place and I can't be leaving my sister, she needs me. It's my cross to bear. You best to be finding someone else who can give you a normal life or go follow your dream of becoming a journalist."

I grabbed his arm after he'd opened the gate.

"I believe in fate, Michael. If we weren't meant to be together or at least give it a go, then why am I here now? I had no intention before yesterday of meeting you. And can you honestly say you had forgotten all about me until we met again on the bridge?" His brow furrowed, and I watched his eyes search the distance.

"I'll never forget your beautiful face, Sally. But that's the way it is. Nothing can come of this."

I surprised myself with my knee jerk reaction. Maybe I felt he needed to be shaken out of his thought rut.

"Now you listen to me, Mate. This is beginning to sound like a melodrama! We can find help for your sister. Katherine really should be counselled by a professional, you should know that. You don't need to be her keeper for the rest of your life, for God's sake wake up. You may never find true happiness if you don't take charge of your situation. Stop feeling sorry for yourself. Get back to university and finish what you started. We may be able to find somebody in the village who will help take care of Katherine. I'm talking to you as a friend Michael. I will help you, please don't waste your life." He seemed to hear me, then he turned and said:

"I'll think about it, Mate." With the word mate accentuated in the Australian drawl, I saw a glimmer of hope and the humour I suspected he still had. But that was all he said.

No one will ever believe this story I told myself, after we'd kissed and said goodbye. I told Colleen but not Marjorie. I chose not to, not until things had been sorted out with his young sister. Colleen was a great confidant, especially when we had to join ranks against Millie. I must say though; Colleen didn't seem entirely happy about the prospect of Michael coming to London to live. For what reason, I wasn't sure, and she never really told me. Maybe she was jealous and fancied him for herself?

*

On our way back to London I reasoned with myself silently. I'm still young, if Michael chooses his sister above me, there will be plenty more fish in the ocean, although my heart was unconvinced. However, I did intend to keep my promise by trying to find help for Katherine, so I prayed Michael would take the path back to London for his own sake.

After working out exactly where Miss O'Mara fitted in with our beloved Colleen Thompson, I was able to ask for her help in finding someone suitable to move in with Katherine. Hopefully, they would help her come back to reality, or else allow her to stay blissfully in her own dream world. Whatever happened, it didn't matter as long as someone other than Michael became Katherine's main carer.

We left Rose Cottage, happy that Marjorie had found herself a new pen pal. She'd promised Miss O'Mara she would send a ticket for her to sail to Australia, insisting she stay with herself and Jonathon.

We finished our farewells to Miss O'Mara on a very happy note. It was not too long, only one week in fact, before Miss O'Mara found a saviour to care for Katherine.

Unfortunately, all attempts by the Psychiatrist, who'd been hired by

Michael, had been unsuccessful in helping Katherine return to reality. Although, after three months, Katherine still seemed more than happy living with Miss O' Mara's relatives, especially when they moved into Katherine's cottage and played the game of find the ghost. As long as they believed her stories and played her games, she remained content.

I took satisfaction in the thought that my plan had been successful, even more than I could have imagined. Katherine had actually told Michael, now that she had friends living with her, he should return to his studies at Cambridge University. Apparently, Michael only had six months left before he graduated as a Doctor. He happily followed Katherine's advice and returned to London where he lived on Campus, so we were able to see each other quite regularly.

Chapter 2

War Brewing

After Millie returned to our London flat, triumphant with her stint in Switzerland, I introduced her to Michael at a dinner party, which Colleen and I hosted in her honour. It seemed Michael was the only man she could not charm. He saw straight through her and
besides, I *think* he loved me.

One week later, Millie took up the offer to go to France and sing in the opera, Les Troyens. We felt relieved. Not only had Millie left us for a while but Chad Renwick it appeared, still had her under his control. We found out later that Millie was able to escape his clutches sometimes and continued to be the fem fatal, especially in France where love reigned supreme.

It wasn't long after this that Millie rang, and I had to sit and listen to her about just who'd showered her in diamonds and pearls and who'd threatened to kill themselves if she didn't kiss them. Shortly after this conversation, Colleen came home exhausted from work. Still smiling at the memory, I told her what Millie had just said to me over the phone, about men dying if she didn't kiss them, Colleen responded with a dead-pan look.

"Oh why don't they just fuck her? That might be worth dying for. Goodnight Sally I'm buggered."

Sadly, we said good bye two weeks after that special dinner party to our darling Marjorie. She was reluctant to leave after seeing how her eldest daughter Millie behaved. Flaunting her charm and sexuality around like it was a bowl of sweets for everyone to enjoy. I held Marjorie tight assuring her not to worry. Millie was her own person and her fame would save her from whatever drama she found herself in. She could do nothing wrong in the eyes of the press. They were more inclined to cover up her dalliances than write about them. I knew this for a fact, as I was rising in the ranks of journalism. My notoriety in London stemmed from my social column, which was popular and well received by the celebrities whom I wrote about, probably because I chose not to hit below the belt with gossip. Instead, I left the reader wondering about my delicate innuendos. Let them create their own gossip.

Just before Marjorie boarded the ship, I finally had the chance to give her the letters and photographs I'd held for her to pass on to my parents. I watched through tears as my one solid link to home disappeared up the gang plank. I chose not to stay and wave Marjorie goodbye, I really needed to study for my final exam and knew if I stayed any longer, I would cry until my eyes were swollen and I wouldn't be able to read my notes. Colleen was unable to be there to say goodbye, she was at work in the Hospital and Millie, it seemed, was too busy in France to even ring her mother to say farewell.

On my return to our apartment the phone rang and then came the news.

"I've left France Sally, I'm in Zurich. I'm staying here in Switzerland. I've met a Swiss-German man of high ranking. He lives in Zurich, but he comes from German Aristocracy!"

Apparently, he was helping Millie to star in the operas in Germany. He was a close friend of Will Meisel, the famous music / operatic composer . Millie sounded a changed woman when she spoke to me. She seemed totally charmed and consumed by Klaus Stromberg's aristocratic standing, strength and good looks. She had literally fallen at his feet. For once, it was not the other way around. I became amused at the thought. However, Chad Renwick would not let her go entirely.

"I have maintained Chad as my manager, but nothing else," Millie informed me - coldly.

The seemingly sincere love which she held for Klaus Stromberg oozed through the telephone receiver.

"Sally I've never met anyone like him. I'm unable to think of anything but him. He's so strong. He keeps me from being the silly little twit you know I can be at times. It's like he's captured my ego and soothed me into feeling like a real woman, not just a social butterfly, flying around gathering in false claims of love and adoration. This is real love Sally. I truly love him, and I will never leave him."

I believed her, but this man was Swiss-German. Although he'd lived all his life in Zurich, he was nonetheless, German. He must be a Hitler sympathizer.

I was so naïve. Why hadn't I got wise then about how infused with hatred, the air was in Germany. How bloody stupid of me. I should have told Millie this and maybe she would have left. I'd hoped all this talk about war would blow over, so I'd stuck my head in the sand. It was probably the fact that my parents were taken away from me to fight in The First World War, which left deep scars of abandonment. I think this prevented me from seeing the reality of the war brewing between Germany and the rest of Europe. The fact was, I simply didn't want it to happen.

It was a magnificent late summer's day in London, the third of August 1939. We were lucky to have a small court yard at the back of our apartment building. I sat on my cast iron chair with a strong coffee in hand, reading the morning paper. The main news was all about the frustrating talks Prime Minister Chamberlain was having with Hitler. War now seemed inevitable between Germany and Poland. There was talk about an evil master plan to expand Hitler's power over the whole of Europe.

"Oh fuck, I hate bloody war!" I said aloud.

I'd heard via information through my job at The Times, about the breakdown of the peace talks but I'd paid little attention to it. I was too busy with social events assigned to me, which I thought were more important articles. The truth was, Prime Minister Chamberlain was having a continuous verbal battle with Hitler over threats against Poland. It had now become serious and of course, if Britain and France went to war, then Australia would fight alongside them. I needed to talk to Dad. I could phone him from my office, as the newspaper kept a direct line open twenty-four hours with Australia. I took off for work and a phone chat immediately.

While driving to the office reality sank in and with it came the worry that I should perhaps go home. The only reason for staying in London was Michael. He was reluctant to leave England or Ireland, as he was close to his sister whose mental condition had not changed. Michael had now been accepted into the Middlesex Hospital London. Whenever we spoke of the impending war, he guaranteed me he would join the Royal Military Medical Corps and go wherever he was needed if war broke out.

"Ireland's only a skip and a jump from England and if those bloody Nazis' get here, then they'll soon make it to Ireland."

Oh God, how I loved his strength, although sometimes I could strangle him. He was so set in his ways and his ideals and he'd never show affection to me in public. However, when the lights went out it was a different story. I thought he must love me, otherwise he would never have come back to London to finish his studies and to be with me. But he'd never said the words; I love you Sally.

On the occasions I travelled with Michael to Ireland, it made me happy to know Katherine seemed to enjoy my company and to accept the relationship between Michael and myself. However, sometimes I found it hard to understand

Michael: he was aloof one minute and demanding my attention the next.

Whatever project I was in the middle of, he didn't seem to care; he needed me then and there. This was beginning to cause problems in our relationship. He thought I should give up journalism, marry him and have his babies. However, I'm very much my mother's daughter and no man was ever going to dictate to me what I should or should not do. Anyway, I knew I had more to offer the world than to be only a wife and mother, especially now. And after all, Dad had waited for Mum to finish her studies in medicine before they were married, so I expected similar. After the First World War, Mum came home and stayed only one month before returning to London for another year to further her studies in plastic surgery. That's when Mum had left me for the second time. Strange how I accepted her leaving me. I suppose Marjorie was my surrogate mother. She had raised me along with her daughters, Colleen and Millie, who are like my sisters not my young aunties.

When I arrived at work in the London office, thankfully I was the first person to reach the telephone. Dad's voice was crackly over the line. We spoke quickly; time was of the essence as he was about to leave for Canberra. When he told me he'd returned to the Army, I fumed at the thought and replied:

"Yes, of course I understand Dad. How could Australia possibly do without your heroism, I'm sure I don't know?" I was angry that he needed to put his life on the line again. He didn't appreciate my tone.

"I hope you're not being facetious Sally. This will be a world war and millions of innocent lives will be lost because of this bloody mad-man Hitler."

Dad had more knowledge about Hitler than I did, especially in what they suspected he was capable of. Maybe Hitler's madness would escalate beyond all their expectations, the way Dad spoke.

We talked briefly about the family, and my brother, who was extremely upset he couldn't join the army. That would be something: a ten-year-old boy on the front line. Dad then quickly told me that Aunty Clare, who was still a capable theatre nurse, and Uncle Angus our genius doctor, were at the ready to join the ranks again and go wherever they were needed.

"Mum, I'm pleased to say, has decided to stay home and sit this one out," Dad said.

I could hear Mum in the background wanting to talk to me.

"Sally I have to go; I wish you'd come home and get the hell out of London. Please come home before this thing explodes. I love you darling take—" Mum had obviously grabbed the phone off Dad.

"Now Sally, I demand that you come home, it's too dangerous in

22

Europe and please tell Millie and Colleen to do the same. Get out now, I love you, I—" The line cut out.

A row of anxious reporters had gathered behind me, waiting for me to say goodbye. I simply handed the receiver to a fellow Aussie work mate without looking at him. I felt tears welling. I sat at my desk, head in hands and cried my eyes out. Phil Bourke, another Australian and one of my senior colleagues approached me.

"Are you okay Sally," he placed his hand on my back, I nodded yes.

"I'm sorry but I have to ask a favour of you. Berty's taken ill and I have a deadline to meet. Someone has to go to the press conference with Prime Minister Chamberlain. I know you've just spoken to your parents, and you're upset, but we need ya MATE."

He knew if he offered colonialism, he'd bring me round. I smiled through my tears.

"Okay Phil … It'll take my mind off my own worries I guess."

I drove home immediately, dressed in an appropriate suit and dabbed a little make up on. I then made my way to Parliament House.

The pushing and shoving, with everyone trying to be seated in the first row to ask questions and take photos of Prime Minister Chamberlain, reminded me of the after Christmas sale at the Harris Scarfe department store in Adelaide. I'd only experienced private and very civilized interviews with Royalty and Celebrities before. I'd never been part of the eager journo's charge like now. As soon as I was seated, my hand went up automatically, even though I hadn't planned a question. Then the director of the proceedings looked straight at me and said:

"Yes you. The pretty blondie."

I didn't know whether to pull a face or ignore his un- professional remark. Instead I stuttered.

"Sir—uh –Sir, Mr Chamberlain. My name is Sally Darcy—London Times." I then gave the master of proceedings a quick venomous look, before turning a Mona Lisa smile on the Prime Minister.

"When Sir, will you be addressing the nation? It seems to me this would be far better than attending a bun fight between journalists, who may just misquote you."

This remark caused an immediate uproar, not from the Prime Minister, he only grinned. I'm sure he would have liked to laugh though. The other journalist verbally attacked me, but I stood my ground. I meant what I'd said.

This pending threat of war had gone beyond the journalists needing to be recognized in their field for giving the best story on what the Prime Minister said or didn't say. I knew all about creating innuendoes, where the words coming from someone's mouth could be twisted on their journey to become the written word.

I called out, trying to be heard above the rebuffs.

"I'd like to know your answer Sir!"

"Well, Miss Darcy, I will be taking your advice but only when all avenues of peace have been explored. And let us hope my address to the nation will be good news, that the impending war between Britain and Germany has been dismissed."

"You are confident then Sir, this war will not go ahead?" This question I slipped in during the silence as the journo's wrote down Chamberlains words.

"No, I am not confident Miss Darcy, I'm hopeful. Thank you." He then looked for
more questions from other participants.

I must say, I surprised even myself at my composure and lack of nerves in speaking with the Prime Minister, face-to-face, and on such a crucial topic. The questions from other journalists then educated me about the world of bustling headline news. I was addicted to significant reporting on my first mission. It certainly wasn't boring. It held such importance for the nation, not like my silly gossip column. Awful as it was to admit, after being congratulated on my first attempt at serious news, I hoped Berty would remain sick in bed with the flu for a long time.

The boss-chief-editor was so impressed with my efforts, he insisted I accompany Berty in the future to further my experience.

Chapter 3

Stay Calm and Carry On

One month later, on the third of September 1939, Prime Minister Neville Chamberlain did in fact address the nation. The message he put across was that he had a clear conscience from his efforts to broker peace between Poland and Germany. He had now been informed, that Hitler had not only begun his unprovoked attack on the Polish people, but he was convinced Hitler would not stop there. Hitler had lied about giving Poland proposals for peace. There were never any documents given, or subsequently found. Great Britain and France were now allying in this war against Germany. We, the English citizens, were asked to do our duties in the war effort with calmness and courage. *'Stay calm and carry on'*, were the words written on red posters hanging all over London.

I took a deep breath and made my decision. My family were notorious for never running away from a fight, that's if it was worth fighting for. And this war, I was now convinced, was definitely that. I would remain in London and be part of it.

*

For the first few months of the war, England remained unchanged, other than the building of air raid shelters and underground bunkers. Other preparations were the handing out of food ration cards and calling for able-bodied men to protect her shores and sea ports. Women began working in factories, learning how to make bullets and machinery, readying for the war effort. In between, they were saying sad farewells to their sons, boyfriends and husbands. Many of the landed aristocracy opened their manor houses and castles to countless children, protecting them from the assured bombing raids to come, or even worse, invasion. If needs be, these cherished homes would also be used as hospitals for returned injured soldiers.

I had only once visited the manor house located in the Cotswolds and owned by my Father. It had been left to him by his biological grandfather, Harold

Birch. The manor house was managed by an old friend of the family, a Mrs. Ruby Tompkins. She and her daughter Emily along with Emily's English husband ran this manor house. He'd been blinded in the First World War. They had it running profitably, as a fine hotel, welcoming guest from overseas to experience the beauty of the English countryside and a taste of the life lived by the squires. Fox hunting, duck shooting, and trout fishing were the main attractions. The guest's evenings, after a silver service dinner, were filled with entertainment from local players and musicians. I remember one time when Millie, under duress, sang at the Manor house for one special evening. It had been under Grandfather Jonathon's insistence. Apparently, it was Emily's birthday. Millie hated having to go there and sing for Emily. She was still exclaiming her disapproval when she arrived home after her performance.

"There's something about Emily and Ruby that gives me the creeps. I cannot imagine how they ever came to be involved with our family!"

I must admit, I too wondered how it all came about. I think it was because, not one of us Darcy's wanted to be responsible for such a large property in England. But it did seem odd, that although Ruby Tompkins assumed airs and graces, from time to time a common expression or an uncouth word would filter through her speech. However, I also knew and had respect for, how Ruby and Emily had worked tirelessly in caring for injured soldiers from the First World War. And although Ruby was well into her sixties, I wondered if she'd do the same in this war. I suspected so, she seemed the type of woman who was endeavouring to make amends for her past, whatever that may be. She also wanted to climb the proverbial ladder of success and acquire influence in the community. Maybe I was imagining this, but her bonding with our family would always be a mystery to me.

Once Chamberlain had announced Britain was at war, I begged my boss to allow me to be a war correspondent, especially since Michael had kept his promise and gone to do his duty as a Doctor in France. I, like my mother, needed to be close to the man I loved. It now gave me an insight into how Mum must have felt in the First World War, after Dad had departed for Cairo. Reluctantly my boss granted my wishes, especially after I'd reminded him.

"I am the daughter of the First World War hero, Patrick Darcy!" I then proceeded to give him my self-opinionated character references.

He finally gave permission, on one condition; my speaking French had to improve before he'd send me to France. And it did dramatically, especially after my friend Julia Nior, a French Model who lived next door to us in London, began my serious French instruction.

Julia was the most beautiful woman I think I had ever met in my life. My mother and grandmother were stunning but this young woman, in my mind, was absolutely exceptional – perfect in fact. I loved her straight black hair, which she kept styled in a short bob. Although it dated her back to the twenties, it accentuated her large brown eyes, which peered from below a heavy fringe. With her full sensuous lips, she pronounced the French language like an instrument of pure harmony. I was forever waiting for Michael to tell me he had fallen in love with Julia. He was like me, always in a trance whenever she spoke or moved, well glided really. Every movement was effortless and graceful. Thanks to her insistence, I eventually pronounced the syllables and nouns, as they should be when speaking the most beautiful language in the world. Not bad for an Aussie girl I thought! I'd learnt quickly, probably because of my previous French lessons at a private school in Adelaide. Since our first meeting, Julia and I had become close friends. We had such wonderful fun together, particularly, amidst the London night life.

Once my fluent French had actually tricked my boss over the phone and as a result I was allowed to pack my bags and travel to France. There I would write firsthand about the desperate heartbreak of war. While I travelled to and from France within that first year of the war, my duties were made plain and clear by the Chief.

"Just stay safe Sally. Wait for the story to come to you. No front-line battles, do you hear me?" I nodded.

I'd been corresponding from France when 'The Battle for France' began and been lost to Germany. Charles de Gaulle actually addressed that nation saying:

"We have lost the battle but not the war!"

The French Military were to remain fighting on many fronts and Michael chose to stay with the allied troops until his return to England later in 1943. While in France, I saw very little of Michael, as our jobs took precedence over romance.

It was another memorable day, the seventh of September 1940 when I returned to London to write then about how the English people were coping. I didn't think the reality of war had really hit home to most of them, not until the bombing began later that same day. The bombing of London happened almost one year to the day since war had been declared.

When I arrived in London, our apartment welcomed me with the aroma of home baked biscuits. I had nearly forgotten Miss Applegate still lived with us. She was sent home from Switzerland by Millie when things became agitated over there in early 1939. Millie was not sure in which direction she was heading. However, she must have made her decision for she moved in with Klaus Stromberg and his family and was living at their Grande Chalet in Zurich.

I stood in the hallway for a moment, breathing in the delightful safety of my home. Miss Applegate, after hearing the door slam, ran to greet me with open arms.

"You're home Sally, I'm so happy I could cry," and she did.

I laughed, "Come now Miss Applegate, I'll always come home. Don't ever worry about me. I'm like my father, indestructible!"

She dried her tears and sniffed away her disbelief at my ridiculous claim.

"Oh, that reminds me Sally, I have some letters waiting for you. Here they are. I thought it silly to send them after Colleen said to expect you home soon. You must tell me, how is Michael?" (She always liked Michael). I hung my hat and coat on the hall stand, placed the letters down and took her by the arm.

"Let's have a cup of tea with those biscuits I can smell cooking. Then I'll tell you all about Michael."

The kitchen felt homely and warm. Her voice soothed me like a lullaby as she shared her daily routine, ending with:

"Everything has changed so much Sally. We have to be so careful and frugal. I do hope we win this war, I'm so sick of the rationing."

When Amy Applegate hung her head and sipped her tea, I felt I had to tell her how bad things really were in France and elsewhere on the continent. Perhaps it was her pettiness at having only to worry about being frugal, but her comments cannoned me back into the reality of the war in France.

I went on to tell her of the bloody and awful deaths I'd witnessed there, mostly young men – very young men. Those men would no longer tell their sweethearts they loved them, or hug their father on his birthday, or do some favour for a mum. I told her how one day I held the hand of an Australian soldier, just before he died. He grimaced up at me and choked out the words.

"You're nearly as pretty as me wife. Here give her this will ya love."

Soon after those words, he closed his eyes and that was it. I cried onto that silver locket with the name Patricia inscribed. I then opened it to see her picture. My tears were mixing with his blood on my hands. I still have the locket, which I intend to return personally when I go home to Australia.

After telling Amy that particular story, I needed to put the sadness aside. Placing her hand on mine, her eyes awash with tears, Amy told me how sorry she was I had suffered watching young men die before their time. Because of her reaction, I tried to make lighter work when describing some of the horrors I'd seen. Then, after some pleasantries and confirming that Michael was doing well, even though the doctors and nurses suffered from exhaustion, we moved on.

We spoke of London and the feeling which surrounded me as I'd walked home to the apartment that morning. London's heart-beat seemed to be thumping with the anticipation of direct war. Although Hitler at present was only aiming his guns at ammunition dumps in England and searching out hidden air fields full of war planes all waiting in the ready under camouflage, the inevitable was expected when speaking to Londoners. It was only a matter of time before the city would be hit.

I must have looked as weary as I felt when I'd finished my last mouthful of tea, as the observant Amy Applegate suggested I take a rest.

After reading an army-edited letter from Dad, and then one from Mum and a last one from Millie, I accepted Miss Applegate's suggestion to take a nap.

The love-smitten Millie wrote about her heartbreak with the annoying disruption of her opera performances, but of course only until the war ended, when all things would return to normal. Millie had written, *I shall then return home to Australia with my love*. I thought this may never happen, or at least never be welcomed if she had married a German.

I snuggled into my bed, which was on the first floor. Soon after, a knock on the door came from Amy. She'd forgotten to tell me where the nearest air raid shelter was, 'if you need it', she added.

"I'll be with you of course Sally, but just in case." There was silence then before she added, "Have a good sleep my dear."

I took little notice of where Amy said the shelter was. I was a war correspondent. I needed to be amongst the action, to report firsthand what I witnessed. There would be no safe haven for me. Anyway, despite being constantly reminded of the war in France, I could not bring myself to take on the certainty of London being bombed – not today. My falling blissfully to sleep was surely proof enough that this preposterous idea held no place in my mind.

By late afternoon, the whining sound of air raid sirens stirred me from sleep. I rolled over thinking I was dreaming. However, Amy was on the ready and shook me violently.

"Wake up Sally! They've arrived. I can hear their engines.

There's hundreds of them. Quickly, we must go to the shelter. Hurry!"

Within seconds I heard the first explosion, it rattled the building

29

like a chocolate box. I looked at my watch, (the gold watch my Grandmother Bernadette gave me), it read five o'clock.

Surprise and horror minced my thoughts. I grabbed my trench coat from the hall stand, which always held my pen, notebook and passport. I pulled my French beret on and tried to run but stumbled while putting on flat shoes. Amy ran towards the front door calling for me to hurry, I ignored her. I had other plans. I'd get a bird's eye view from our rooftop. Amy turned to follow me, screaming for me to come with her. The next bomb came close. The stairwell swayed, and I stood still waiting for it to collapse. The fearsome screaming of the fighter engines filled the air.

"I'm a war correspondent I need to tell the world Amy! You take care of yourself and I'll take care of me." I finally managed to convince her she was not responsible for me. I ordered her to go.

The fear in her eyes before she left would haunt me forever.

For ages, it seemed, I stood alone on top of our building watching London's horizon become surrounded by fire and flames. Grey-green smoke, tinged pink, streamed upwards clouding the first stars. Minute after minute, the bombers hurled death charges at the city. Exploding with deafening accuracy, hundreds of lives were being taken. I stood high above it all, dumbfounded and in shock, but at the same time in awe of the sickening beauty. Everywhere I looked massive explosions of red coloured the sky. I imagined the human carnage lying in the streets matching the flames of destruction – the devil's own colour. I truly expected at any moment to be blasted off the roof. I became frozen to the spot as I witnessed the total destruction of the world; imagining I was the last woman standing. I needed to report what I'd seen, so I wrote frantically, in the light of London ablaze.

Then, as suddenly as the noise of the bombs falling had begun, there came silence. Only fire engines and ambulances could be heard. The fleeing attackers gave peace to my ears but not my heart. I searched the city line to decipher which of our great monuments had been hit or saved. One stood out like a beacon, it was Saint Pauls Cathedral, lit up by the glowing redness. It seemed to send a message; we are wounded but not defeated! What better structure to remain standing after the bombing, than St. Pauls?

I hurried downstairs and began running towards the hospital, praying it was still there and I would see Colleen. I needed to know before anything else, even before helping people in the streets, that Colleen was alive. I panicked at the thought of losing her, my best friend. My life would begin to fray, my toughness weaken, and I wouldn't be able to carry on with my job without her. It

30

was in moments like this that I began to realise just how much she meant to me. All throughout my childhood, Colleen was always there for me, a genuine caring soul just like Johnathon, her father. Colleen possessed angel like qualities rarely found in human beings. What she also possessed, was a wonderful dry sense of humour which bordered on satire, especially when anyone was behaving melodramatically like our Millie did – often. Colleen had the unique ability to see things for how they really were and deal with them through her intelligence and compassion.

Finally, I reached the London Middlesex Hospital. I'd pushed through rubble smoke and flames to get there. My heart soared when I saw the entire building unscathed. I laughed out loud and thanked the Lord.

The corridors, as was every spare inch of the hospital, was occupied by incoming victims from the bombings. Looking around, I thought it may be impossible to find Colleen, until I heard her commanding voice above the moans of people in agony. She was giving orders in her usual firm manor, although with calming overtones. I then caught a glimpse of her auburn hair, I ran to hold her tight, delirious in the realisation she was alive. She soon released me.

"Come now Sally I'm alright and thank God you are too." Her tired eyes smiled for only a second before she spoke kindly, as if I were a young child again and under her command.

"We could do with some help here. Go with Sister Fran, there's a good girl. She'll show you where to scrub up and then you can help wash and bandage."

Following Colleen's orders came easy; I'd done it my entire childhood. Under her supervision, I'd bandaged and washed dolls all day long, it was my specialty. I smiled thinking of those carefree days and how it was her only wish to become a nurse. Funny I thought how each of us girls had been lucky enough to know our path early in life. Surely something important and meaningful must be accomplished with the three of us being so determined and knowing in our hearts exactly what we were meant to do. Perhaps now our actions were proving this right.

I found out the following day, Amy had died, after being hit with shrapnel whilst running to the nearest shelter. Colleen and I were to learn she had no surviving relatives. We were the only ones who attended her funeral, which we organized and paid for. Little enough compensation for her love and caring I suppose. She was sadly missed, but fondly remembered. Our dear Miss Amy Applegate – God bless her.

Chapter 4

Doing My Best

I remained in England for nearly two years after that fateful night. My time was mostly taken up travelling the country side, talking to people and writing stories about their personal war efforts. Also, how they felt about the sacrifices of sending their children away to the countryside and abroad for safety, or losing a husband, or son to battle. I inspected buildings and homes which had been bombed and consoled children who'd lost their parents. I helped find homes for the elderly, who after returning from a bomb shelter found their home in ruins. I sang happily along with the locals in their pubs, songs especially written for Dame Vera Lynn, in an effort to lift the spirit of the nation. Those songs would forever bring tears to my eyes. I danced the jitterbug with many soldiers, yes, it was not all bad. We had to find humour and strength in order to maintain our free life style, after all, this is what we were fighting for. We celebrated wherever and whenever we could, never knowing if it was for the last time.

I did manage to take a trip back to France in the late spring of 1942 mainly to track down Michael. It was through the French Resistance that I was able to contact him. Our meeting was brief, with only one night of love making. The love we'd shared before that night, I felt was still there, but the passion had almost died. I just put it down to this bloody war. Michael's face showed the strain of his constant battle to keep young men alive – most times in vain. His eyes had sunk into lifeless shadows and the small laughter lines which used to compliment his spirit, had carved deep chasms around his eyes – they were lines of weariness. He seemed almost devoid of emotion. It was as though he was in a personal battle of loss. To me, it seemed he hadn't realised this war was bigger than all of us. I thought he'd made a huge mistake by taking it personally and I told him so.

"All we can do Michael is to give what we can and no more. Don't lose your mind or soul over what you cannot possibly change. Please look after yourself."

I left, feeling that if Michael didn't slow down, he would eventually kill himself. He needed to take a break. I pleaded with him.

"Get out of here Michael. Go back to England, or better still, go home to Ireland for a while."

I walked away not knowing if my words would ever get through to him. It nearly broke my heart to see him that way.

After my short time spent with Michael, I needed to go and see the atrocities for myself and to write about the horrible truth; the extermination of thousands. Through my French and Polish underground contacts, I was able to go to the outskirts of Auschwitz. It was an in-and-out, and a very dangerous thing to do. However, I felt somewhat safer because of my war correspondent's paperwork and badge, even though it was deemed 'mission impossible' at first. Eventually, I was shown firsthand the horrific scene of mass graves, filled with skeletal bodies. The graves sat just outside Auschwitz's massive brick walls. There we hid, watched and listened to the camp guards laughing and talking as they threw the bodies into the graves, as if they were throwing out their garbage. For as long as I live that scene will never leave me.

I returned safely to London, four weeks after I'd left Poland. I found our apartment building still standing. I gave a sigh of relief; at least I didn't have to go underground to the main railway tube to sleep as so many people did. I could sleep in my own bed. Colleen was at home and extremely pleased to see me. It was one of the very few days she'd had off work, so we celebrated into the early hours of the morning. We walked to every pub, still open and drank straight whiskies in everyone; then drowned the whiskies with a beer chaser. We danced our feet sore with some officers at their private club, then refused their romantic advances and left to continue pub crawling, as we call it in Australia. When all the pubs had closed, we returned to the Officers club and stayed until dawn. It was then that we realised not one bomb had dropped on London overnight, or if they had, we were too drunk to notice. Running through the streets of London, we called.

"The war is over; it's the end of the war!"

Still inebriated and celebrating the fact we were still alive, we kissed every man we met. Sometimes when I look back, I still feel embarrassed at our behaviour, but war does crazy things to your mind. As the alcohol infusion slowly wore off, Colleen and I ambled home and slept for eight hours straight. Colleen was back on duty by eight pm, with a smashing headache and I thought she'd blame me. Instead, she thanked me for the best booze up she'd had in years. We'd needed it.

It was one week later, when I heard from a friend who wrote for the European Society column, that Millie was believed to be missing somewhere in Switzerland. Her closest confidant (Millie's shadow, Chad Renwick), was left not knowing where to turn. Chad had finally been dismissed by Millie's lover, Klaus Stromberg, who had turned on him venomously without provocation or reason, according to Chad.

Chad had returned to London after that but before leaving Switzerland he'd tried to contact Millie one last time. She was nowhere to be found. Chad, of course, thought the worst and reported it to the Police. He also contacted the Australian Embassy in Geneva. The Police went on to question the Stromberg family, who assured them, Millie had returned to England. The Police had taken their word, probably because the Stromberg's were one of the most influential families in Switzerland and seemed to have a strong association with Hitler.

The only letter I'd received from Millie in the past two years was the one Miss Applegate handed me on the day before she died. It said Millie was in rehearsal preparing for a commanded Opera. Whatever that meant? And then of course the telephone call I received with her admission of remaining in Switzerland and performing opera to whoever wished to enjoy it, until the war ended. There Millie went again with inuendo's. It couldn't be an order from Hitler? Of course not! Though I thought it strange she hadn't contacted me again. However, Colleen had received periodic letters to say how very much in love she was with Klaus and she would not return to London until after this stupid war had ended. Colleen actually commented that she thought Millie to be in a sort of dream state and far removed from reality. Millie had simply shrugged the war off by saying it was none of her concern. All Millie ever wrote about was the love she had for the magnificent Klaus.

Millie's disappearance was also confirmed by another journalist, whom I knew well, and who also worked in Switzerland. This information was given to me, before it made the *London News* headlines. I straight away sent a message home to Mum and asked her to break the news to Grandad Jonathon and Marjorie. I vowed I would travel to Switzerland via France and search her out. Please don't worry, I'd written. But the fact remained I was worried. My imagination was running riot. What if those bloody Nazi's had told the Stromberg family to be rid of her, or Hitler had run out of patience with the Opera Company in their attempts to please him and had all of them shot. I knew for a fact that Hitler's seething hatred for anyone who excelled in the arts, was due to his artistic talent being shunned when he'd entered his painting into a competition. Ridiculous I know, especially since Switzerland was neutral. Or was it? Hitler I'm sure was still holding influence over that country.

After a week, I found Chad, or actually he managed to find me first. He confirmed it.

"Yes, Millie is definitely missing," he said, hanging his head almost guiltily.

We made a date to meet at the local pub the next day. Chad seemed uneasy at first and I wondered if he was exaggerating the disappearance of Millie and it was just that Klaus Stromberg was trying to be rid of him. However, Chad stuck to his story. While we ate our lunch, I was able to question him for nearly two hours. Finally, he said to me:

"Why do you think I came back to London Sally, I don't want to die under a bloody bomb, which is what London's all about. I came here looking for Millie. Stromberg said she'd returned to London and even the bloody Swiss Police searched everywhere and couldn't find her. If she was in trouble, surely she would have gone to the Australian Embassy in Geneva?"

I couldn't argue with Chad's logic. I made my decision; I'd go to Switzerland as soon as possible and find her. London was still being mercilessly bombed by German air raids and I must say, part of me felt like a traitor leaving our wounded city. But I knew I must undergo this mission for my family's sake. My mind and plans were quickly sorted.

My usual contacts made it possible for me to be transported to the closest point on the French coastline and that was Calais. From there I would travel by land across to the French Alps and then on into Switzerland. As the crow flies it was not that far, compared to Australian distances. My idea of parachuting into Switzerland from a war plane as the quickest method, I thought a good one. However, upon meeting the commanding officer and voicing my suggestion, I was met by his stern re-buff.

"Are you bloody mad, you shouldn't even be doing this. This is not what women should be doing!"

"And what exactly should women be doing Sir?" I asked.

He mumbled something about sewing up parachutes and not jumping out of them.

"But I can't sew Sir," I said, laughing out the words.

"Well you'd soon bloody well learn if you were my daughter!"

I chose not to comment; my sense of humour was obviously not appreciated in such official company. Plus, his ridiculous attitude towards women in this war was so out of date. Everywhere, women were becoming fighter pilots and spies within the underground networks, not to mention killing the enemy in hand to hand combat. They were running factories, driving trucks, becoming linguists and intelligence officers and playing so many important roles. This commanding officer was a dinosaur.

My tongue in cheek plea for a parachute jump into Switzerland was heard by Berty, my English Warco mate, who'd just entered the room and was standing right behind me. Berty was the journalist who'd been ill the day I interviewed Prime Minister Chamberlain, I'd taken Bert's place from then on. Bert helped convince the chief Editor, plus this Commander, of my talent for the ridiculously impossible, plus my lineage of bravery.

"Sir with all due respect, I've ridden alongside Miss Darcy in point to point races. She has shown, if you don't mind me saying so, just what she's made of. Especially when she beat all the men in a horse race, then later that day won the tennis match, and that same evening, Miss Darcy became our champion chess player. It is most doable for our Miss Darcy. Yes, indeed Sir, most doable," Berty concluded.

After Bert's testimonial, I was duly credited with permission to undertake the mission.

You could say, I held the respect of most men who knew me in England, and what I liked about the Englishmen was, they gave praise where praise was due. Unlike most Australian men, who thought a woman like me to be a challenge and invariably held my talents against me?

The next day I had a meeting with my Editor and Chief of, 'The London Times.' He agreed that I had the balls and the credentials to do the job. I'd told him I could also do a spiel on the French Resistance at the same time. However, his orders were explicit.

"Stay away from the front-line Sally, just take a back seat in this mission of reporting what you see." He then continued with his head lowered to avoid eye contact. "I hope and trust you'll find Miss Millie. She has a sublime voice, yes simply sublime."

The very next night, I'd made my way to the British headquarters and was about to leave, when Berty came through the door.

"Berty. What are you doing here, this is a personal mission!"

"Oh no it's not! The chief wants me to go with you Sally. You may need help with the French Resistance story. This could be one of the biggest scoops in the war so far. He's asked me to go with you and help, well, keep an eye on you."

He dramatized the, 'keeping an eye on you,' with his face up against mine and then went on to say.

"Anyway, we *all* want you to find your Aunty Millie, she's our pin up girl and many here in England love her you know."

"You mean every man loves her?" I smiled. "Okay Berty, but stay close, we may be in for the time of our lives."

"You don't mean jumping out with a bloody parachute, do you Sally? I'd rather row the Channel in a bath tub!"

"There will be no jumping out of planes! The Commander yelled. "You would be shot down. The Swiss are taking aim at any aircraft entering their air space. Haven't you heard about the mistaken bombings on Switzerland by the allies?"

I smirked when looking at the expression on the commander's face. My sense of humour seemed to ruffle feathers occasionally. I was delighted it did.

I had never obeyed the chiefs' orders about staying out of the firing line. I'd always found a way, usually by conning an officer, who'd encouraged me to tell it how it really was for them and their men. And so, I'd join the soldiers on many occasions at the front line. I simply told the boss my article had been relayed to me by officers and of course the injured men, some whom I knew Michael had saved.

Chapter 5

Back to France

The darkest of nights awaited us as we approached Dover. Only a golden sickle of moon branded the sky, however, it soon disappeared when the clouds rolled in, leaving not a shadow anywhere. Once in Dover, we made our way by jeep to the English shore line where we were introduced to four men, who were all English Special Services, except for the driver of the boat, Alain, a young and very handsome Frenchman. As we were about to embark, Alain took my arm to help me on board. Our eyes met for a moment before he placed a lingering kiss on my hand. It sent a tingle through my senses. Once we were all aboard, the timber fishing boat chugged off from the English coast.

After making the acquaintance of each man, speaking in English, we all began to speak French. I then found out that our so-called French fisherman, Alain, was a crucial part of the French Résistance. He was most charming, and I scolded myself for forgetting Michael for a moment, especially when I sat close to Alain as he steered the boat. Then he said:

"My mother is one of the forces behind a special unit of the French Resistance, so I respect and admire women. They are stronger than men on the inside but are to be treated like delicate flowers on the outside." He turned his perfect profile to face me, and asked, "Is it not so my friend?"

My heart skipped a beat. I didn't want this to happen, I was here on a mission I told myself. I need no distractions, but then smiling into his beautiful hazel eyes, I answered coyly, too coyly for me.

"I suppose so."

"I am wrong then? This disappoints me. I thought I knew women very well," he said while tilting his head to one side.

I laughed at myself and his response.

"No, Alain you have it right, very right indeed."

"Aar, I am so 'appy." he said with an animated sigh of relief. "You will stay with us at my 'ome near Calais. I will then take you to my Uncle who lives in Saint Quenton. 'E will arrange transport for you to the Swiss Alps. We 'ave many connections there, they will 'elp you find your Aunty. The road may be full of danger, but I 'ave 'eard you are brave, and you speak French very well for an Australian," his face lit up with a smile. He was beautiful.

I agreed with him in French. "Yes, I speak French okay, so I'm told."

He nodded his approval.

"The Australian Soldiers are loved and respected by the French people. They are true warriors and 'ave saved thousands of lives in both wars fought in our country. My mother will welcome you with open arms. She 'as told me the story from when I was a little boy, of 'ow she fell in love with an Australian soldier in the First World War. But unfortunately, he was killed two days before the war ended and before he could marry my mother. My father found her crying at 'is grave. You see, 'e'd come to the burial site to visit a fallen Australian comrade. My father consoled 'er, and the rest of the story is 'istory. So, we 'ave great love and respect for you Aussies!" His eyes saddened, as he told me his father was a merchant fisherman before he drowned at sea. This was when the vessel he was on became engulfed in a horrific storm.

I don't know why I did it. Maybe I felt I needed to after his story, but I kissed Alain on the cheek. His hand immediately went up to the spot and with melodrama, he said:

"I shall never wash my cheek again."

I laughed until we saw lights from another boat coming towards us. Alain was quick to act. Grabbing my arm he gently pushed me to the floor.

"Quick all of you crawl to the 'iding place," he whispered. The others followed immediately.

We'd been shown loose floor boards under a sea-grass mat. Inside was a space large enough for five people plus canvas, fishing crates, life jackets and the disgusting stench of a thousand rotting fish and prawns. It hit me like a gas explosion when I lifted the boards. This deception had been planned as an immediate deterrent for anyone who found the opening. We had to suffer the foul fumes until the coast was clear. I can honestly say now, this experience put me off eating prawns for a very long time.

"False alarm, another French fishing trawler," Alain said after he'd knocked on the trap door.

The Calais Harbour was quiet when we landed. Only the sound of gentle waves splashing against small fishing vessels that sat dwarfed beside German war ships was heard. The German guards who patrolled the coastline could be easily distracted by the young locals. The women were more than happy to provide 'special services' for the salvation of France. Most times, the girls added a sleeping drug to the officers' wine, making the promise of sexual intercourse null and void.

Alain went first to see if the way was clear and then returned to hand everyone, including me, a net full of fish to carry ashore. My hair, I'd pushed up under a cap and I wore baggy trousers and a waterproof jacket over a turtle neck jumper. The jacket had enormous pockets which held my war correspondent papers, passport, plus any personal items I may need, including French money. Berty was dressed the same.

We made our way to the fishing co-op, which held the catch in refrigerators, until collected in the morning, and then we walked with Alain to his family's home. It was quite a way and extreme tiredness overcame me by the time we reached the charming white-washed cottage. Alain then informed us:

"In our place 'ere, we 'ave a large timber barn at back. It shelters a tractor, two 'orses, a milking cow two goats and many chickens. Our property consists of one 'undred and thirty acres. Some of the acres 'ave been cleared to sew crops and vegetables, plus grape vines. The rest of the land is taken up by a small forest and a stream."

It all sounded wonderful, but I needed to bathe. My clothes stank of dead prawns and had to be washed immediately. I had to laugh though, thinking this smell would be a deterrent from interrogation, had I been caught by the Germans.

Alain's mother, Suzan, welcomed us with zealous charm, that is, until she caught the drift of my stink. She turned to Alain with dismay.

"You struck trouble Alain?"

"No Mama, it was just another fishing boat, but we could not take any chances."

He smiled at me before Suzan whisked me away to the bathroom. I spoke to her in French for some time; she then kissed me on both cheeks. This gesture, I'm sure was her approval of my sincere attempt at their poetic language.

I stripped while Suzan took my clothes away and threw them outside. They'd be processed at a later time. The perfume of the lavender soap she handed me on her departure, took me back to my first home named 'Wildflowers'. Marjorie and Colleen Thompson would be forever boiling up Lavender to make soap. We, as children inevitably smelt like little lavender blooms. I thought this could be my last moment of luxury before I travelled into the unknown to find Millie. So, I soaked up the glorious perfume along with the warm bath which soothed my body and soul into peaceful reverie. Suzan arrived with a warm towel, a little too soon. She also carried a lovely floral print frock and a woollen wrap.

"Merci Madame."

"Come Sally, I 'ave some chicken soup ready and the bread 'as just finished baking."

I needed no second invitation, I was ravenous, as were my new friends. I approached the table to see them eating heartily and they immediately excused themselves for beginning without me.

"No, no, please," I said. "I had the luxury of a wonderful soothing bath it was heaven. I'm nobody special to wait for, we're all equals in this."

Suzan poured wine for me and then raised her own glass to drink a toast,

"'Ere is to the French Résistance and the defeat of the German Army!"

We raised our glasses and clinked.

"Here, here, we chorused," and I gulped the delightful warm liquid.

Our dinner was mostly eaten in silence, then Suzan showed the men to the barn. It was the last time I would meet them. They were on a secret mission of some sort, which they dared not divulge. I knew only their names and who was to say if their names were genuine.

When we were alone, I spoke of mundane things with Alain, I was trying to keep a lid on my arousal due to his sensuous looks. Thankfully, Suzan returned to the room, for I don't know where he might have led me, most probably where I'd have liked him to. I smiled at the thought and then stood to bid them goodnight. Noticing Berty had fallen asleep on the couch, I went to wake him, but Suzan stopped me with a shoosh, she then covered him with a feather doona. Anyway, Berty looked too comfortable to move so I kissed him on the cheek. He smiled and snuggled further under the cover.

Sometime during the night, I was woken with a soft, lingering kiss. Startled at first, I sat up then felt a hand gently cover my mouth.

"It is me Alain," his voice was low, "you are so beautiful Ma Cherie,"

I literally melted with those words. My heart said traitor, and my body said take it while you can. Who knew what was in store for us. I had to admit, at first sight I was extremely attracted to Alain and more so later when he gave me his opinion of how women should be treated. I just loved how he thought.

I breathed out my words. "I have a man in my life Alain. He's a doctor working close to the front line here in France."

He retorted quickly.

"I am a man, working for the French Resistance." He then softened,

41

"Did you 'ear what you just said Ma Cherie. You 'ave a man, not love a man."

"I love him Alain, I can't be unfaithful."

"Are you engaged or married to 'im?"

"No. We were going to wait for the war to end."

"Exactly. Sally my love, you are waiting, let us not wait to 'ave this moment of pleasure, there is so much pain and struggle in the world. Making love is for the moment; loving someone is forever. You don't 'ave to make love to me Sally just accept my love and I promise, you will enjoy my gift to you. Then you will be taking from me not giving of yourself. You will then stay faithful in your 'eart to your man. It is simple, let me adore you."

His soft lips kissed the nape of my neck sending a welcome message to my sexual desire. I whispered in his ear.

"I shouldn't be doing this."

"You are not doing this Sally I am, but I will not force you, I would never do that, I am just asking you to relax and enjoy my love."

I succumbed happily, and it wasn't long before he had me crying silently. Alain's silken touch released total euphoria. Not one inch of my skin was left un-loved or un-caressed. I had an orgasm within seconds and told myself it was because I hadn't had sex for over a year. Michael was unavailable and no casual sex for me; I wasn't that type of girl. However, my self-lecture became unconvincing after accepting Alain's love. From what I'd heard, he seemed the typical French lover. I'd never made love to a Frenchman before, but if Alain was typical, then I felt all women worldwide should have this experience, at least once in their lives.

Alain slept alongside me for the rest of the night. His body moulded into mine, giving comfort to my yearning. Sleepily I awoke as the apricot sunbeams began to filter through the curtains. Morning had arrived far too soon, but I delighted in the reality of lying folded into Alain's masculinity, and more than happy it had not been a dream. I sighed with the satisfaction of knowing that we were surrounded by the terror of war and still, there remained so much pleasure in making love – there always would be.

Suzan came into the room carrying a breakfast tray for two – unfazed.

"Good morning, I 'ave made fresh croissants."

The tray was placed on the table next to the bed. It held a bowl of homemade strawberry jam, croissants, coffee and cream, plus fresh apples. She'd paid no attention to her son's presence in my bed. She did however warn him:

"You should not dilly dally Alain, as you 'ave to ride to the next village and reach it before dark. You cannot break the organized transport to the Swiss Alps."

Suzan then left with a knowing smile on her face. Yes, this was France alright, love reigned supreme. It seemed all was accepted and forgiven in the name of love. Once Suzan had left, Alain turned to me, his hands reaching up to gently caress my face.

"Are you 'ungry Sally?"

With his provocative eyes alluding to something more satisfying, I asked:

"Can we eat the apples and croissants later?"

That morning I returned all the loving I could to this charming Casanova. We both cried out with the ecstasy we shared.

Chapter 6

The Mission

Alain hitched his magnificent Cleveland Bay horses to his hay cart. Their feathered legs pacing in time on the spot, ready for the pull. Breathing in their unmistakable smell, I was transported to happier carefree times. I longed to ride a horse and feel free again.

"Hello mate." My arms automatically wrapped around this giant horse's neck. I didn't want to release the embrace, until Alain laughed.

"It seems I 'ave a competitor for your attention Sally."

"Horses will win every time, sorry Alain." My voice was muffled by my closeness to the horse's neck.

I chose to wear the floral frock Suzan had given me, she was a little smaller than me, so the dress clung to my curves. She also gave me a canvas tote bag for my personals. As we said farewell, I thought how much I admired her courage and unmistakable knowledge of separating trivia from importance. Suzan had been responsible for rescuing hundreds of Jewish families, especially children, from Poland and neighbouring countries. She'd also aided in the killing of many German soldiers, which I was told was by nefarious means.

"God bless you," I called out.

"Is there one?" Suzan called back. I chose not to answer.

Berty hopped up and sat on top of the hay, looking every bit the French peasant while I sat alongside Alain in the driver's seat.

A mellow autumn day offered me a sense of living forever. If it were no other time but war, our journey would be heaven sent. I sat listening to the clip clop of the horse's hooves and wallowed under sun beams and fleeting shadows filtering through giant maple trees. I kept telling myself, stay in this moment Sally for if you do, the memory will fill you for a very long time.

Half an hour into our journey, and while travelling along the country road, autumn leaves were being whisked up by the breeze. They soon began falling softly. Somehow it reminded me of the dying in this war; each one floating in space before reaching its destination. This foliage and the bodies of the dead would replenish the earth; life would remain eternal. With this realisation my heart saddened. If I died on this journey, I would not leave a soul to take my place.

"What 'ave you been thinking about ma Cherie? You ave been very quiet," Alain said.

"Oh nothing, I was just admiring the autumn leaves." I said convincingly, before looking behind to see Berty sound asleep on the hay. I laughed.

"That bloke could sleep anywhere, anytime."

"It is a good way to be, is it not?"

Each time I gazed into Alain's amazing hazel eyes I fell a little more in love. I became hypnotized when he spoke.

"I am so 'appy we have two more days to enjoy our slow trip to Saint Quentin Sally. I will be sad to leave you there, but you will be taken care of by my uncle. 'E will take you to Troyes. We have comrades there, they will make arrangements for you to go inland to Lyon and then to Mulhouse. That's not far from where you begin the journey over the Alps to the Swiss border. You will 'ave to cross the Jura ranges. It is one of the lowest parts of the Alps and there are many trails, it is not so 'ard. There are also many resistance groups who live in the caves and refuges. They know what goes on in Switzerland. They should be able to 'elp you find your aunty."

He then held my hand while he placed a lingering kiss on my lips. I felt no guilt.

We'd travelled without speaking for some time before German army jeeps rumbled towards us. My heart beats echoed above all other sounds, witnessing my nerves. Alain remained calm.

"It is too late to divert from our course now. Remember, you are my wife and Berty is your brother. We are to deliver this 'ay to my Uncle in Saint Quentin. My mother 'as packed some 'omemade jam, it is a form of bribery. I will give it to them. Do not look at them Sally, just look bored and look ahead. Can Berty speak French well enough do you think?"

Berty answered. "Yes I can, I've been speaking French nearly all my life."

"That is good Berty. But be silent unless you are spoken too."

My heart pounded, like a hundred pigeons trying to escape. The first jeep slowed down then stopped. The officer sitting next to the driver asked in English where were we heading. Alain shrugged his shoulders and in French said.

"I do not speak English Monsieur."

The hard-faced officer sitting in the back seat asked Alain the same question in French. Alain smiled.

"We are going to deliver this 'ay to the German 'orses, which are stabled in Saint Quentin. My mother has made some homemade strawberry jam. I am sure she would like you to 'ave some."

Alain jumped down from the cart and handed the officer sitting in the front seat, the four jars of jam. He then smiled and tipped his hat. The General looked suspicious and told his offsider to ask in French, who Berty and I were. When asked, I answered in hurried French, trying to sound matter of fact.

"I am his wife," I said while nodding at Alain and then I turned to Berty, "and this is my brother Sir."

He relayed my answer to the General. The General's glare told me he still had suspicions, but it was obvious he was in a hurry. I could see the back of their jeep was laden with boxes of wine and produce. After glaring at Alain and giving me a smile, the General motioned his hand for the driver to move on. Alain remained on the ground smiling and as the three jeeps passed by, Alain wiped his brow, sighing with relief as he jumped back into the cart.

"You know Ma Cherie that was the first time they aven't asked to see my papers, or interrogate me, you are my lucky charm." He kissed me on both cheeks and squeezed my hand.

"Darn right she's lucky," said Bert. "She stood alone on the roof of her London apartment building, in the very first London Blitz. Said she needed to watch and report the whole bloody thing. Nearly everything around her went down but not Sally. We call her in the office, the lucky Boomerang!"

"What is exactly a Boomerang?" Alain asked quizzically, seeming unfazed by Bert's information. I answered quickly, after assuming Berty would not be able to explain it properly.

"It's a piece of wood carved in the shape of a sickle. The Australian Aborigines use it to hunt their prey. When they throw it and if it doesn't hit its intended object, it comes back to the thrower. It saves a lot of walking."

"This is incredible you must show me 'ow it is done Sally."

"It's a bit hard unless you come to Australia and ask an Aboriginal to show you how it's done."

His eyes and voice softened; "I intend to."

I smiled uncertainly. This sounded like a proposal. I'd come to believe that in war, all things were of the moment. I made no plans for the future, so I gave Alain no hint of my thoughts. However, my heart was telling me, this union could definitely work.

We'd travelled for nearly five hours. There were no further encounters with the German's, before we reached a small farm. Alain's friend and fellow underground member grew sunflowers and sorghum on his hundred acres. I delighted to see the shimmer of yellow-faced flowers drowning in the deep golden sunset. Alain trotted the horses up the driveway, while my senses bathed in the late afternoon glow.

A pleasant evening was shared with his friend and that family. As usual, they served tasty, hearty food before an early night was called. The family explained, they would begin their harvest at dawn, and we had to be on our way before then.

The next evening, and after another trouble-free day on the road, we slept in a barn belonging to another of Alain's friends. After I was introduced as Alain's wife and a fellow resistance fighter, the woman of the house ignored us and yelled at her husband.

"This war will come to its end without you trying to 'elp and be killed! Oo is going to plough the fields then ay?"

We were not offered a place at her dinner table; instead she almost threw the bread and cheese at us, before she shut us behind the double doors of the barn. However, the horses were given top grade oats by this woman. It seemed she hated warfare, but even more, she detested her husband taking part in the French Resistance. She had no vision of peace, just survival.

Half an hour before sunrise, we harnessed up the horses and pushed on. The wife had at least given us enough bread and cheese the night before to do us until we reached Saint Quentin. Alain assured me we'd be totally spoilt when we arrived at his uncle's farm.

The day once again had greeted us with perfect autumn weather. I didn't mind at all riding in a horse drawn cart, in fact I loved every minute. I felt a little guilty with this degree of happiness, especially after hearing Alain's car had been confiscated by the Germans.

By late afternoon we'd bi-passed Saint Quentin and after another three quarters of an hour, the small village of Remau Coopel came into sight. I thought it yet another quaint French village, before noticing some of the buildings still showed the scars from almost being blown off the map in the First World War. The town's people watched, in a forlorn fashion as we passed by. Our horses' iron-shod hooves created a clonking echo when hitting the cobblestone road. That echo of emptiness matched the people's faces. There was no question that the German soldiers who'd stopped us some two days back, had been here and taken most of the villager's produce. This was yet another raid by Hitler's intruders who'd promised France it would be free of pillage and tyranny. That promise would only be kept if all the people collaborated. To collaborate with the Germans was toying with evil if you asked me and it seemed the bulk of the French people would agree. Notwithstanding, some were happy to make themselves seem more important by aiding the enemy. Because of this, their lives were made easier. However, their fellow countrymen suffered because of them. But I'm pleased to say, I think most kept up their own type of resistance against the Germans.

Once we'd arrived at Alain's Uncle Pierre's small but prosperous farm, we were welcomed heartily. After entering this tastefully furnished cottage, I noticed Uncle Pierre had the same features as Alain. Large soulful hazel eyes, perfect nose, high cheek bones and full lips, just made to be kissed. I loved the fact that they chose to wear their hair longer than most men would, giving them the air of the artist – the non-conformist. Both men were true romantics I was sure. I was then introduced to Alain's Aunt Bridgette who was a most attractive blue-eyed blonde, and as I would find out a little later, a superb cook. Before night fell, and while the men discussed important plans, Bridgette showed me their secret cellar.

"This is where you need to 'ide Sally, if there is any trouble."

The hiding place was outside and under the chicken pen. The stench of chicken poop I was sure would prevent anyone from finding this underground cellar. Bridgette's curves swayed along with her long blonde hair as she walked briskly in front of me. Once we reached the inside of the chicken pen, she bent over to shift the ample straw. This lay on top of a door which allowed us entry into the cellar. I noticed a further pile of straw was glued to the top of the door for camouflage. Bridgette took the five steps down in front of me and then told me where to find the matches to light the lantern. It was a massive dugout. It held enough wine, dried fish and meat, plus pickled vegetables and preserved fruit to keep a family of ten alive for six months. In the main house they also had a large kitchen pantry stacked with food, mainly as a decoy for the German raiders. Bridgette told me she'd become a very good actress and laughed before she began to act out her ruse.

"I beg you Sir, please leave us with just a little to eat, or we will surely starve, then your supply of the best produce will end." I laughed – she was good.

Most times it worked, and the soldiers would leave them a day or two of supplies. I was amused at her portrayal of a damsel in distress. Then speaking in French, I told Bridgette what a great attitude she had especially with the way

48

things were at the moment. She seemed delighted with my compliment and returned by saying she would never have known I was not French; my accent was so convincing.

"Ah yes," I said. "It was my beautiful French friend, Julia Noir, who lived in the same building as me in London who taught me the correct pronunciation."

Suddenly Bridgette surprised me by hugging me tight and crying tears of delight.

"I know Julia. Her mother, Jacqueline, was my best friend when I was young and lived in Paris."

How incredible that Bridgette and I held this common link. It truly was a small world. After talk of our mutual friends, Bridgette exclaimed she was also a great Opera fan and knew well of the famous Millie Darcy and of course my quest to find her. I felt Bridgette would be an advocate for my cause, unlike Suzan, who seemed single minded about only saving Jewish families. Bridgette's feelings it seemed, were holding on to great hope for the future. She believed we would definitely see all things return to peace and happiness, like it was in the past. Bridgette was just what I needed; a perpetual optimist.

Her pretty blue eyes sparkled with tears when she announced in unequivocal terms.

"We will find Millie Darcy. Yes, we will. We will 'ear her beautiful voice again and again." Bridgette shone with pride. "I too would 'ave liked to be an Opera singer, I love to sing and act." Clasping her hands together and sighing deeply, she then said. "Just to meet Millie Darcy would be a grand memory for me to cherish."

"Yes, we will find her Bridgette. And I will ask her to sing, especially for you."

To find somebody, with so much joy and hope for the future lifted my spirits. For no apparent reason, we giggled when grabbing two of the finest bottles of wine off the rock ledge, plus a bottle of port. I listened to the bottles clanking a tune in Bridgette's arms, while climbing up the ladder and through the manhole.

Upon our return to the house, Alain and his uncle Pierre, plus Berty and a new-comer, Phillip, were sitting around the kitchen table. They'd been discussing the latest influx of Jewish citizens coming from Poland to be hidden in the Swiss Alps. They would remain there until arrangements could be made for their passage to America. The men said they hoped it wouldn't interfere with our guides being able to give us enough time to go and collect Millie. I stopped

49

Alain right there.

"You said collect her, does that mean you know where she is?" His gaze centred on the wooden table, his eyes not wanting to meet mine. I stiffened and prepared for the worst. "Is she dead, maybe injured, Alain?"

Alain lifted his head and smiled reassuringly, his hand reached out to mine. "No Ma Cherie, no she is not dead, or injured, it's just...," he looked down again.

"What is it then, tell me what it is, I can't bear the suspense!"

Alain answered carefully, seeming to consider my feelings.

"It's just that Phillip 'as come to give us some information. Millie is living with a German officer and 'is family in a Chalet in the Swiss Alps. She may not want to leave. She may be a Nazi sympathizer."

I knew Alain well enough by then to know he hated saying this, so my anger was softened by his empathy. However, I spoke emphatically.

"But you don't understand Alain, Millie went missing from the Stromberg's home. I know who they are, and they told the Police she'd returned to London. The Police searched the Chalet and found no trace of her. Anyway, she would only stay there for the love of a man, not to join the Third Reich. I know that for certain and I know who the man is, he's Klaus Stromberg. I don't think either of them are Nazi sympathizers, definitely not Millie. She told me over the phone he was helping her to convince Hitler the Opera's should continue throughout the war. She is a love-sick fool that's all. We need to get her out of there!"

Suddenly, tears welled in my eyes. Alain's voice was low and sincere.

"You may be right Sally, 'e may 'ave been forced to be an officer in the German Army, most of the Swiss Germans 'ad no choice, especially the aristocrats. 'E may be on our side, just waiting for the war to go either way."

"Are you sure you want to do this Sally?" Alain asked kindly. "The risk may be too great. Millie is safe with the Stromberg's; we know this much. My best friend Marcel lives in Switzerland and 'e as contacts. A young woman who works in the chalet 'as told 'im, Millie is being kept safe by the General's family. She 'as never left them. Millie must be mixing with German Officers, 'aving dinner with them. She may be pretending to be on their side for 'er own safety. It would be too dangerous for you to find out at this stage Sally. I beg you to return to England and wait until the war 'as finished. Whichever way your Aunt is leaning, she will be kept safe by the man who loves 'er."

This last statement was of little consolation. Although, if the decision was left entirely up to me, I think I would have left Millie there. After all, the

Swiss were neutral. But the ramifications from my family would be another thing. I would have to deal with their emotions and opinions on whether I was thinking only of myself in abandoning her. What if she were being held a virtual captive by this Nazi loving family; afraid to move, say or do something which may incriminate her. Why did this family tell the police she had returned to London? My mind spun like a wheel, not wanting to rest on any decision. Alain squeezed my hand.

"Let us 'ave dinner and some wine Sally, we can discuss it later."

Bridgette had remained silent while busily preparing our dinner. She then bustled in and began serving. We ate a wine infused variety of field mushrooms, cooked with cream and bacon on homemade pasta, along with a giant glass of red wine and hot crusty bread with cheese. I didn't feel much like eating but after forcing the first mouthful down, my taste buds exploded into orgasmic pleasure. I knew I should give thanks to our chef, but words could not properly explain the taste sensation, so clumsily I said.

"My God, but you French know how to cook. How do you make something so simple, taste so bloody good?"

Their laughter was a blessing after such a serious pre-dinner discussion, and then Bridgette said with a sensuous wink.

"It is made with love Ma Cherie."

I smiled at her comment and kept eating. I didn't want to lift my head from the plate. I was enjoying my food too much and just a little embarrassed by her innuendo. My last mouthful was savoured like a lover's farewell kiss. I then helped Bridgette clear the table and she gave me dessert spoons to hand around. I asked her (not that I was hungry), what she had prepared for dessert. Instead of telling me, Bridgette showed me the apple Tartan baking in the oven. The magnificent aroma, so similar to Mother Matilda's apple pie, caused my eyes to glisten with the memory. Bridgette noticed and patted me on the back.

"Sally, why so sad?"

"I'm just remembering an old friend who made the best apple pies ever. But I'm sure this Tartan will be every bit as good."

After dinner, we began discussing plans on how to travel through the Alps to where Millie was living or being held captive. No one really knew for sure, it was all hearsay. What I did learn however, was that the different groups of French Résistance soldiers were very well informed in so many ways in this war. Although there were few women who took part in the French Resistance, the ones who did, including Suzan, Alain's mother, were well respected. Damsels in distress, such as me, were well cared for too. However, Alain seemed reluctant for me to proceed with this mission. I struggled to understand his reasons. Whether it was the fear he may lose me, or whether he thought the mission to be a frivolous exercise to save someone, who in his opinion, did not need or deserve saving.

I paid no attention to my assumptions and stuck to my point of view during this meeting. I believed Millie was only there pretending for safety's sake, to be a sympathizer. Personally, I had to get her out of whatever situation she was in and without risking my own neck. Phillip, I felt was on my side. Perhaps it was because he was an Opera buff and greatly admired Millie. This meant her fame and popularity was the common denominator, the real motive for her rescue. I wondered then, if it were 'little insignificant me' needing rescue, whether I'd be left to face the circumstances on my own. No jealousy on my part, just amusement at human nature. So, whatever reason it was that drove me to attempt and hopefully complete this mission, I was onward bound not the reverse. I refused to wait for Alain's approval. Anyway, he would not accompany me as he too had other battles to deal with. He was an expert with explosives, so was the main instigator in blowing up the German vans which travelled about the country picking up the signals of hidden allies' radios. So far, he'd demolished fifteen of these German vans.

The bottle of port we'd brought up from the cellar was enjoyed by all before we bade Phillip good night. He said he'd return in the morning before daybreak, along with another comrade, Jon-Paul. Jon-Paul was an ambulance driver who could take us all the way to Mulhouse. This would take three days of driving, or two, if we had a good run. We'd be disguised as sick infectious people in the hope it might deter German investigation. It was all settled. However, in that instant my heart filled with fear. I realised I'd be mixing with some of the most wanted and searched for soldiers in France. I began to have reservations. But how else could I have accomplished Millie's rescue? If I'd gone in the front door of that chalet, I may have been a greater threat to Millie or endangered myself. Especially as I knew nothing about the Stromberg family or just how close Klaus was to Hitler. I could only hope that more information about her situation would be revealed as we travelled through the Alps to where we believed she was. There would surely be time to pull out and return if word came through that she was determined to stay with the Stromberg's until the war ended. I just had to try, at least once, to reach her for my family's sake and my own moral reckoning.

Phillips eyes sparkled with enthusiasm. He kissed me on both cheeks before leaving and said sincerely.

"We will bring 'er 'ome. Do not worry Sally."

Suddenly, I had the feeling he would leave me behind. I remembered then, him suggesting during the meeting that perhaps I should not go and perhaps he was right. But then I'd replied:

"No, this is my duty, and I'm positive Millie will not leave unless I am with you. I know her very well."

Phillip had agreed with me then. However, I now had more than a sneaky suspicion about the way he said. 'We will bring 'er 'ome do not worry'. I began to think he'd made up his mind to leave Berty and me behind. I chose to jettison the thought. Surely, I had convinced them that Millie would not go with them without me being there.

Not too long after Phillip left, I became extremely tired. I longed to stay awake, so I'd not be left out of things, but my eye lids felt like stones and my body weak. Before I knew it, Alain gathered me up in his arms and carried me to bed. I remember smiling up at him, thinking he was the most beautiful sensitive man I'd ever met. With my last ounce of strength, I pulled his face down and kissed his lips. That was the last thing I remember before the mid-day sun woke me.

Chapter 7

Left Behind

Dazed and still half asleep, I tried to lift my body off the bed. I felt as if I'd been drugged and I had. My head spun in an aching mess. I lay back down and cried. Instinctively I knew they'd left me behind. I hated men, why did they do this to me? Don't they know who I am? I'm tougher and stronger than they think. My sobbing became loud enough for Bridgette to hear. I felt helpless while she rocked me back and forth in her arms.

"Sally, dear Sally, it cannot be 'elped," she said with that amusing French vernacular of dropping the h. "The men thought it safer to travel without you. They will bring Millie 'ome 'ere and then we will get the two of you back to England safely. Please don't cry. It is for the best. Come, 'ave a cup of tea with me and we can talk."

"My head aches, I feel sick and angry." I said sniffling. "They don't understand Bridgette. Those arrogant bastards! They don't know who I am. I'm made of steel and Millie won't go with them anyway, not without me!" Almost ashamed, I then admitted, "I also wanted to write about the journey and my time spent with the French Resistance."

"There, there Sally. We know all about you and what you wanted to do and that is why the men thought of everyone's safety, especially yours. If you were caught by the Gestapo aiding and writing about the Resistance, they would soon find out from you 'oo our members were. It would not be fun, and your Aunt Millie would be questioned too. Come I will give you something for your 'eadache. You need a nice cup of tea."

I was angered at her patronizing assumption that I would give forth information on members of the Resistance. Stroking my back, she said thoughtfully.

"I know you would not give secrets away Sally, not at first, but the torture they use would make anyone talk."

I digested the picture she'd painted, while I sipped on black tea, sweetened with honey. I used the constant sipping to deflect from speaking my mind. I knew it was not Bridgette's fault and she should not bear the brunt of my anger. I then asked her as I'd just remembered.

"Where's Berty?" Bridgette's eyes showed the fear of telling me he'd gone with the men.

"Well, Sally, I don't want you to be upset, but Berty went with them."

I exploded.

"Those fuckin' chauvinistic bastards! This was my mission. How dare they!" Raging, I paced the room. I had to think clearly, control myself, and not let my feminine ego run riot.

"Okay" I said, "I'm going to find my own guides, I have money, somebody will take me. Or else I'll just use my war correspondent's badge."

Bridgette's pleading to calm me fell on deaf ears. I dressed hurriedly and ran from the house. Then I continued toward the village, looking behind every now and then to see if she'd followed. She hadn't, I was alone. Breathless and gasping for air, I slowed up to walk as I went down the hill leading into the main shopping street. Thankfully, the village was quiet and there was no sign of the German soldiers returning to go on one of their raids. I'm sure the supplies we'd seen laden in the back of their jeeps would last at least a week.

The first place one would go to ask for help I thought, should be the tobacconist. They usually know all that is going on within their village and of course they would know who I could rely on as a guide. I opened the framed glass door and slightly jumped at the sudden loud ring of the bell. The Tobacconist would have been about sixty years old. His black beret sat to one side, exposing grey hair and his moustache was stained orange where a cigarette hung from his bottom lip. He was speaking French into a wall phone.

"Yes, yes, I will tell 'er. I think this is 'er now. "He hung up the phone, turned and smiled. "Are you Sally?"

I nodded yes and stepped backwards. I was a little surprised he'd asked. He kept smiling, obviously amused at my nervous disposition.

"It is alright Mademoiselle, I 'ave just spoken to Bridgette. She thought you would be smart enough to come 'ere. She wants you to take some tobacco 'ome and she says she as some good news. So please you must go now." He said this while wrapping the tobacco in newspaper. "You must go 'ome to Bridgette, I know what you want, but I cannot 'elp you Mademoiselle Sally."

I stood frozen with the feeling that perhaps I was being tricked again. I was at their mercy, unless I decided to take on my correspondent status and throw my fate to the wind. Yes, I could look after myself, I didn't need them.

Before I had another thought, tobacco man handed me the parcel, took me by the arm and led me smartly out the shop. He then went inside closing the door. That's it; they're always closing doors on me. Why?

I began walking lethargically up the hill that led to Bridgette's home. I'd honestly thought I could trust her, and she would be a close confidant, but she too seemed to want to block my passage over the Alps. Should I trust what he'd said, or should I turn around and head back to Calais, hitch a ride on a fishing vessel and get back to reporting the war from England?

I was obviously not welcome within the French Resistance. I kept walking and unconsciously headed towards Bridgette's. Finally, somewhat calmer, if not completely down and out, I arrived into her welcoming arms.

"Sally, I 'ave just phoned Alain's mother Suzan, she says to wait for Alain, 'e will take you over the Alps, 'imself. It is good news no?"

My eyes must have looked disbelieving, as my mouth stayed shut while Bridgette defended her statement.

"Yes, yes, it is true Sally! Suzan promises she will send Alain to you, 'e will borrow is friend's car to drive back 'ere. You must wait ma Cherie, 'e will come to you. He loves you." She kissed me on both cheeks. "Come inside. I will cook you a proper breakfast."

Five days and five nights passed and still no Alain. Bridgette tried several times to phone Suzan, his mother, but there was never an answer. Bridgette's face looked lifeless as she hung up the receiver for the tenth time.

"'E must 'ave travelled alone through the night. Nobody would possibly know straight away if 'e's been taken by the German's. We will 'ave to wait for the Underground to receive news, as to what 'as 'appened to 'im and Suzan."

My mind raced with indecisions as to what I should do, or even feel. All I knew was I needed to walk alone in the woods and allow this devastating news to sink in. I needed to speak with God. Allowing my mind to transcend to the ethereal realm had always been easy for me. As a child I'd been brought up on the word of the Lord and found great solace and peace when talking to our invisible creator. I told Bridgette this and she said she understood. She hugged me before I left through the back door that led to the woods.

Sunlight streamed through what was left of the last autumn leaves clinging to the trees. The rays felt warm upon my skin and for a moment I travelled home in my mind. The crunching of dried leaves under my feet took me further back in time. I was a young girl again and Millie, Colleen and I were playing hide and seek in the bush adjoining Granddad's property. The same crunching sound was a giveaway as to which direction we'd run. The secret to not being found was to find a good hiding place quickly and not move your feet at all. It was fun and so the memory put a smile on my face and a kiss on my heart. I wished I was there, and all that had happened since then had been a bad dream. These thoughts sent me reeling into melancholy. Feeling sorry for myself was something both my parents would chastise me for. Maybe this emotion came from being left by my parents so often as a child. Whatever the reason, I did have the habit of falling victim to this self-indulgent mood. I had to force myself back to reality and ask the Lord for guidance.

The giant elms stood stoically around me; separate yet close together. Birds twittered amongst the ground-leaf searching out worms. I noted one Elm stood all alone, allowing it to take full advantage of the sun. The space around it begged me to rest. Under its leafless branches I took up this silent offer and slid my back down the trunk, grateful for the warmth it held. I sat.

Closing my eyes, I drifted into memories of Millie, of all the trials and tribulations my life had held being brought up with such a prima donna young aunt. Without a doubt, she would know what she was getting into, but at the same time, hold the cunning to get out of whatever predicament in which she found herself. I felt this war held the same scenario for her; she'd find her way out. After all, she was probably much safer than I was at the moment.

Was it a need to prove my worth to my parents that I'd become so angry at being left behind by the men? Was I just trying to prove how brave and accomplished I was? If only I could talk to my father just to let him know I tried to go and collect Millie. It seems this country had its fair share of chauvinists who would not allow me to take part in the fight, or were they being chivalrous? Now my darling Alain had gone missing. For some reason, maybe it's when you love someone you seem to know if they're safe, or not, I felt deep down Alain was safe. But where in the hell was he? Why hadn't he come to me?

In my mind I chose to leave the Millie fiasco behind and trust in the French Resistance to do the job. My thoughts then drifted. It truly amazed me how many resistance workers there were in the countries surrounding France. These networks sent out vital messages to each other in order to keep up the never-ending battle against the Nazi's. Realistically, my coming here in the first place was probably my gung-ho ego trying to get two stories in one. I should have waited for the carrier pigeons to relay the truth about Millie and forgot about the inside scoop on the Resistance. This quiet time, with my back against the elm, settled my inner arguments. I would now wait for the return of the men and whatever news they brought with them regarding Millie. However, one question still remained, and it led me to believe she was definitely being held against her will. Why on earth hadn't she written me a letter just to let me know she was safe? Why wouldn't she want her public and her parents to know, if not me, that she was safe and just holding up in a neutral country? I would have to put that question aside until further information came my way.

I had so much going on in my mind and now Alain had wedged himself into my heart. I knew there was nothing I could do, except pray, so I finally made peace with myself. Knowing all I could do was wait, I began walking back to the house. There must be a reason for me being here at this point in time I thought.

Chapter 8

Accepted

As I moved closer to the back of the home, I saw through the kitchen window two German soldiers. One slapped Brigitte's face and she screamed.

"I do not know where 'e is!" The soldier threw her to the ground.

I felt helpless, what should I do? Then I remembered seeing two rifles and a pistol with ammunition in the underground cellar. I could only see two men inside the kitchen and wondered if there were more soldiers waiting at the front of the house. Trying to be invisible, I crept from one tree to the next, until I caught sight of the army jeep parked out the front. The driver sat back, leaning one arm on the door and with his free hand he was smoking a cigarette. I made my way to the underground cellar, carefully checking; watching all the time to make sure they couldn't see me through the window.

The chicken's remained almost silent when I entered their coop – thank God. I carefully lifted the door to the cellar and crept down the five steps, where my fingers danced along the shelf to the left of the entrance. I found the matches and lit the lantern. Breathing a sigh of relief, I picked up the pistol and loaded six bullets. Back home I'd rarely miss a rabbit. Dad called me, 'Dead-Eye-Dolly,' when I'd shoot as many rabbits as he did on our days at Bulkawa, the family property. Holding the loaded pistol firmly in my right hand, I began to climb back up the stairs. With every step taken, after I'd left the safety of the cellar, I assured myself; *you can do this Sally. You can kill the enemy. This is war*.

Brain washed and full of false courage, I stood behind a tree and planned my next move. Before I could act, I realised the loud voices coming from inside the house had ceased. I crept slowly towards the door with my heart pounding and my hand clutched firmly around the gun handle. I reached the kitchen window and stood to the side, leaning my back against the wall. I turned my head, just enough to see through the window. Bridgette was lying on the floor sobbing; the officer standing above her wore an evil self-satisfied grin. I recognized him, he'd been in the convoy that we met on our way here. He was doing up his trousers. Bridgette had obviously been raped. Her dress was torn about, and a bruise had already risen on her cheek bone. However, I felt grateful she was alive. Then I heard him say:

"I will return later Frauline."

He strutted like a rooster to open the front door – the victor. I waited to hear the jeep drive away before I ran inside to where Bridgette lay weeping.

"Oh Bridgette!" Throwing myself on the floor, I held her close and whispered. "I went to the cellar Bridgette I found the pistol; I was going to shoot him, I want to shoot all of those bloody Nazi bastards." I held her limp frame tight, until her sobbing slowed, and I felt her hand caress my back.

"It is all right Sally, this is war, and this is what 'appens in war time. I was unlucky, or maybe I was very lucky, the men were not 'ere and you were not 'ere as well. I knew 'e 'ad been waiting to rape me for a long time. 'E was one of the officers who always came 'ere to raid our pantry. When Pierre was not looking 'e would give me a wink and pat my bottom. I never told Pier. 'E would kill 'im and then we would all die. I knew 'e wanted me, and it would only be a matter of time before 'e found the opportunity. I will be safe as long as 'e does not tire of me." Bridgette sat up and let out a huge sigh before snuggling her pretty head into my shoulder. We stayed this way until finally Bridgette lifted her head and said:

"Let us not think about this anymore Sally. They came looking for Alain. 'E must 'ave gone to his friend's 'ouse to loan the car from 'im, so as to come 'ere quickly to see you. They were 'aving a meeting with some Resistance members at is friend's 'ome that night and there was a tip off. Alain was seen, but 'e escaped. 'E is probably 'iding in the countryside somewhere. It is not safe for you 'ere anymore Sally. We must get you back to England, I will arrange it."

I sat back stunned. All this woman could think of was my safety after she'd just been raped and humiliated. Bridgette's eyes pleaded with me, to let it all go; let it be forgotten. She needed no words; her expression spoke her feelings. And so I told myself once again; here I stand helpless amongst heroes. However, this would not be the end for me. I must do something, anything to help. I tried to explain to her how I felt.

"Bridgette, you must understand what I'm trying to tell you. I feel my life would be worthless unless I'm able contribute in this war. There must be something I can do. I'm sick of just writing about the war. I want to do something to prevent the killing somehow."

Bridgette scrambled to her feet, moaning in pain as she did. I watched her walk stiffly towards the bathroom, she said nothing. This to me was patronizing in itself. I quickly sprang to my feet. Taking giant steps, I caught up to her and took her by the arm.

"Look at me please Bridgette. I need to be validated in this war, I can help. You know I can, please let me stay and be part of it."

She shook her head.

"My beautiful Sally, there are already too many dead 'ero's in this war, please do not be another one. Go 'ome 'ave babies. We will win this war and you will give birth to the children who will enjoy this freedom. Now please let me bathe my wounds." Bridgette gently pushed my arm away, turned and before entering the bathroom, she said:

"You must go to the cellar now Ma Cherie and 'ide until I am ready to talk to you about the plan to get you 'ome. If the Soldiers come back, you will be tortured and killed if they find you 'ere. Your war correspondent badge will not protect you in this 'ouse or this country anymore. They know 'oo Pierre and Alain are now and they may remember you from when you were in the 'orse and cart with Alain." She sighed deeply, "I think that German bastard wants to believe I am an innocent party. I tried 'ard to convince 'im. I said, 'ow do I know what my 'usband does? I don't care where 'e is; I am just 'is slave. Yes, this is what I said Ma Cherie, it is what I 'ad to say for all our sakes."

I left knowing Bridgette was right about everything, especially when she said the soldiers would return. However, I would not wait hiding in the cellar forever and for what? To see the men captured on their return, or for me to be sent forcefully back to England. I refused to wait and discuss my return to England with Bridgette. If I did go back to London it would mean, I'd been defeated on all counts. I would do things my own way, since she'd refused my help. I wrote Bridgette a note and left it tucked under the bathroom door where she was sure to find it.

Dear Bridgette,

You cannot imagine how sorry I am for what has happened
to you. I thought this to be a relatively simple mission, where
I needed only one guide to help me reach Millie. I know
now it was wrong of me to ask for your help with such an
un-important mission compared to what you people do. I
admire and respect each and every one of you, I do not wish
to be a burden and so I will leave and find my own way
home. My only wish is for any news of Millie or Alain, to
be sent to me at the Times Newspaper in London. I pray for
your safety, as I know you will for me. I have borrowed a

*scarf and a coat, one day when this war is over, I will return
them to you.*

Yours sincerely and forever, a grateful S.D.

Not really knowing which way to turn once I'd left Bridgette's home, I placed trust in my instincts that led me back to the village. I took to the path through the woods which ran parallel to the road. I was certain if anyone could help me with a guide over the Alps, it would be the tobacco man. All the feelings and experiences I'd suffered over this past week had changed me dramatically. Feeling totally confused and alone, I walked briskly. Luckily the road was quiet. I saw only one elderly couple walking arm in arm, their shopping trolley dragging behind. They stopped to take a breath, the old man's eyes then creased as his smile gazed lovingly at his wife. His lips puckered and placed a kiss on her cheek. They could not see me, but I felt empowered by the love they shared, despite the chaos that was taking place all around them. I watched and waited behind an elm tree until they were out of sight. I thought of what my mother would have said.

"While goodness and love outweigh evil on earth, we will survive."

The tobacco man's back door faced the woods, so I tried to make my entrance from there. Unfortunately, it was locked. I stayed close to the wall, walking sideways until I came to the front of the shop. The coast looked clear, so I quickly went inside.

Tobacco man almost laughed.

"Not you again!" he said, "Ow can I 'elp you today Sally? More tobacco for Bridgette?"

My throat went dry and I stammered, I couldn't speak. I was trying to tell him what had just happened to Bridgette. However, I began agonizing over who I could or couldn't trust. I really hadn't discussed his loyalty with Bridgette, although she'd telephoned him and told him about me, so he must be trustworthy, if not sympathetic.

His large frame seemed a blur through my tears, as he walked to me, gently placing his arm around my shoulders. He then gazed through the window to the empty street before I was ushered out to the back room.

"Tell me what as 'append."

Once again, my words faltered. "Please, find ... find me a guide over the Alps."

"No, no. It is more than that on your mind. Tell me, is Bridgette all right?"

I had to trust him. Tears trickled down my cheeks and my breath shortened. Within a moment I'd managed to control myself. I explained what had happened. He sat heavily in his chair, slumped and pulled his beret off to scratch his head. Looking up at me with empathy he asked.

"Is she going to be all right?"

"Bridget is brave; she will be fine. But she said this is why I could not possibly stay in France. I would bring more danger to them."

He shook his head, I assumed in agreement with her statement. I jumped in quickly:

"But what is far more important to me, is to pre-warn the men, Pierre, Phillip and Berty. They'll come home to a trap. We must get word to them!" I then went on to fill him in about Alain. How he was missing and had hopefully escaped capture by the Germans. How he must be in hiding somewhere. "Do you understand? That's why the Germans came here looking for him at his Uncle Pierre's home. I'm passionate about helping the Resistance. Please, I need to help in any way I can. I want to stay here and fight with you."

He stood and shook my hand.

"My name is Jon; I am the father of Jon-Paul the Ambulance driver. I will 'elp you get back to England as soon as I can. But first we must get word to Pierre about the trap. Jon-Paul will be 'ome tonight. It is too risky to try sooner to get word to 'im. Phones may be tapped. They will be on the lookout for anything suspicious."

I was shocked. He didn't seem to comprehend what I'd just said, so I repeated my plea again, along with the information about me being a war correspondent.

"Yes, yes, I know." He spoke impatiently, "but it will be much safer for you to return to England."

The frustration, the forever feeling I had to be nurtured, preserved, or patronized was infuriating. My Aussie brashness couldn't be contained.

"NOW YOU LOOK HERE MATE, I've just about had enough of this. I've been ignored, left behind, told exactly what to do and when to do it ever since I set foot on French soil. NO MORE! Do you hear me? I'll give you only one option now. I'm staying here to help you in the resistance fight. And you may not know this, but there is a French man out there somewhere, whom I happen to love. His name is Alain Laurent! I would like very much to find him. I've witnessed the sickening mass murder of innocent women and children by these Nazis in Auschwitz. I have a deep need to act in this war, to be useful. I will not be sent back to England, not yet!" My foot stamped in time with my last words. I hadn't done that since I was a child and it was only once, when

Mum grounded me from going with Dad on an overnight cattle muster. This foot stomp I think tickled Jon as he smiled knowingly.

"You know Ma Cherie, I would 'ave loved to 'ave 'ad a daughter, but unfortunately my wife died giving birth to Jon-Paul." I felt his tears moist upon my cheeks as he kissed me.

"Now I can see 'ow I would 'ave liked 'er to grow up, just like you."

Chapter 9

Reunited

In war time, or any extreme circumstances where the pressure is on, I think we perform at our best. With help from my new friend Tobacco-Jon, T-Jon as I then referred to him, I dyed my hair black and cut it into a bob style. I looked hard into the mirror, trying to see a resemblance to my beautiful friend, Julia Nior. There was none. T-Jon fossicked around and found a pair of thick framed spectacles. Thankfully the power wasn't too strong and only hindered my vision and movements slightly. They did the trick, I now looked goonish and awkward

"Not a good look." I said, turning to him with a stupid expression on my face.

It had been only minutes after convincing T-Jon that I wanted to join the Résistance that he began searching for hair dye, scissors and the spectacles. I noticed his sadness as he caressed his wife's old clothes before he handed me her plain grey dress and a dark brown cardigan. Her clothes fitted me perfectly, including her nurse's uniform which might come in handy. Luckily, they hadn't changed that style at the hospital since T-Jon's wife had died. After my transformation, I appeared a very unattractive woman.

False passports were a thriving trade in the war. It was not difficult to have my photo taken, looking nothing like the real me. My new passport had been completed by evening and cost five hundred franks – cheap I thought. Later T-Jon and I walked to the local café where we shared a bottle of red wine and vegetable soup served with crusty bread – delicious. A romantic song played in the background, putting me in a mood where I wished for all things to return to normal. No more war, only romance.

Cigarette smoke veiled the couples who seemed as if they were also in the mood for where the music was leading them. After waking from my short daydream, I returned to my uncertain reality. I had a more secure even happier feeling now I was accepted into the French Resistance by T- Jon at least. A strong purpose for life had suddenly filled me. Not wanting to interrogate T-Jon, but at the same time needing to know what he'd done about sending a warning to the men, I worried then began to ask. He placed a finger to his lips. There'd been a time when he'd left me earlier that evening and I could only hope it was to contact his comrades. T-Jon placed his cigarette stained fingers over mine. He looked me full in the face.

"One thing you must learn, Louise (this was my new name, Louise DuPont), we never talk of such things in public."

I laughed far too loudly after feeling all eyes were staring at me. I hoped my laughter suggesting sexual innuendo, had disguised any suspicions from the couple sitting directly behind who may have heard me. You never knew who was your friend or your enemy in a public place.

T-Jon's reason for taking me to this charming café was to see if I would pass the test of being a fair dinkum French woman. Of course, we only spoke French and when he first introduced me to Eugene, the owner of the restaurant, I was Louise Du Pont, a daughter of a male friend of T-Jon's, who lived in Paris.

I was assured from Eugene's response, I'd passed the test. With my French accent close to perfect, it also helped that I could remember an address in Paris where I told him we lived. 37 Ave Cardinal-Lemonier-Paris. I knew Paris well, so any question about my fabricated father, Franck Du Pont, or places around Paris came easily to me. Eugene's reaction was warm and friendly, if somewhat sympathetic because of my looks. The old-fashioned clothes, black, heavy-rimmed spectacles and a very bad haircut, made me unrecognizable from the Sally Darcy of the previous night.

We left the restaurant and walked into the chill of the night. Peace and darkness blanketed me from my concerns about Alain. It was always this way with me, the cover of night held no fear. Instead, it gave me happiness to think that no matter what had happened, the sun would always rise in the morning. I remember Mother Matilda telling me when I was a child, 'night time is when the Lord works his miracles so that all things will be put right by the light of day.' What a wonderful thought for a child to sleep on.

However, before sleep, I needed to find out how Bridgette was and whether her German rapist had returned to take his pleasure once more. T-Jon was not keen to go anywhere near her house at this point and assured me Bridgette would always play her cards right. She would put up with what she had to, for the sake of her country and fellow countryman. I had to agree, for I had been a witness to this. Notwithstanding, I pleaded and begged him to let me go alone. I would go through the woods to her home, while he went to meet with his comrades and inquire if there had been further news about the men. I would then meet him at his shop an hour later.

"I promise to be careful. I won't do anything to cause trouble, no matter what I see or hear, I promise."

Reluctantly he wished me farewell, with a warning to stay invisible and to return to him in one hour as promised.

With my courage up, due I'm sure to being accepted as a member of the Resistance, I forged through the woods, taking the same path I had walked earlier in the day.

A full moon gave light enough to see through the shadows of the trees. For the first time in this war, I felt I belonged. I wasn't the poor little kid looking in the toy shop window. I owned the toy; it was all mine. My plan was to first look into the house to see that the coast was clear. I didn't want to frighten Bridgette with my new look, so if all was well, I would call out to her and enter through the back door. I was anxious to know if she would recognize me and whether she would also accept me as one of them.

Nervous but not frightened, I approached the back of the house. The kitchen light was off, so I crept close. Suddenly a light shone through Bridgette's bedroom window, located next to the kitchen. When close to the window, and in no danger of being seen, I heard Bridgette say:

"Are you sure you did not tell anyone you were coming 'ere Sherman. I do not want anyone to know just 'ow much I want to be alone with you. 'Ow I long for you."

His voice sounded confident. "No of course not my love, I knew you wanted to be alone with me from the very beginning."

"Oh Sherman, I 'ave to show you 'ow much you mean to me. You know if the young lieutenant was not 'ere this morning, I would not 'ave fought you. I would 'ave gladly given myself to you. This is what drives me insane, your power over me."

What she'd just confessed to this Nazi, outraged and sickened me. My hand automatically went to my mouth preventing a loud gasp.

Sherman was none other than the German officer who'd raped her. I thought this can't be true, she doesn't want him. How could she? Moments seemed to turn into eternity. My pulse raced, and I was sure my heartbeat could be heard for miles. I dared not look, especially when I heard him moan. No, she can't be doing this, she just couldn't be. Please Bridgette stop, my mind screamed. My stomach convulsed with the thought of them entwined. Bridgette had certainly fooled me. Who could I trust in this country?

These thoughts were jolted back to reality by a loud thud. Something solid had fallen heavily in the bedroom. A second later, the sound of breaking glass hitting the wooden floor, shattered the silence. I dared a look through the window. Sherman was lying motionless on the floor with a dagger in his heart. Blood oozed from the wound. His eyes were glazed with an expression of shock and horror. Thin slits, passing for his mouth opened and a gurgling sound broke the quiet. His head suddenly flopped to one side and blood trickled from his gaping mouth.

I stood frozen, watching Bridgette. Her hands clutched at her heart. It took her time to realise she had actually killed him. With a sudden turn of her body she looked towards the window. I pulled back realising if she saw me, she may not recognize me. It would be a major shock to think a stranger had witnessed the killing.

"Bridgette, Bridgette it's me Sally."

Would she recognize my voice?

Before I could manage another sound, a large hand went over my mouth. My heart sank, I twisted my head violently to see who it was. Alain's smile held back his laughter. I'd forgotten the way I looked. He kissed me passionately before he said:

"I had to make sure it was really you Sally but now I know. No one in the world kisses like you."

Why was I so deliriously happy? After all, we were caught in a very serious situation here. Bridget had finally given that bastard what he truly deserved and now Alain was safe in my arms. Of course, I was happy.

Alain had just missed seeing me that afternoon when I'd left Bridgette's home. But Bridgette assured him she knew where I would go. Later it was confirmed to them by another confidant within the village that Bridgette had been correct. I was still with T-Jon - I hadn't left.

Alain explained their plan once we were inside the house. Sherman's murder had been organized by Bridgette and Alain. The lure of love and easy seduction had led Sherman to his death. The thought of Bridgette longing for him, fed his ego to the extreme. His dreams of the beautiful alluring Bridgette, whom he'd lusted after from the moment he'd laid eyes on her, had finally come true. Bridgette had confessed to Sherman on the telephone she would be all his, now and forever. She had begged him for more of what she wanted – total dominance. Although, it was Alain who was supposed to take Sherman by surprise and kill him while he and Bridgette were in a compromising position, obviously Bridgette harboured enough hate and revenge to do it first.

Now the three of us were bound together. Quickly we wrapped

Sherman's body in a tarp, cleaned up the evidence and then carried him outside and into the back of his army jeep. A deep ravine, some two hour's drive from the village was where Alain planned to push Sherman's jeep and body. The ravine was also not too far from a cave where the Resistance members met.

It was decided that Alain and Bridgette would stay in the cave and I would return to T-Jon and tell him what had happened. Then I'd stay with him for the night and meet Alain and Bridgette at the cave the following night. T-Jon of course would have to take me there.

The three men, Berty, Phillip and Pierre had been warned not to return to Bridgette's home. Our little group would meet them near Camon in the French Alps, then together we'd climb our way into Switzerland.

This stream of surreal events had happened so quickly, my mind had trouble consolidating what had taken place this day, let alone that evening. I felt right in the thick of the action and prayed I'd be able to help in the way I'd promised. Maybe it was nerves, maybe it was sub-hysteria, but before leaving Alain and Bridgette to return to T-Jon, I began laughing. Holding Bridgette close to my chest, I confessed between laughs:

"You certainly fooled me Bridgette; you should win an Academy Award for your performance tonight. It was truly amazing. I only wish I'd seen you plunge the knife into that mongrel. You know I thought he was moaning from pleasure. I felt sick to the stomach with that thought. Thank God you killed him."

With my words, Bridgette broke down. She sobbed hard into my shoulder. Oh my God, how bloody stupid of me. This poor woman had probably never contemplated killing anyone before; whether he was our enemy or not, she'd taken someone else's life. This beautiful kind woman in a moment of pent up hatred, had actually stuck a knife in him and stood to watch him die. I felt the horror of her mind begging her gentle heart for forgiveness.

Alain hugged us both, whispering, "I'm sorry ladies, but we must leave. Bridgette you will be alright. Our plan went a little 'aywire, I should 'ave killed 'im. It does not matter now 'e is dead and that is 'ow it should be. You are a strong woman Bridgette; 'e was your rapist – our enemy. Please do not feel guilty. Now let us go, please."

Chapter 10

In Up to My Neck

I watched until Alain and Bridgette drove out of sight, I then made my way back to T-Jon's shop. The back door was left unlocked and the light on. I called.

"T-Jon."

"Is that you Louise?"

I hesitated for a moment.

"Yes." The name Louise was still new to me, as were my looks. The thought suddenly struck me; my darling Alain had taken no notice of how unattractive I looked. His feelings for me were obviously much deeper than my appearance. It put a smile on my face. To be loved by a man, perhaps unconditionally, was a rare comfort in life.

T-Jon and I discussed the drama which had just unfolded and how imperative it was to go as soon as possible. Even though Alain had said we should meet them tomorrow night at the cave. T-Jon was of a mind to go right now.

"It would be safer for me to take you now Louise, before the Germans come sniffing around tomorrow."

I had to agree, plus I longed to be in Alain's arms as soon as possible. His kiss had fuelled my love for him. No man had ever kissed me the way Alain did. He made me feel I was the most desired woman on earth.

The grandfather clock on the wall struck midnight.

"The magical hour," I said once the chimes had finished.

T-Jon held me at arm's length and looked directly into my eyes.

"I know you love Alain very much and I 'ope it is not the only reason you 'ave put yourself in great danger, Louise?"

I laughed and said in English with a French accent.

"Ah you 'ave read the story of Cinderella."

The wrinkles around his eyes creased with mirth.

"Of course I 'ave and I believe in fairy tales, so let us go Sally, I mean

Louise. I 'ave our pumpkin carriage waiting in the shed."

French Citizens were rarely allowed to keep their cars during the German occupation. If T-Jon's car had been found, it would have been confiscated immediately. He opened the double doors of the stone garage to show that the entire inside was filled with cardboard boxes, old furniture and rubbish of all descriptions.

"Where's the car?"

T-Jon wasted no time in removing the camouflage.

'It is well 'idden under this enormous pile of shit."

"Jesus," I said, "It may not even start!"

He smiled cockily.

"Of course it will Ma Cherie, it's a Mercedes Benz!"

"You traitor," I quipped before helping him to retrieve the glorious machine from under its cover.

I breathed in the special smell of expensive leather, turned in my seat and smiled at T-Jon as we drove peacefully out of the village. I should have been extremely tired after such an eventful day, but my senses were invigorated. I became aware of the stars surrounding the moon.

When I was a little girl, I believed the moon was actually following me because when we stopped, it would stop too. So in my child's mind, the moon belonged to me. After a long interval of silence, T-Jon asked.

"What is going through your mind my child? Are you regretting being a part of the Resistance already?"

"NO." I flew at him, "I've been counting the stars and remembering when I was a little girl. I thought the moon belonged to me then because it always followed. I wanted to lasso and own it, like a balloon on a string."

"Ah yes, this is what we are fighting for, our next generation, so they too can lasso the moon." He placed his large hand gently on my arm. "Try and sleep Sally, we 'ave a long way to go. It should take another two hours or so. 'Ave a nap while you can."

I tried to rest, but the bumps and pot holes of the goat tracks we seemed to be driving on, gave me no peace. My watch told me we had been on the road for nearly three hours, when T-Jon began to slow the car. He was straining to see out of the window.

"I always 'ave trouble finding the right track to drive down at this point. From somewhere near here we 'ave to get out and walk. Yes, yes, 'ere we are. This is it!"

We pulled up; God knows where. The woods and undergrowth were extremely dense and wet. I'd packed my canvas back-pack with personal items, including the floral dress which Suzan gave me. I used the back pack in front of my body to push my way through the scrub.

T-Jon walked alongside me for a while and then took the lead when we came into a clearing. A wide rock ledge shimmered silver under the moonlight. He picked up a rock and threw it over the ledge, then whistled loudly. The tune seemed contrived. A warning to tell them who it was I guessed. Within moments, Alain appeared holding a lantern. His welcome smile warmed my heart. I adored him. He scampered up from the landing under the ledge and handed T-Jon the lantern. He then kissed me like there was no tomorrow. (If I close my eyes now, I can still feel that kiss.)

We followed Alain inside the well-hidden cave. It was amazingly civilized. Contained within was everything we'd need to survive for months. It was deep and wide enough to house fifty people, a rare find indeed. I hadn't been to this part of France before and I asked impulsively.

"How far are we from the Alps?"

"Not too far", one of the men inside the cave replied.

I was then introduced to the other Resistance members. Martial was the first; he was very young, probably about eighteen years old. And then Oliver, another young man who looked like a boxer in that I mean a crooked nose, scar on his left cheek bone. I later found out he was and a very good one. Then Timothy; he was Martials father, they looked identical. Black wavy hair, olive skin and beautiful brown eyes with long thick eye lashes that most women would die for. The other two men were much older; I'd say in their mid-seventies. They were introduced as the twins who owned the two hundred acres around the cave. Paul and Peter were their names. They'd never been married and at first, they seemed put-out with me being there. I say this because they hadn't raised their heads to look at me when we were introduced. However, when we sat as a group to catch up on news the twin brothers boiled the billy and made us all a cup of tea. They offered the tea and biscuits to Bridgette and me first. They gave it along with their shy toothless smiles and a nod of the head when we accepted their simple offerings. I loved them from that moment onwards.

T-Jon drank a large mug of strong black coffee and headed back to Saint Quenton. Alain escorted him back to his car in case he became lost. He needed to reach the village before daylight in order to hide his car in the garage under the garbage. It would take time on his own to set up all that rubbish again. We heard from him the next day over the radio.

"I am 'ome safe and so is my son Jon-Paul."

Jon-Paul was part of a sub-cell of men in the underground movement who'd been waiting for the past two days for another large group of fighters to join them. They would bring many types of guns and hand grenades with them when they joined us. The ammunition supplies had been strategically dropped by the American allies. The word had been passed to us that a large garrison of Germans were to enter the French Alps in two days' time. The German's mission was to hunt out and capture the French Resistance members who were aiding and abetting the Jewish families hidden amongst the Alps. These French Resistance men would join forces with other groups amongst the foothills. Alain told me they expected nearly a thousand members to be ready and waiting. Hopefully this would drive back the major onslaught from the Germans. I voiced my enthusiasm to be part of the mission.

"I can shoot the eye out of a needle and I was a champion discus thrower at school. I'm sure my aim with a hand grenade would be just as accurate." I felt a little annoyed and uncomfortable with the looks the men threw at me when I said this.

Just as I was about to have another go at convincing them, Bridgette's arm went around my shoulder and she looked at the men coldly.

"Two more 'ands would be of 'elp. I 'ave already stabbed a German to death, I can kill again, and I am also a good shot. 'Ooh do you think shoots the rabbits that we eat for dinner?" The men's expressions lightened, and they laughed. Despite their initial reluctance, they then accepted Bridgette and me into the fold.

The next evening, we heard rocks being thrown on top of the cave ledge and then the familiar whistle. By now I knew the signal well. Every time somebody left the cave the same tune had to be given upon their return.

Twenty men and one woman then filed into the cave after the sound was heard. They'd brought with them food supplies, ammunition and guns of all descriptions, including many Germans pistols. When I picked up a pistol and examined it, visions of Dad holding my hand while I fired at a line of tin cans flooded my mind. After that introduction to Dad's gun, I became a good shot. As usual, I loved to show off to all who'd take notice, especially when shooting rabbits. Now this similar pistol was for killing the enemy. I shuddered. The memory and the new realty were at odds in my head.

The plan was to travel to the Alps early the next morning. The twin brothers owned a large cattle truck and because they slaughtered and donated their well-bred cattle to the German army, the truck was used regularly and known to the army patrols. This way the truck received special clearance to wherever it was headed. As we were loading up in the morning, the brothers explained.

"Giving the Germans our cattle is a small price to pay for the real work we get done. We are truly fortunate to be able to 'elp."

The guns were loaded first and then us. We lay under piles of hay and straw in the back of the truck. The brothers had definitely played their cards right in this war. They were never under any suspicion of wrong doing – thank God.

This new troop of freedom fighters, including one woman named Sandra, had joined us during the night. They would help build the defences against the German patrols once we reached our destination. Alain, Bridgette and I, after the fighting was done, would continue on to a chalet which sat directly on the border of the French-Swiss Alps. This was the destination where we'd made plans for Pierre, Phillip and Berty to meet us.

The straw which had completely covered us in the back of the truck (with plenty to spare), seemed to work its way into every clothing seam, body crevice and nostril. Thankfully, none of us suffered with hay fever. After travelling for some time, I felt the truck slow down to a snail's pace, and then heard a German voice ask in mispronounced French:

"Where are your papers and where are you going?"

Peter answered. "We are going to a friend's place. 'E is in need of 'ay for the oncoming winter."

There was a pause, obviously Peter had handed the German his road pass, or his papers and then Paul added.

"Our friend 'oo is in need of the 'ay gives his fattest cattle to the German army kitchen I might add."

"Continue", I heard the German say. We then moved on quickly. Collectively we breathed a sigh of relief and hay dust along with it.

With apprehension, I began thinking about what we were doing to aid the victims of this war. I'd known since the beginning that Switzerland could only give refuge to so many undesirables, according to the Third Reich. The rest, unless they were rescued by sympathizers and transported out of the country by ship, cars or other means, or hidden in the Alps, would surely meet extermination. Whether their lives were prolonged in work camps, or quickly taken by gassing; death was assured. The gas method I would have chosen without a second thought, if choice was in the offering. Discriminately, they were selected to undergo inhumane medical experiments, or worked and starved until they literally fell down dead and were thrown into mass graves. This horror fuelled my hatred against the Germans like nothing else ever would. I knew this to be a different war, different from any other in human history because it was the demonic power of one who stood against the free world as we knew it. Of course, Hitler had his backers, and some had become as mad as he, but it was he who had sown the seed that was appealing to the dark side of human nature. His converts may never have entertained such evil had they not been coerced or convinced. Puppets or not, they were obeying or dying.

While travelling the many miles hidden in the back of the truck, I remained mindful of why we were fighting. I was about to make my contribution in a small way to the down fall of this maniac and hopefully survive to write about it.

Chapter 11

My First Fight

By the time we'd finished our long bone shaking journey, my body felt like I'd been fighting ten rounds with Oliver the young boxer. The truck pulled up amongst a pine forest bathed in clean fresh air. I blew my nose which cleared the straw dust. I then breathed in that most delightful fragrance.

The Alps stood majestic above us; snow-capped and awe inspiring. How wonderful it would be if I were here on holiday with my family, rather than lugging guns and a back pack almost as heavy as me and then be ready and willing to kill another human being in the name of freedom.

We moved quickly behind our leader Henry. He was a short, thick-set man with dark hair greying at the temples. I'd spoken at length with him in the cave during the past night and his accent intrigued me.

"Are you French or English?" I asked.

This began a long conversation about his parents. His mother was English-Australian and his father, French-Spanish. He had a wonderful happy-go-lucky personality which was attuned to my Aussie sense of humour. Henry had travelled to Australia six years earlier to visit his grandfather who lived in Adelaide. I delighted to hear that his grandfather had served in the Light horse, under my dad's command. This to me was a rare gift, to be able to talk to somebody about my dad, especially after Henry told me his grandfather had given him his own story about the Light Horse. Within his story he sang the praises of a young Lieutenant-Major, Darcy. Henry's grandfather had been the oldest member of the Light Horse, apart from the officers. Henry's plan was to initially stay only one month in Australia, but he stayed for six after his grandfather became ill and then passed away. He spoke of mutual places and even acquaintances we both knew. I for one, was pleased to be led by Henry in the upcoming fight. He had a good soul and an ingenious mind. It didn't surprise me when I learned he was an Engineer.

Henry moved us without hesitation to a high vantage point and we soon settled amongst the rocks and bushes before setting up our radio. Our timing had been perfect. It was confirmed; the German troops would begin arriving the following morning. Our scouts were then sent out to count numbers of our members who'd settled into hiding in nearby terrain. There were many other Resistance soldiers strategically scattered and positioned where the refugees were waiting. They'd dug in much earlier, closer to where the Americans had dropped our provisions. We loved the Yanks for they were a saving grace for the French Resistance and the Jewish families in hiding.

Our small group was to be one of the forward attack cells along this mountainous line of defence. If we were killed, the chain of Resistance volunteers would continue to move into the breach until the last man or woman stood. Our aim was to become snipers, picking off the Germans as you would in a duck shoot, until we were overrun or escaped. Henry was in charge of the machine gun, which would hopefully kill off the first wave of pursuers and then scatter the rest into cover. Sooner or later they would have to raise their heads, hopefully to have them removed by our elite shooters, possibly even me.

During that first night, before our battle began, I was grateful to have Alain's warmth on one side and a sleeping Bridgette on the other. We'd snuggled together against a rock ledge sharing a thick woollen blanket, (the one I had insisted on putting in my back pack). While drifting off to sleep in Alain's arms, I thought of being on an overnight muster with Dad, singing songs around the camp fire until my eyelids flickered like the flames and sleep lulled me into dreamland.

It was just before dawn, when I woke to the vibrations and then sound of army trucks rumbling on their approach. Within a few minutes, our night watchman alerted us on his radio.

"The Germans are 'er."

My instincts it seemed had clicked in moments before his watchful eye had warned us. Sometimes Dad would say, 'Sally, you have better hearing than my cattle dog'. I never told him, that I'd learnt to truly listen from our Aboriginal stockman, Mulga. I could place my ear to the ground and tell how far away the cattle were and in what direction they were heading.

"The white fella doesn't listen. 'He can't see the bush even when he travelling through it." Mulga had said. He'd then laugh; his white teeth contrasting against his black skin. At first, I didn't understand what he meant. But he soon had me remembering the number of goannas and kangaroos I'd seen when we took a short walk-about, plus how to tell a cow was in calf before anyone else knew. Mulga taught me so many important lessons; not only how to make things easy when working and living off the land but how to survive if I was ever lost. His advice about following my instincts had become an invaluable tool for my survival on many occasions.

For instance, one night during the London bombings when I was on my way to visit a friend, I had a feeling or premonition, that her building would be bombed. I ran to the nearest phone box.

"Get out of the building and tell all the people there to do the same. Go to the underground railway shelter now. Please do what I say! You're going to be bombed!"

It was one hour later when the air raid began that her block of units was completely crushed. There was talk then that I may be a spy, otherwise how did I know. It took some time to convince them I'd simply learned to follow my instincts. It was the same when I stood on top of our unit in London to witness the first bombings. I knew I would survive. But
would I survive this Resistance stand now?

We had suspected that our position was the main point of entry for the German's to begin their search across the Alps, so we'd gathered the main forces to this point to help us hold this position.

A familiar voice came over the radio to alert us.

"Stand your ground until you see the whites of their eyes, then let them have it."

I found that familiar cowboy and Indian remark amusing and started to giggle. Alain gave me a stern glance, as if to say, this is not funny Sally. It seemed to others that I laughed in all the wrong places. And bugger me, if I didn't need to pee right then. I stood to go behind another rock to do a wee when Alain grabbed my arm, thinking I was offended by his angry look.

"Let me go Alain, I need to pee."

Bridgette placed her hand over her mouth to stop herself from laughing.

"Stay down," he whispered.

"I will," I whispered back.

I knew it would take the Germans sometime to be ready to climb and reach us, so I'd take my only chance to wee while I could. The expression on my darling Alain's face as he let my arm go, even though angry, showed just how handsome he was.

When I settled back down beside him, we were ready. With guns in our hands and across our knees we watched formations of German soldiers encroach upon the foot hills. The way they'd spread out when commencing their climb, made it easy for Henry to annihilate the first wave with his machine gun. We noticed that many who'd missed being killed by that first spray of bullets, were soon shot down by other marksmen in our group. I think I was responsible for killing at least five. I didn't have time to count or feel anything before we were given orders to move further up the mountain. After the first surprise attack, the forward soldiers in the German group retreated quickly down the mountain. They took cover behind their trucks and probably called for backup. This gave us time to re- trench and be ready for the next wave of their attack. We threw ourselves behind an enormous boulder some two hundred metres up from where we'd come out of our shallow trench and quickly dug in.

I don't know if it was nerves, or adrenalin, but while re- loading our shot guns and pistols, the three of us smiled, then kissed each other. Alain remarked once we were settled
and ready again.

" Well done ladies, I am so proud of you."

Bridgette, now a real warrior said: "And we're proud of you too Alain, aren't we Sally? Oops, Louise."

Alain noticed the blonde roots showing on my scalp. He immediately pulled my beret' down over my hair, securing it above my eyes giving me a rakish look.

"I think we should call 'er Sally-Louise, with this kind of appearance," he said as he winked.

We had short moments of comedy like this to release the stress. It was needed in this life or death situation. It reminded me of Colleen and how she survived the nursing game with her wry sense of humour.

The sniper shooting continued throughout the day. The enemy's bullets constantly peppered us, along with hand grenades thrown at random, two of which landed close to our bay. They needed to be smothered or thrown back at the enemy. Dad had told me how he'd experienced grenade bombardment in the trenches at Anzac Cove, in the First World War. Select soldiers were chosen, to be in charge of smothering, or throwing back, the hand grenades. The smothering was done with hessian sacks, filled with mud or sand. This of course didn't prevent the charge from exploding but it lessened the fall-out damage. Alain was extremely angry with me when I picked up a close grenade and hurled it back. He made me promise never to do that again.

I laughed. "And If I don't do that again, you won't have the chance to be angry with me – ever!"

Alain just shrugged his shoulders in defeat and smiled.

Henry's machine gun needed a continuous supply of water to cool it down.

By mid-afternoon he'd run out, so he sent young Marshall to the nearest cell for more. While making a quick dash to bring the canvas water bags, Marshall was shot in the leg. I volunteered to replace him, but Alain insisted I was a better shooter than a water carrier: I needed to stay where I was. Maybe he was right. I'm sure I shot and killed two of Alain's would be assailants, when he took over and kept dashing back and forward keeping Henry supplied with water.

As twilight began merging into night, a cease fire became mutual, or so it seemed. We then concluded we may have had a small victory over the German assault in this section of the French Alps, if only for a day. The radio informed us, while it sang our praises just a little, that we'd only lost five men and could easily withstand a stronger attack. After listening to reports sent out from the various resistance groups, I remarked:

"I hope the French don't get too cocky and think this fight may be over."

"It is far from over Ma Cherie, I only 'ope we don't 'ave to fight 'ere for the rest of our lives," Alain said.

The way Alain looked at me when he'd said those words, gave me reason to prod Bridgette with my elbow. She was savvy and began to rise.

"I am going to talk to 'Enry. I like 'Enry, 'e is part Aussie and I like Ausies." She winked at Alain, then continued, "I think it must run in the family, 'eh?"

I told myself, I must stop wishing for things I could not have, like making love to Alain right now. My eyes must have given my thoughts away, because he asked:

"Are you thinking what I am thinking Ma Cherie?" I laughed a little, raised one eyebrow and said:

"I'm sure I am."

With Alain's soft lips on mine I ached with the knowing that this would have to do for the time being. I could not possibly make love while I was dirty, out in the open and with still enough light for the others to see us. With his lips resting on my neck, he whispered.

"I will wait Sally. I would wait for eternity for your love. This is not the right time or place. I just want you to know 'ow much I adore you. We 'ave the rest of our lives to make love."

His last sentence sent a shiver up my spine. How close were we to the end of our lives now? Closer than most at this point in time, I suspected. Soon it would be dark, and I had our blanket to cover us, but right now I needed his love more than life itself. We could be dead tomorrow.

"Alain."

"Yes ma Cherie?"

"I'm going to get some water to have a wash. I'll be back in a moment."

"Be careful Sally, I will keep an eye out for you."

I'd safely reached Henry's hiding place where Bridgette was being entertained and of course there was a plentiful supply of water. As I crouched down to join them, something caught my eye. A glancing shimmer of light bounced off what looked like a metal helmet. I froze then I ducked down throwing my body at Henry and Bridgette, knocking them flat.

"Shoosh, I saw something. It looked like a German helmet. Hurry! Give me a hand grenade Henry."

Quickly, Henry handed me the grenade and I pulled the pin. I think I killed at least a few Germans, as many let out screams of pain. It gave us enough time to man our positions once more.

Before this dusk uproar, we'd settled down in the late afternoon making four close, but separate groups of fighters. Other groups spread themselves along many ridges. The Germans, we knew then, had obviously planned a surprise attack by picking off the front markers during the night – us.

I scrambled back to Alain.

"No rest for the wicked my love," I said before I lunged behind our rock and kissed him on the cheek.

"What 'appened?"

"They're out there Alain. Just as well I went to see Bridgette when I did, or I would have missed seeing that German creeping up on Henry."

Alain shook his head.

"So it was you Sally who threw the grenade, was it not?"

"What did you want me to do Alain, put my hands up and surrender?"

He laughed, "Only to me Cherie, only to me."

Chapter 12

A Safe Haven

Our small, but nonetheless important battle, ended in just over two weeks. It had ended as suddenly as it had begun. Whether those particular German soldiers were ordered to leave and fight more important battles somewhere else, we never found out. We only knew they were never given any substantial back-up from their superiors.

Bridgette and I had proved ourselves to be fine combat women. In those two intense weeks, we'd earned the respect of our fellow Resistance fighters. We probably killed as many of the enemy and took as many risks as the men. I could go on to complain about, how cold, hungry and exhausted I was during that time, but it would fall far short of the stories we'd heard from the allied trench soldiers. Sometimes they were up to their knees in mud, unable to sleep, wet to the bone and living off bully beef for months at a time. At least we were high and dry most of the time. We did experience some rain, but it came during the day and by nightfall we were dry again. At the end of those two weeks, Bridgette, Alain and I wished our comrades farewell, as most of those men would stay for a while longer, just to be sure they'd secured our precious ground. We shared many hugs and sincere words before continuing on our long climb into Switzerland.

Two days later, after our hardest climb, we stood at a focal point in the Alps, with Bridgette and I wrapped in Alain's arms. There we took time to admire the snow-capped Mont Blanc Massif, which lay ahead. We could feel the winter chill beginning its unrelenting journey down from the snowy summit. Autumn was coming to an end, there was no mistaking that.

"Not a good time to be climbing around the Alps Sally-Louise. Winter will soon be hampering us or killing us."

Having said that, Alain led on. The three of us trudged along with our heavy back packs and began our climb over Col de Balme. This would eventually take us just over the border into Switzerland.

I could have whined a hundred times that day, as we walked, climbed, slid and fell; but I didn't. My feet were completely numb with the cold, actually, all my extremities were. I was a filthy tired wayfarer, looking for a hot bath, hot food and a soft bed. Five hours into our climb, I just had to rest, or I would have passed out. Alain saw my exhaustion and wanted to grant me longer, but he urged me on gently.

"I am so sorry my love, but we need to reach my friends chalet today, before night fall."

Of course, I obeyed him and tried taking my mind off my own worries by admiring our spectacular surroundings. Whenever Alain or Bridgette brought my attention to an out- of-this-world view, I cried and laughed at the same time. I just could not explain the feeling of being in some place so outstandingly beautiful and then having to rush through it to save my life. It seemed ridiculous. There was also the soothing thought, that if we were found and killed by Germans and this was the last place on earth I viewed before I went to heaven, then I was sure heaven could not possibly look any better. I will try to explain the splendour of those mountains, valleys and glaciers, with their richness of colour contrasts, but I don't
think I can do it justice.

White, almost blue- snow caps draped over the mountain like icing melting on a warm cake. The valleys, dark and foreboding, sent a warning of danger: one erroneous step and you become a sacrifice. And the rich greenness of the pines, giving life to a scent that was intoxicating, it engulfed me. This wilderness stretched your imagination to the limit. Any wonder these Alps, which span eight countries, send silent invites to the masses who feel drawn by their call.

"This is nature at its best," was all I could say between breaths.

I think if my mum were here to see me when I laughed and cried at the same time, she'd say; 'Sally, you're just crying tired'! And she'd be right, but I wouldn't admit this fact to my darling Alain, or the beautiful Bridgette. They amazed me with their boundless energy and climbing agility. I truly wondered why I seemed the only one to be so bloody tired.

Finally, bedraggled, limp and starving we reached the welcome sight of a chimney wafting smoke. Soft light glimmered from the timber Chalet's windows, giving out a warm welcome. It simply beckoned us to enter. I wanted with my last ounce of energy to run at this amazing lifesaving chalet and kiss its walls. However, Alain told Bridgette and I to stay hidden behind a large bolder and watch for his signal that the coast was clear. It was only due to his hard

83

pushing that we reached the chalet by sundown. The fading light would not only give him cover, but enough light to still see danger. He approached carefully, ducking behind trees until he was close enough to sneak up and look through the small window.

When finally, Alain waved his arm for us to come, my sigh of relief was audible. Again, I laughed and cried, but this time, I thought I knew why. It was the overwhelming joy of finally reaching warm safety before complete nightfall.

This refuge, or chalet, was owned by the Furrier family. Their son, Marcel, had been a childhood friend of Alain's. Through family ties, they would see each other on school holidays. That's when the boys met and struck up their loyal friendship

Marcel was not at the Chalet that night. He lived in Zurich with his Swiss-born wife, Jane. He too was a member of the Underground movement in Switzerland but was able to pay his parents frequent visits. Tonight however, it was only his parents, Robert and Edith who welcomed us. We were then introduced to four other French Resistance members whom Alain knew. They would be staying overnight in the barn, before making their way back to France early the next morning. This chalet sat only two miles from the Swiss border. It was in an out-of-the-way place, far from any jeep access, so it was deemed reasonably safe from the Germans. Edith and Robert ran a small dairy farm, mainly producing cheese. It was far easier to transport boxes of cheese down the mountain than daily supply fresh milk to the neighbouring village.

The massive wooden barn sheltered their cows in the winter, it also held a large room set aside for the cheese making. To one side of the barn, they'd built a shelter for holding twenty Barnevelder chooks, a Dutch breed, which produced large brown eggs. As you may guess, our first dinner with Edith and Robert was a delicious cheese omelette. Our entrée was a tasty bowl of vegetable soup and our dessert was the famous Swiss apple tartan served with clotted cream. What a wonderful treat for weary travellers, especially after first luxuriating in a hot bath. On our arrival, Edith had told us she'd boiled plenty of water beforehand, so we could bathe in her cast iron tub. She was a very intuitive woman I thought. No, not really, on reflection she'd been informed by Alain on his radio the time to expect us, and what we craved.

I was sent to heaven bathing in that fragrant warm tub, then even higher with our delicious hot meal. The combination relaxed me into a pleasant weariness, too weary to take part in conversation. I kissed Alain and Bridgette and bade our new friend's goodnight. My bed was made from wooden slats and on top, sat a feather mattress and a feather doona. Before drifting off, I thanked the Lord for his mercy. A deep sleep then swept me away for the entire night.

Near to waking, I had a dream which transported me to Bulkawa, where Mum was attempting to cook an apple tartan. Alain was with us, laughing and drinking red wine as we sat watching her struggle with the pastry.

"I can do this, I don't need any help," she said determined and obviously trying to convince herself as well as us about having a talent for cooking.

She'd always been spoilt with live-in cooks catering to her every whim; she'd never held any interest in learning culinary skills. I wondered why my subconscious would throw this dream at me now. However, it did put a smile on my face. But then after waking fully, I wallowed in melancholy for the rest of the morning, that is until Edith let the chooks out for a run and I found it really amusing. I began to belly-laugh.

"It looks like a chook race Edith. You should put numbers on them, so we can lay bets."

"What a good idea Sally!" She strode out ahead of me and after counting the eggs said: "It looks like cheese omelettes again tonight!"

I didn't mind at all but there was one important thing I had to ask Edith first. My dream had reminded me about how my family would be struggling with the fact that I was now missing as to them it would appear, I was. I knew Edith's radio was far more powerful than the one Alain had so I asked.

"Edith, could I possibly send a message to my family on your radio. They live in Australia?" Before Edith could answer, I added quickly. "I also need to send a message to my friend who's a doctor in England." I assumed by now, Michael would have returned to London.

Edith placed the eggs in her basket and hurried me into the cheese shed. Once inside, she explained that I would have to give her the information of names and places and then she would relay the information to her contact. They would then pass on my message. Edith then walked towards an ancient cupboard that seemed stuck to the wall. Inside lay shelves full of stinking cheese. Edith reached her arm under the middle shelf and something clicked. She pulled the shelf out towards her, exposing a Radio and transmitter which sat on a plank behind another small, well camouflaged opening. She then went about relaying the coded words and waiting patiently for an answer. Before too long I heard a man's voice. They passed on several phrases to each other, which to me were unfathomable, then she placed her hand over the receiver and said:

"I can only give a short message to your family Sally, just to say you are safe."

My heart sank a little; I really needed to tell more, especially when trying to explain Alain to Michael. I suppose informing them of my safety was good enough for the moment. Once my message had been translated and confirmed, they would then do their best to get it to the right people. Relief filled my heart; at least my family would know I was still alive.

Edith and I then laboured for a short while in her flourishing vegetable garden, pulling out weeds and digging chook manure into the soil. Later we picked carrots, potatoes and onions to add to our evening meal. As we worked together, I told her my stories of Australia, Hawaii and how I'd grown up with my grandfather in Adelaide whilst my parents were fighting different battles in the First World War. My mother, saving lives, while my father was killing the enemy. Edith seemed delighted and intrigued. When I'd finished, she told her own story, making special note of how much respect and gratitude the French people held for our Australian soldiers, especially during and after the First World War.

After so many weeks of intrigue, not to mention the murder of Sherman and fighting the enemy in close combat, this time in the garden seemed almost surreal. Funny how I just referred to killing Sherman as a murder but of course it came under the heading of killing the enemy in wartime. I needed once again to strip my mind of those things and enjoy our short time here in this relatively safe chalet. Soon we would be greeting Pierre, Berty and Phillip. They had been in hiding some miles away, further along the ridge nearer to Italy. They'd begun their journey to join us here two days ago and were expected to arrive around lunchtime.

Bridgette had been having heart to heart talks with Alain about killing her rapist, Sherman. I could only imagine her anxious mind would be twirling in all directions at the thought of meeting up with her husband Pierre again, after that event. I tried personally to calm her from her worries.

"Pierre is sure to look at you the same as he always has, and that is with great love and understanding. He knows about the powerless predicament of women during wartime."

Bridgette, however, was convinced beyond all of our assurances, of an opposite response.

"No, I am sure things will never be the same between us, ma Cherie."

Bridgette had been busy with the household duties and set the table for lunch while we'd been in the garden.

The bread Edith kneaded early in the morning and put aside to rise, Bridgette had placed in the wood-fuelled oven. The aroma was sensational and reminded me of when I was at school and the baker delivered the bread. He'd drive his horses up close to the school's kitchen, which sat near our classroom. When he opened the back door of his wagon, our classroom filled with the same heavenly aroma. We would lift our noses into the air and literally breathe it in.

"What a feast," I declared, after Edith placed the hot bread on a large wooden carving board.

I stood beside the table, drooling over the many different cheeses, dill pickles, cold meats and sausage. These had been hung and cured in a room near the cheese house.

"If those men don't arrive soon, I'll just have to start without them!" I said.

Edith's beautiful Border collie dog named Jack had been lying calmly beside the fire watching us prepare the lunch. With one bound he suddenly jumped up and began scratching at the door.

"Are they 'ere Jack?" Edith asked, while opening the door.

We looked outside from behind the dog but saw nothing. However, Jack was off, running towards the track leading up the ridge to our Chalet. Alain had been collecting and chopping firewood with Robert, so they were behind the chalet, in the opposite direction to where the three men would come from.

"I can't see anyone Edith?" I said.

She just gave me a side-long glance as if to say, something is wrong. And soon I knew why. It seemed this dog never wasted his energy behaving like this, unless the strangers arriving were enemies, or they were friends in danger, possibly sick or wounded.

We ran towards the track, keeping under tree cover. Then to our horror, we saw Phillip and Berty almost carrying the blood-soaked Pierre up the final climb. Bridgette cried out and rushed to him. The other men stopped to get their breath, then Phillip explained.

"We ran into a group of German soldiers. They were disguised as civilians. We think they were sussing out our 'iding places. One of them, Pierre recognized. 'E was one of the soldiers who 'ad once or twice raided your pantry Bridgette. 'E knew Pierre straight away. Pierre walked away pretending 'e didn't recognize 'im. Pierre then took us aside and said we should take 'igher ground and keep the Germans under surveillance. When the time was right, we would shoot them."

Berty then spoke.

"I think the German's had the same idea and it became a race to see who would get the advantage. They thought they'd won by shooting Pierre but then we cleaned them up entirely." Berty then gave Pierre a friendly tap on the shoulder and said: "He'll be alright won't you old mate, just a graze really?" Berty then smiled at me, "I say Sally it's so good to see you. You look radiant!"

God bless Berty. Talk about a true Brit and a stiff upper lip, he was the expert.

Bridgette and I took over helping Pierre to the chalet, as Berty and Phillip were both pretty exhausted. They'd been hefting Pierre up those steep inclines for miles. Alain and Robert came in the back door, just in time to see us all traipsing into the Chalet. Sighs of relief and exhaustion filled the room. After washing, most of us sat down to the table and food. Bridgette rushed Pierre off to have a bath and seemed relived she didn't have to face him about her own dilemma. Instead Pierre was the one needing her compassion and support.

It turned out Berty had been right. Pierre's wound was little more than skin deep, although blood flowed freely from it and therefore it had caused him to eventually feel weak.

Bridgette decided in her wisdom that he needed to drink cow's blood. So she came back to us in the kitchen, leaving Pierre to languish in the bath. She stood at the doorway, a pleading look on her face, then asked for a cow to be bled.

"This is to 'elp Pierre regain 'is strength." We stopped eating and looked dumbfounded, then Alain spoke.

"Yes of course it can be done Aunt Bridgette, but will 'e drink it?"

Berty then offered a little common sense.

"Well, I'm not really an expert on such matters Bridgette but the body does have a way of recouping. Maybe, with a good rest and perhaps eating cooked calf liver, that is if you have any?" He looked at Robert who nodded his head. "Well then, I'm sure Pierre will be back to himself in no time. Of course, to stop the bleeding, as we tried to do on our journey, is of the utmost importance. With our walking and climbing, his blood pumped even faster. But now he's able to rest for a while, that alone should stop the flow and so will a clean bandage."

I think with Berty's assurance that Pierre would soon mend, delivered with his very upper-class accent, convinced Bridgette. Berty then added:

"Well, I'm sure that's all settled then. Let us continue eating and reclaim our own strength, shall we?"

I sat silently throughout lunch and listened to the chatter about everything and anything, but nothing was said about Millie. My anxiety waited patiently to be informed by Phillip, about news of her. Previously I'd only heard vague, short bursts of confusing information over the radio. I needed to know the finer details. I still held a little anger with the men for leaving me behind, especially as they'd returned empty handed.

I was frustrated that I hadn't received word from home on whether or not they'd actually heard from Millie. I also tried several times to think of the words I'd say to Michael, when telling him about Alain. I'd fallen so deeply in love with Alain, I couldn't possibly return to Michael. But the words I thought to say never seemed right. Besides my message was simplified by Edith to say, 'I'm safe Michael'. I knew I would never be truly safe until this war was over but that was true for all of us.

Our lunch was enjoyed slowly. When we'd finished, Edith gave me a reprieve from the cleaning up, so I could talk at length with Phillip and Berty about their attempt to bring Millie back. We settled down comfortably in front of the glowing fire, even though it had warmed up outside. The chalet still held the chill of the previous night. A moment of silence passed before we all began talking at once. I had the feeling the news of Millie was not good. This would account for their shy unwillingness to begin telling me what they'd un-covered. I was wrong, well sort of. It seemed at first, they were still a little ashamed and embarrassed at having left me behind, so they began to apologize. I assured them it was over – forgotten. But I urgently needed to know their story about Millie from beginning to end.

Berty gave a huge sigh of relief, then went headlong and somewhat excitedly into the string of events which led them to Millie and eventually back to Edith's Chalet. This included helping several Jewish families escape their doomed return to Germany, after they were refused entry into Switzerland as refugees. The Swiss quota for refugees had already been filled. However, there were many good Samaritans within Switzerland who helped to hide or transport these unfortunate people elsewhere. Not all of them were hidden in the Alps. Phillip told me about a large paper mill factory on the outskirts of Zurich that was owned by a Swiss millionaire. Apparently, he'd closed the mill down and boarded it up with a sign that read, 'DANGER DO NOT ENTER.' This was his attempt to distract intruders. But really the factory was a safe haven for some fifty Jewish families.

Berty continued his telling with so much information. He told me about the false passports and travelling papers being distributed to Jewish people, so they'd avoid capture. Switzerland, although remaining neutral, also held many sympathizers for the third Reich. The act of aiding and abetting the Jewish refugees held grave risks for the helpers. Instead of simply going against the law of the country with its refugee intake quota, where mild punishment would be metered out, it now meant death to these Jew collaborators if caught.

Berty also told us that while in Zurich they'd experienced an air raid by the Allies. It appeared Switzerland also had its fair share of unintentional bombings from English and American fighters. Germany too, accidently over-ran bombing raids on France and dropped bombs on Switzerland. The bombings were completely accidental and sincere apologies came from all sides. It still infuriated the Swiss Government. On many occasions, they pursued and shot down the culprits with German made ammunition no less. An enraged Hitler, after finding out his German planes had been shot down by his own anti-aircraft guns, warned Switzerland they stood in real danger of a full attack if they continued with such actions.

Berty was about to go on with more of his, Swiss News bulletin, but I stopped him. I just had to hurry him up with any news about Millie. I thought he was stalling, but I also knew that if they'd found her dead, Berty would have told me on our first meeting. So I begged him to tell me later of all the war news, it was only Millie I was concerned with now.

Suddenly, Berty's eyes lowered to the floor. He spoke with much less fluency and excitement.

"She's, she's still with her General and his family, well mainly with his family in their Grande Chalet in Zurich. She refuses to leave Sally, even though the General mostly spends his time in Germany. He's one of Hitler's right-hand men. Millie told our confidant, Hilda, that she held no conviction one way or the other in this war. She only cares about the man she loves and her desire to return to her opera career when the war ends.

My stomach convulsed. I felt ill. The blood rushed to my face so rapidly I felt like I would explode. I seethed with anger. For a full minute I stood ridged, then paced the room as I began to curse her. Alain then appeared in the doorway. He'd obviously been hiding. I'm sure he knew the news before I did and guessed my reaction. I could not be angry with him, why would I? I needed him. As he drew close, I flung myself onto his chest and cried like a baby. After some moments of consoling hugs, I regained my composure and delved into the how and why from Berty.

"From whom did you receive this information Berty?" He remained calm and spoke with careful deliberation.

"Well, you more or less understand now how the underground works, Sally. One of our confidants is Frederick Potowski, he's Hilda's Uncle. Hilda is one of the house maids who works in the chalet where Millie is living. Hilda was able to relay the message to Millie that we were in Switzerland and on the ready to get her out of her situation and then return her to England. This young lady, Hilda, said that Millie was most indignant with her reply, which was: 'I'm staying here no matter what. So you can tell those men to leave Switzerland immediately. I won't be going with them'!"

"Did Hilda ask Millie why she hadn't written to her parents, or to me?"

"Oh yes, that was the other thing. Millie gave her a letter to post home to Australia. It was only a short note Hilda told us. She knew this because Millie had asked her to wait while she wrote it. I'm sorry Sally, but she didn't write anything for you."

I then asked myself a question am I bloody stupid, or am I just trying to convince myself that Millie would not and could not possibly be a Hitler sympathizer. The thought suddenly crossed my mind then about all the hedonistic acts this woman had pursued in her life. The world had always revolved (in her mind), around Millie. This war was no exception. It was an interlude in her life, that's all. A bloody interlude until she reigned supreme on the world's stage once again. She had no thought for others or those working to make the world free. And for her to write only a short note to her elderly father who worshipped the ground she walked on, just a short note. How could she be so cold, so removed from empathy? How could she forget her own parents and not feel for them and know of their heart-ache in thinking they'd lost their daughter. This was the thing I found unforgivable. I made a silent vow to myself then. I would dismiss all thoughts of Millie now. I wouldn't care about her anymore. I gathered myself and stood tall.

"I thank you both. And now I must say, I'm pleased you left me behind. You were right to do so. Because if I were anywhere near Millie after her refusal to leave, using such selfish motives as she did, I think I would have strangled her with my bare hands. And God knows, I've wanted to do that several times in my life. I think it would have been the final straw! So, I thank you with all my heart for your attempt at bringing her back."

Then I laughed. There I went again, laughing at the most inopportune moments. I wondered what was wrong with me. Was it the relief of knowing that finally, I was not responsible for Millie's actions? I didn't really know why I was so happy lately. I was laughing at almost everything. What I did know was, I needed a drink of alcohol desperately and hoped by asking Edith for one, I wouldn't offend our host and hostess. Edith was obviously clairvoyant.

"Would anybody care for a wine to celebrate out time together?"

Robert then stepped in with an offer that bettered this.

"My friends, I 'ave a fifty-year-old port, just begging to be opened!"

This was what the doctor ordered. After swilling the first glass down while standing, I sat comfortably to savour the next. My rush of anger had subsided. Now my cheeks glowed with the smooth silkiness of the port and the warmth of the fire. I'd thank Pierre later as he was asleep, recovering from his ordeal.

Chapter 13

I'm Pregnant

We enjoyed another two glorious weeks with Edith and Robert. Part of me, the selfish part, wanted to stay in their chalet forever, as long as Alain stayed with me. However, that was not possible. We had been summoned to help the French Underground prevent the German's sea-going attacks on England. This involved blowing up war ships when in port. So, before the heavy winter snows fell, making it almost impossible for us to walk back down the mountains into France, we said goodbye to Edith and Robert.

In those two weeks of living together at the chalet, we had a wonderful reprieve from the war effort. Bridgette and Pierre seemed to have solved any friction which may have a risen from Bridgette's rape dilemma. They had become close and affectionate again. Berty taught Phillip how to play chess, in between writing his wartime memoirs. Alain and I made love at every opportunity. I also held a close secret, one which finally explained to me the reason for my tiredness and constant laughter. I was pregnant; well at least I thought I was. I had missed two periods but had no other signs like morning sickness; only tiredness and laughter. Funny how sometimes uncontrollable mirth can be caused by a hormone change in pregnancy. I'd been asking myself why, in this time of war, I laughed so much when there really wasn't much to be happy about.

The only thing I wasn't sure of, was whether to tell Alain or not. I knew if I did, he would treat me like a precious gem and that I didn't want. I'd be in this fight until I had to give birth and then I'd keep fighting for my child's sake. So I kept my condition close to my heart. Only I and my unborn son knew about this inner bonding. I felt it was a son but had no idea why.

The day we set off for France again, the sun shone so brightly it seemed to ignite me from within. Perhaps it was a sign from God that our way back down the mountain would be hazard free. Our radio kept us in touch with Underground movements. We were told (in secret codes and words), we'd be picked up by the twin brothers and taken back to the cave. From there, the brothers would drive us to Calais where we would meet with another member of the Resistance.

Because Alain was a specialist in deep sea diving, he was to attach the bombs to the German War ships. This would be Alain's most dangerous mission so far and it worried me. I had to convince myself, not to think negatively. Only think of what a great triumph it would be for the Allied forces. I shed any negative thoughts by coercing positive ones to smother them.

All things went to plan with our climb down the mountain including our timing. The very moment we reached the floor of the French Alps, the twin brothers were waiting for us. The only thing disturbing me a little was the two cows that the brothers had tied in the back of their truck. Peter explained when he saw my look of intrigue.

"The cows are a decoy. We think the Germans are getting a little suspicious."

Of course, I laughed. I'd laugh at anything. I'm sure Alain was beginning to think me mad. Paul looked at me with a puzzled expression.

"If you promise not to laugh out loud Sally, you and Bridgette can climb in the back behind our seat and 'ide under the blanket. The men will 'ave to 'ide under the straw between the cows. We will say to the German's if we are stopped, that we 'ave milking cows to deliver to General Farmersburg. 'E already knows we are delivering them to 'im."

I laughed again, thinking Farmersburg was a made-up name. Peter shook his head.

"It will 'ave to be tomorrow when we begin the trip to Calais Alain, the rest of you will 'ave the 'ospitality of the cave until Alain returns."

My heart skipped a beat, or more like a great thud. I suddenly realised Alain was the only one going on this mission. I asked him, with a little anger in my voice:

"But what about us, aren't we supposed to go on this mission too?" Alain pulled me gently to his side.

"Ma Cherie, this one is only for me. I am the only one who can dive. I know all about the explosives and 'ow to attach and set them off. We will only need two men." His smile gave me some assurance. "Do not worry my love. I will return to you. You will be kept safe. Berty will return to England and Phillip will go back to Usson and keep fighting. Pierre and Bridgette will stay with you in the cave, until the time is right for them to return to their 'ome."

With my head tilted, I said. "But I thought we would stay as a team and work together?"

"No Sally, this will be the end of my fighting for the resistance," Bridgette said, as she held me close. Then she whispered. "We know you are pregnant Sally. I will look after you."

This was not what I wanted. I wanted to be right beside Alain all the way. I didn't want to leave him, not for a minute. Oh shit, it's my hormones racing, I'm not thinking logically. I pulled away from Bridgette.

"So you all think I'm pregnant do you! Well I'm not!" I lied. It seemed to convince them for the moment. After all, I'd had lessons about lying from Millie. She'd done it all her life.

Alain seemed very disappointed. "Are you not pregnant Sally?"

"No I'm not! And another thing. I'm going to Calais with you Alain. Maybe I can be a distraction; you know a decoy or something – anything. I don't want to wait in agony not knowing whether you will survive or not! And if you don't take me then I'll surrender to the German's and tell them everything I know!"

I stood defiant, then suddenly shammed by the dreadful realisation of what I'd just said. I hung my head and waited for their shock to voice itself. Instead, there was deadly silence. Looking at each other, as if they were all agreeing to a mental telepathy message, Alain said:

"She is pregnant for sure. Do we all agree?" Every head nodded.

"Oh, bloody hell," I said before I burst out laughing – again.

And so, the original plan took place, just as Peter had explained it would. My darling Alain was gone for only two weeks, but to me it seemed an eternity. We later found out, Berty had returned safely home to England and Phillip continued to help, wherever and whenever he could, the Resistance fighters.

We'd also heard from T-Jon and Jon Paul. The Germans had literally turned Saint Quentin upside down in their search for Sherman. Luckily, they took no prisoners or suspects in for questioning. Everyone it seemed had an alibi. And for the soldiers to upset these villager's, would be like robbing their own bank. Their supplies of some of the best produce for miles around would dry-up if they manhandled the farmer's. Sherman's jeep and body, as far as we knew, were never found.

We stayed safe and reasonably warm within the brother's cave that winter. Sometimes a different group of resistance members would come and join us before being called out to fight the never-ending battle to free France. And sometimes Alain would leave to commit his usual trick of blowing up the enemy vans equipped to detect radio waves. He and his team travelled all over France in their search for those moving vans.

The heavy snow had begun to fall in early November and prevented us from achieving a great deal of fighting; most of the time staying safe. Each member of our small group were well known by the Germans and hunted, except me perhaps. But I couldn't risk exposure, especially in my state. Being found out and interrogated would have been easy in my pregnant condition. I was an emotional cocktail of volatility and I stood out somewhat.

Thankfully the radio stayed functional, so we were able to keep tabs on where the groups were and what they had achieved. After waiting for far too long to hear about how Suzan was faring, the day finally arrived when Alain received news over the radio that his mother, Suzan, had been captured. That fateful night was when she was attending her local resistance meeting. She was taken to Breendonk, a detention camp in Belgium. There she would be interrogated by the SS. I blamed myself for her capture. After all, our initial plan to save Millie was, at the time, deemed unnecessary and frivolous and voiced that way by Suzan.

Alain with all his love and sincerity comforted me into believing it was not my fault. He assured me that Suzan had been under surveillance by the Germans for a long time before her capture, so it could have happened at any time. As far as our informers knew, Suzan was still alive, but for how long no one could say.

That night, Alain and I waited for the others to go to sleep. I knew he needed desperately to be alone with me and unload his personal pain. This was another part of him I loved. When somebody really needs you, it becomes one of the greatest components of love – an honour. I soothed him first with words and then in the best way I knew how. We melded into each other's bodies, becoming one. It seemed different somehow; different from any other time we'd made love; I felt that something sacred had been joined into one entity.

The next day Alain and I lit candles and prayed for Suzan. I personally spent many moments each day, kneeling and praying in front of those tall thin flames, which I had to keep lighting, then snuffing out. I wanted to preserve our meagre stock, but I wished I could keep the candles alight for her.

Over the next three months of winter, the brothers kept us supplied with food and water. Every now and then, we needed a shower, so we would dare to walk to the twin's home, hiding along the way from anyone who might see us. The hot shower awaiting us was well worth the risk. The German soldiers rarely went to the brother's home. They had no need to go there and threaten them, as plentiful supplies of produce, as well as beef were delivered personally by the generous two. It was the neighbours, who the brothers didn't entirely trust that we had to watch for. If anyone saw us, and then followed us back to the cave, our safety would be compromised. The brothers were certain that nobody, except our underground movement, knew of our hideaway.

During those long cold months, I began to write about my time in this war, along with memoirs of my childhood. I stopped every now and then to watch as my stomach rose and fell with the baby's movements. My most treasured moments were when Alain placed his head on my belly, listening to the heart beat of our son. He delighted when feeling him kick and move around. I felt like I'd become the Madonna in those months. Nothing was too much trouble for anyone, and the twin brothers spoilt me with home maid chicken soup, fresh baked bread and biscuits.

Alain and I discussed where I should go when my time came nearer to giving birth. The child needed to be kept safe above all else. This baby was the future for which we fought. It was decided, after talking with Edith and Robert over the radio; we would make our way slowly back to their chalet, in the first week of spring.

There I would stay until I gave birth. It was of great consolation to me that Robert was related to the doctor whose practice was in the Swiss village closest to the chalet. He informed Robert that he'd be on call if anything should go wrong.

Edith's son Marcel, and his wife Jane, would come as soon as we sent word to them that the baby and I were ready to travel. They would then take us to Zurich to live with them until the war ended. Other plans we'd discussed seemed too full of danger. Even to try and get back to England held too many hurdles now. Of course, I could have gone straight to Switzerland to be with Marcel and Jane before the baby was born, but I was not familiar with them. Besides, I really liked Edith and Robert and felt comfortable in their home.

Bridgette had decided she too would stay with me at the chalet and then live with us
in Switzerland, as it was impossible for her to return home. It may never be possible if the war didn't go our way I thought. Pierre would stay with us until we reached Marcel and Jane's, but then he'd return to France and fight with the Resistance.

Even with all the love and care shown to me, I still had many moments of melodrama when I blamed myself for all the troubles forced upon my dear friends. It seemed to me from the very beginning, I was an impediment in their fight against the Nazi's. I was to blame for Suzan being captured. If Alain hadn't gone to his friends home to borrow a car that evening, so he could be by my side, he would never have been spotted; therefore Suzan would not have been questioned and taken away to the work camp. For my gung-ho approach of needing to join the Resistance, I chided myself in private. It was my guilt trip. The truth is, I wanted to be part of the heroics because I needed to be more like my Dad. I'd camouflaged my guilt by pretending to be Joan of Arc, and God knows I was a far cry from her.

And now I'd become a real burden; pregnant and useless. Just as well the laughing gas that appeared to have accumulated in my body during pregnancy lasted throughout. It helped camouflage my heartache over my ego's meddling. There was also the Pierre fiasco too. If he hadn't left his home to help Phillip find and bring Millie back safely, he'd have been home and relatively safe and then Bridgette wouldn't have been raped. All things may have appeared normal to the German raiders when they came searching for Alain. But with Edith's husband and Alain's Uncle also missing, I guess it seemed suspicious to the Germans. And with Bridgette not knowing where Pierre was at the precise time of questioning, their suspicions grew into certainties.

However, Alain gazed lovingly into my eyes and often spoke gently, his words of comfort and assurance.

"We cannot change what was meant to be Ma Cherie." When he said that, my faith returned, and I felt truly blessed to have found this angel of a man.

Chapter 14

My Love is Missing

Our plan to return to the chalet for me to give birth went smoothly. Although sometimes I felt the strain of the long hard climb just might bring the baby on too soon. It didn't happen. We made it to Edith and Robert's chalet safely and awaited the birth in comfort. In the early hours of May 26th, 1943, a healthy baby boy screamed his entrance into the world. He weighed eight pounds two ounces and measured nineteen inches. A mane of black hair, along with his tiny muscled body, made him look somewhat older than a new born. I hadn't needed the doctor, thankfully. The birth was a standard delivery, which only took five hours of excruciating pain. I was blessed to have Edith and Bridgette help me deliver him.

My world then seemed complete as I embraced my son while Alain held my hand, his eyes misty with tears.

"My son," he said, then kissed us a hundred times I'm sure.

Physically exhausted but at the same time, spiritually invigorated, my first need was to inform my parents. Sending a message home to Australia had become common place after we'd arrived back at the chalet. I had before this day; sent several messages to Jonathon and Margi about Millie. All I could bring myself to say was that Millie was well and safe. It was all they needed to know until this bloody war was over and then we could sort Millie out.

I knew once my family had received the news of my marriage and the baby there would be celebrations. I began the message with.

'Alain and I were married by a Catholic Priest two hours before I went into labour. He'd travelled especially fast in order to complete the service *before and not after* our baby was born. We now have a son and named him Peter Paul Laurent. Laurent is my married surname. I will explain later the reason for our choice of Christian names.' My message was somewhat longer than usually allowed, due to the joyfulness of the news.

Predictably, from the moment of his birth, we called our baby PP. We then sent a message to the brothers about our choice of naming him after them. After all, they had not only been our saviours, but a God send for hundreds of other Resistance soldiers. We thought it only fitting to name him after the twins, Peter and Paul.

After sending my message, I returned to bed and slept soundly for five hours before Alain's kiss woke me.

"'E's crying darling I think 'e's ungry."

Alain stood above me with PP in his arms, rocking him and cooing like an old woman with her first grandchild. I laughed between yawns. When feeding my darling boy, I thought how natural this mothering business was. You give birth, you feed them, they sleep. You watch them grow and teach them all you know. I held PP close, placing butterfly kisses on his head, feeling a maternal and spiritual bond, which I was sure would last a lifetime.

True, the umbilical cord had been cut, and yet it was not broken and never truly would be – not ever. This was how I felt.

Alain became the mid wife in those first few nights after PP's birth. He stirred before I did whenever the baby woke. He'd then lay his head on my shoulder watching his son suckle my breast. The closeness of my new family overcame all my senses, it was truly amazing.

On a fine morning, a week later, Alain came to me just as I'd put PP down to sleep. He'd been speaking on the radio with the Resistance. His expression told me the news; he'd been called to do a job. This time however, it seemed simple. He would meet with a group in the Alps, nearer France, and there he would be introduced to a Dutch woman, Frieda Belinfante. She had been the mastermind in blowing up the population registry in Amsterdam. Alain's eyes sparkled with pride at what she and her colleagues had successfully accomplished.

"They have saved thousands of Jewish people from being officially found out Sally. No records – no proof," he said. "Now she needs a guide to bring her over the Alps into Switzerland. The Resistance has already rescued her from Belgium and taken her to the French Alps. I need to guide her to Geneva and then she will sail to America."

It sounded easy to me, one of his simpler missions. I was not perturbed in the slightest at his going. The only thing which sat a little uncomfortably in my mind was a pang of jealousy. Not because Alain would be alone with another woman, no; the fact was she'd committed a wonderful stroke of genius and bravery. I felt inferior and obviously needed to be validated further in this war. Nothing I felt could ever escape Alain's observation. This man knew me better than I knew myself. He sat on my bed, holding me in his arms as I sobbed.

"There, there Sally, I will come 'ome, this is easy, just like taking a tourist for a 'ike. I will buy you a present when I'm in Geneva." He said it like I was a child and would cheer up with the thought of accepting a gift.

"You must forget about the fighting for now, you don't need to compete with other women in being a war 'ero. You are the beautiful mother of our son."

I began to laugh at his in-sight, my head still buried in his chest.

"How did you know I was jealous of her conquests and that I wasn't crying because I was envious of you being alone with her?"

"Because I know you Sally. You are a little warrior, not un-like your father, and one day I will be proud to meet 'im. I knew you could not be jealous of another woman. Not when you know in your 'eart that you are the only woman I will ever love." And he slowly kissed away my anguish.

Alain packed his bag, kissed me again and hugged PP, then he was gone. Every day after Alain left, I clung to our baby, telling him;

"Daddy will be home soon."

But soon never came. After three months of unbearable agony, copious tears, anger and frustration, there was still no word. I almost gave up hope of ever seeing Alain again. I tried to make sense of his disappearance, telling myself all sorts of stories to quell my torment. I'd take long walks and imagine seeing him come walking towards me saying, Sally, my darling, I am so sorry. There were just a few things I 'ad to do for the Resistance. But I am 'ome now ma Cherie'.

This didn't happen. My dreams and prayers were slowly fading, and I knew I couldn't stay with Edith and Robert forever. However, there was still enough fight in me, to keep going, hopefully until the end of the war. Surely that must be soon. I decided after three months of waiting and hoping, it was time to take up Marcel and Jane's offer to live with them in Zurich. Bridgette and Pierre became my fortress, as were Edith and Robert, but they found no answer as to why Alain had not made contact. After all this time and no word, we could only imagine the worst had happened. Our comrades in the underground informed us that Alain had delivered Frieda to Switzerland and headed off alone back to the chalet. This was all the news they were able to deliver. From when they spoke with Alain at that time, he had simply disappeared.

Pierre and Robert had tirelessly searched the Swiss-French Alps border, tracing the same path Alain would have taken to come back. They had undertaken life threatening exploration of glaciers and hidden crevasse regions within the mountains. For weeks at a time they had searched, but to no avail. Alain, it seemed was gone forever.

101

I gave leaving the chalet another month, just in case he miraculously returned, but
after waiting four months for news that he was alive, or someone had found his body, I decided I must leave and move on to Zurich.

After saying sad goodbyes to Edith and Robert, Bridgette, Pierre, my son and I began hiking through the Swiss Alps. We all shared carrying PP in a back sling. He seemed to love the change when seeing our faces from each other's back. We rested whenever we needed to revive our energy and when we did, we thralled at the splendour of the scenery in those early months of autumn.

Walking through the autumn Alps, allowed me some happiness, which had eluded me since Alain's disappearance. As grandmother Sally had gathered Australian wild flowers which she pressed and kept within her secret diary, so I decided to follow her example and collect stunning autumn leaves. On her death bed, Grandmother Sally's diary had disclosed these preserved gifts to her husband Jonathon, along with her life story, revealing her forced abandonment of her baby Patrick (my father), into an orphanage.

The flowers she'd picked, she wrote reminded her of the people she'd loved. I would now do the same and press the golden Grindelwald leaves into my journal; it would hold memories of this journey.

We were lucky the weather stayed perfect for our trek into Geneva and we were able on that first night, to stay in reasonable lodgings. Although we really needed two nights of rest, we decided to push on and take the train to Zurich, where Marcel and Jane would be waiting.

We had little trouble boarding the train in Geneva, as the guards were captivated by PP, so were distracted from inspecting our passports thoroughly. It was a most pleasant train trip, until we reached Zurich, where the atmosphere definitely changed. A more rigid, serious demeanour ruled the people in this city. I was very pleased when we finally reached the safety of Marcel's home.

Upon our arrival they greeted us warmly. We were quickly taken on a guided tour of their impressive Tudor style home, which had four bedrooms and one very large bathroom. I'd known previously that they were unable to have children and it struck me as sad. They were so happy to take PP under their wing. I was relieved at their obvious delight in having all of us come to live with them.

Pierre stayed for nearly a week and then bade us farewell. He would return to France to join the Resistance, as we'd planned. It was a heart wrenching moment for Bridgette, but she made her choice to stay in Switzerland and safety until the war ended. I put myself in her position and came to the conclusion that if it were me, I would have gone with my husband and continued to fight. But Bridgette was not me and much older. I had no right to compare myself with her.

Chapter 15

Switzerland

In the second week of living with Marcel and Jane, I realised I had become a different person. No doubt the disappearance of Alain and the longing to know if he were dead or alive was a major part of what overcame my senses and led me into depression. I know, I've written before, that you always know when your loved ones are in danger. However, in Alain's case, I now felt nothing. No emotion whatsoever; I was numb. Sadly, my baby PP had become a duty rather than a joy. His cries to be nursed and soothed went unanswered by me. Instead Jane or Bridgette would console him. At that point in time I could not bring myself to be the mother I should have been. I was pre-occupied and restless. I heard voices in my head, they kept telling me I had unfinished business. What it was I didn't really know. Maybe it was finding Alain, or maybe it was something else I needed to achieve. All I can say is that I could not lay down my cards in this war, not at this point, and I couldn't believe that Alain was lying dead somewhere. I believed deep inside, just like I had before, that Alain would return one day. But was this wishful thinking? I really didn't know what to believe or feel, so I stayed numb, the easier option. I simply went through the daily routine.

Day after day I watched as my son slowly but surely moved away from me. Jane and Bridgette laughed and played with him. They fed him milk while holding him close to their breasts, rocking him and singing lullabies. My milk had simply dried up. Bridgette said it was due to the trauma of Alain's disappearance. The women took the opportunity to mix a milk formula for Peter-Paul which he loved and then they shared the pleasure of feeding him.

Deep depression had slowly engulfed me. It gave me the helpless feeling of drifting lower and lower into my grave. I needed something, anything to stop me dropping deeper into this abyss. At least I had enough sense left to be aware that this was happening to me. I felt sorry for both my son and myself with the breaking down of our bond; the bond I thought could never be broken.

It was into our fourth month of living with Marcel and Jane that I realised PP had truly slipped away from me. He seemed to prefer Bridgette or Jane to feed and play with him, rather than me. When the day finally arrived where he'd wiggled his way out of my arms to crawl to Jane, that was when I took action. I wrapped him warmly and we went to church where I prayed.

From then on, I walked the two miles in the snow each day to the church, along the banks of the Lake. PP wriggled or whimpered in my arms all the way to the Catholic Church. Once inside I knelt and prayed to God, mainly for my own wellbeing, for without having my senses returned I could not possibly be a good mother. I cried so hard sometimes I'd have to sit PP on the ground next to me, so I could hold my body in case it shuddered apart. I felt my heart had already done this. But I needed to be strong again, to mend and if not entirely, at least enough to get by without Alain.

These times spent alone with PP and praying to God, soothed and helped me. I gradually climbed back out of that black hole, although I felt I was only hanging on to the edge waiting to fall back into the deep dark again. After a week of walking to the church each day and praying, shakily I joined the women again in playing and feeding PP. It felt good and normal but there was still something missing. I began to realise it was the need for me to act in this war, not just sit and play mummy. We'd heard of many victories by the Allies and now the Americans were a driving force. Hopefully the war would now end sooner rather than later. It raised my hopes of someday soon, returning home to Australia with my son.

Our host, Marcel, had not only become a Swiss citizen after marrying Jane, but was heavily involved in the Swiss Underground, something I longed to be part of. One evening, after we'd finished dinner and Marcel was about to leave for a meeting with the underground, I took the opportunity and conjured up the courage.

"Marcel, I hope you don't mind me asking, but I would like to join you in the meeting tonight. I feel my energies are wasted at the moment."

I Looked directly at Bridgette and then Jane.

"I don't mean to imply anything ladies, I'm really grateful for your love and care of
PP. I think everyone knows I haven't been myself since A ...," my voice tapered off, I found I couldn't speak Alain's name.

Marcel's eyes showed a mixture of sympathy and maybe it was assurance that I could be of use. I felt uneasy in the silence that followed, before Bridgette spoke.

"I think Marcel that Sally needs to be involved. She will not be 'appy until she is."

He gave a wry smile and held out his hand.

"Alright, Sally, come with me. There is always something brewing and I'm sure you can be of some help."

I jumped up immediately, grabbing my coat quicker than I did on the first night of the London bombings.

While walking to the meeting, Marcel suggested, it was best not to tell the group of my true identity. I agreed, due to the Millie fiasco. I would remain Louise Du Pont. My husband, Alain Laurent was a close friend of Marcel's and Alain and I had been married just before our son was born. However, I had not changed my passport due to Alain's disappearance. The Australian accent could be explained by my mother being Australian. It didn't really matter, as they would accept me as Alain's wife. They had heard much about Alain and admired his work in the resistance.

Marcel then discussed the operations taking place within the underground movement. I listened before a sudden shiver went down my spine. And then a second shiver, like an electric current. It shocked me into a vision. Alain and his mother Suzan appeared before me. They looked like the living dead, with grey flesh covering skeletal frames. Their eyes were sunken and blood shot, and then as fast as the image came, it went.

I was only just conscious of Marcel asking me something. I took a deep breath and apologized for not answering.

"I'm sorry Marcel, what was it you asked?" He looked puzzled for a moment.

"Sally you look like you've just seen a ghost!"

I sighed deeply. "Yes, perhaps I have. I had the strangest vision. I saw Alain and his mother. They looked dreadful, almost dead. It was horrible."

He squeezed my hand. "We should never give up hope Sally."

We walked on silently until we reached the warehouse where a group of men and women sat waiting for Marcel. The atmosphere seemed positive, almost gripping. After being introduced, I sat listening to their victories and also their future plans, plus the sad news of members lost. They seemed mostly to be an academic group, yet I'd assumed they would be the working-class soldier like most of the others I'd met so far. The strategies designed by these intelligent people would go down in history as saving thousands of lives through basically out-thinking the enemy.

Marcel introduced me, as Alain's wife, Louise Du Pont.

"I call Louise a hero because of her amazing courage in helping to hold off the German's infiltrating our hide-outs in the Alps." He paused to see the surprised look on their faces, and then added. "Louise probably shot and killed more of the enemy than the men did."

I simply blushed, then laughed as I said:

"Shooting comes naturally when you're brought up on a large property in Australia. It's mandatory to be able to shoot straight."

I shrugged off the congratulations, but deep down I was proud and happy. I now had the credentials to be accepted into their group. I needn't beg anymore to be included. This nagging need, to be accepted and an important contributor, was beginning to dominate me again. Why had this war brought about such change in me? Did I have a subconscious lack of confidence in my own worth that only now was becoming apparent? I'd have to think more about this.

Marcel and I kept our secrecy about Millie. As far as our comrades were concerned, I was an Australian and married to Alain Laurent. Of course, the group were informed beforehand of Alain's disappearance, so I was given compassionate hugs and condolences before the meeting began.

A special mission was planned that evening and after two hours it was decided by the group that I would become one of the women decoys. I'd be distracting the guards on the Swiss-German border by flirting my sexuality, never expected to go the full deal, but be convincing. This would be an almost impossible task for me as I was still grieving deeply for Alain. How could I possibly act this out, become the opposite to how I felt. I'd rather be somewhere else; taking my anger and frustration out by shooting the enemy, not playing the charmer. However, as it was all in the name of war, I accepted my mission as graciously as I could. So many persecuted families were relying on the guards to only half concentrate on their forged papers – I had to pull it off.

After Marcel and I returned home we told Bridgette the plan that would go into action the following afternoon. She was not impressed.

"Can't they give you something else to do, Ma Cherie?"

I held her in my arms.

"Don't worry my darling Bridgette I have my flick knife. If the German guards try anything too cheeky, they'll soon regret it."

Bridgette smiled at my naivety and ran her hand over my hair.

"We best try to do something with your 'air Sally; it looks like a skunk's pelt, it will not attract anyone!" We laughed then. It felt good to laugh.

Bridgette sat me down in the kitchen and with a sharp pair of scissors she cut the remaining dark ends off my blonde hair. The result was good, much better than my previous attempt at a bob cut.

My first job, as I called it, happened the very next night. I met with the other women, who with our amateur acting skills, would try to seduce the guards. We'd make believe we were excited about our German soldier boyfriends coming into Switzerland. We pretended the boyfriends were expected to cross the border that night to go on leave for a few days. We'd giggle and flirt with the guards, while waiting for our 'invented lovers'. The guards we hoped would be distracted by our beauty and sex appeal, especially when our boyfriends never arrived. By doing this we may possibly save fifty or more families from extermination. The plan proved to be very successful, but I hated having to suck up to the enemy. I explained at the next meeting how I felt.   " N o congratulations are needed thank you; just give me a real job." My comment was immediately frowned upon. Hang on a minute, one moment I'd done well and now the look of disapproval. Of course, the reason why suddenly dawned. I'd thought of myself first and not the families our team of fine actresses had saved.

I scrambled for recovery.

"No words needed my friends your looks are enough. Thank you for reminding me who comes first in this war and what we are fighting for. Yes, it's not about me, I remember now."

Most of the group applauded, as if I'd said something profound. I'd earned back my brownie points with this admission.

The next operation was, to help blow up a chalet where a group of the German hierarchy would be staying. The Resistance plotters didn't know for sure if their information was correct, but this is what our leader had heard from a reliable source. Hitler himself was said to be attending a dinner, held in his honour at a chalet on a particular Saturday night, then staying over until Sunday.

I knew instinctively which chalet it would be. I held my tongue until the map was laid out on the table and the German Officers were named.

The only regret most of the group had, was that the Stromberg family would have to perish, even though the Stromberg's had by now shown the resistance fighters whose side they were on. They'd been a well-liked and respected family in Zurich, before the war.

Nina, one of the women I had been with at the border decoy, became quite outraged when some in the group stated they were feeling guilty for having to kill the Stromberg's. She almost yelled:

"How can you feel guilty and how dare that family remain in Switzerland? All they have done since the war broke out is give extravagant parties for those Nazi bastards. They should either live in Germany or die!"

I quaked when I heard her voice – such hatred. Of course, Nina and the rest were kept in the dark about Millie's connection to me. Millie remained my secret and after hearing Nina's outburst I was pleased I'd said nothing about that matter. They knew Millie was Klaus Stromberg's lover and suspected she was still there, although apparently nobody had seen her at the Chalet for some time. I didn't know whether to be elated or worried, when I heard one man say:

"Klaus Stromberg's mistress seems to have gone missing."

Perhaps Millie had come to her senses and found her own way home. Or maybe she was found to be an antagonist amongst the Stromberg group, and they'd done away with her. Finding out any news from our radio contacts through the network had been somewhat infrequent lately. Maybe it was because Alain wasn't there blowing up the trucks the enemy use to intercept our transmissions. Communicating by radio for the French Resistance was of the utmost importance. Without a clear and continuous run of plans, the resistance would simply fold up. I was hoping to hear something about Millie's disappearance and if there was any news of Alain or his mother – there was none.

Switzerland, although waving the neutral flag, was far from neutral. It held a seemingly passive war, or more like an argument going on within its own society. One could not trust the telephone, or even the mail system. Secrets had to be kept close for fear of reprisal. I was more than a little out of touch with the outside world now. I hadn't even contacted Michael again, not since I'd sent the message from Edith's radio to say I was safe. Poor Michael, he would probably be shocked by all that had happened to me since I'd left him in France – the then boyfriend in-waiting.

So many events, plans and people crowded my mind as I walked home with Marcel after that meeting. The first thing was the jigsaw puzzle of what had happened to Millie. I would have to use every contact I had in order to find her again. Secondly, the realisation of the incredible mission about to take place in four days' time, frightened and intrigued me. It could be the biggest coup in this war. To actually kill Hitler. Now that would be incredible, amazing, and stupendous! I smiled broadly; the wonderful image of people all over the world celebrating peace again thrilled me.

"What are you smiling about Sally? "

"Oh, just the vision of a world free from Hitler."

Marcel shook his head and replied.

"That would be wonderful, but you know there are still many countries that will have to surrender to the allies before we can celebrate victory."

109

"I know. It's just, well you know. It's like the bully at school, when some little kid finally knocks him out. We all celebrate and feel free from tyranny, don't we?"

"Yes, I know what you mean. Hitler is the biggest bully we have to knock out that's for sure!"

He then spoke seriously.

"Are you going to try and find Millie?"

"Of course I am, and I'll need your help Marcel." I paused for a moment, thinking about the trouble she'd caused. "Although I know at this point in time, it appears she doesn't deserve our help. It seems obvious where her loyalties lie."

Marcel placed his arm through mine.

"Maybe you should not judge her too harshly Sally. You have already told me she's madly in love with Klaus Stromberg and I know him. Before the war, he was a kind gentleman who always leant a helping hand with charities. Years ago, his family set up a generous scholarship for underprivileged youth to be tutored in the arts, music in particular. I still find it hard to believe they are Nazi sympathizers. But if the special evening at their home gives us the opportunity to kill the hierarchy of the German command, then I'm sad to say, their lives will be a small price to pay."

I could not argue, but I worried. If Millie returned to the chalet, she might be killed.

That night in bed, I tossed and turned as several nightmares tormented me. In one dream, Millie was behind bars with flames dancing all around her. I tried so hard to break down the bars to free her, but I couldn't. Then somebody from behind pulled me away into a dark room. I didn't see her perish in the flames. I woke in a cold sweat – hyperventilating. I knew then, I could not let them blow up the chalet, not until I knew for sure Millie wasn't going to be there. The next morning, I confided in Marcel about my dream and told him it was of the utmost importance to find Millie and to make sure she wouldn't be in the Stromberg chalet that fateful evening.

"Maybe we should let the group know the truth about how I'm related to Millie and how at first, before I became involved in the French Resistance, my mission was to find her and bring her home."

I studied Marcel's intelligent face. He seemed to be thinking of varying angles before having to reveal to the group the relationship between Millie and me. Although the group had accepted me, knowing I was true to their cause, if the truth was revealed, would they still feel the same about me and hold

110

sympathy for Millie. After all, she may seem to them to have made her choice by joining the enemy.

Marcel looked me straight in the eye.

"I think Sally that we should try first, to find out where Millie is. She may have been sent away."

I felt faint with those last words and pleaded with him.

"You don't think she has stood up against the enemy at some dinner party and they've sent her away somewhere dreadful, do you Marcel?"

This question was more a wish that he'd say, no Sally, she's probably come to her senses and left, but he said:

"I don't know what to think. We just have to do our best to find her and make sure she is not in the chalet on that particular evening. This information will have to come via my contacts that are not actually within our group. Safe houses we call them, run by older people and although they don't physically put themselves in danger, they receive news about what is going on. They help whenever they can."

I then thought of something. It was so stupid of me to almost forget about the young woman Hilda, who worked as a maid in the chalet, the girl who'd posted Millie's letter and told Millie there were French men waiting to take her back to England. She should be able to help. I then spoke my thoughts aloud to Marcel, who actually knew of Hilda.

"Hilda has left the Stromberg's employ Sally. This was after your men approached her through her uncle. Hilda is the niece of Frederick. He is an old friend of my family. Hilda is not the bravest, or the brightest girl in town but she's smart enough to realise her own pitfalls. She does not want to be part of the underground, for fear of losing her life. I will meet with Hilda and ask if she has any idea where Millie may have gone. This will be without connecting you with Millie of course. If she is not forthcoming, then her uncle Frederick may know something."

I felt relieved and optimistic. My morning continued with breakfast with PP and later taking him to the park in his stroller, a gift from Marcel and Jane. It was a rare occasion when I could escape alone with PP, but this morning was the exception as Jane and Bridgette delighted in joining us for our walk in the park.

Chapter 16

Finding Millie

Springtime in Switzerland was stunning. Lake Zurich appeared like a dark sapphire shimmering under the sun, it contrasted against the snow-white frosting on the surrounding mountains. The parklands gave show to pink and white blossoms along with colourful spring flowers. They danced daintily in the breeze while the side-walk cafés came alive on such magnificent days. We decided after our long stroll to have an early lunch in the Central Café. The tables set on the footpath provided us with a bird's eye view of people passing by, plus the best cheese fondue in the world. These moments of normalcy gave me faith in the world returning to sanity one day.

On that morning, we three women spoke of many things; one was Millie of course. Bridgette being an over-sensitive individual was more forgiving of Millie than me. She had the idea that although Millie may have been coerced to join the enemy, she was just play acting. She'd spoken so lovingly in defence of Millie's actions that I just had to tell her:

"You're an admirer Bridgette, a fan if you like. I understand. But I've grown up with Millie, lived nearly all my life with her, so I'm able to speak through experience. She knows exactly what she's doing. But I have to agree with you, I don't think she would ever intentionally join the enemy. She'd have to be forced or brain washed into it!"

I'd only just finished talking, when Jane recognized a young woman walking briskly in front of our table. Before I could speak another word, Jane called out.

"Hilda, Hilda."

The young woman turned and smiled but kept walking, seeming to be in a hurry. I asked Jane was she Frederick's niece?

"Yes."

I jumped up and ran like one possessed. I reached Hilda while she stood waiting to cross the busy road. I took her by the arm, as I heaved for air.

"I'm sorry Hilda, you don't know me, but I'm a friend of Marcel and Jane's." I paused to catch my breath.

"You are the Australian?" She asked abruptly.

"Yes, I am Hilda."

She then pulled her arm from my grip and made a dash across the road. From behind her I heard her words.

"I'm sorry but I cannot talk to you now."

I ran after her again. When I caught up, she said:

"I cannot talk to you here. I told Marcel I will meet him tonight at my uncle's house. I will tell him then all I know."

"Please Hilda can you just tell me now?" I felt I couldn't wait until then.

Angrily she cut me off.

"I told you I will tell you tonight. Now let me go!"

The people passing by began to stare. Hilda was right: you never knew who would be listening over your shoulder. I calmed myself and smiled.

"It was good to see you Hilda," I said as I waved her off.

To say I was anxious for the rest of the afternoon would be an understatement. Night finally fell, and Marcel and I left for Frederick's home. We walked along the banks of Lake Zürich, absorbing the magnificence of the evening. Many other couples were doing likewise, and it was nothing unusual in this neutral country. But I wondered how many underhanded deals were taking place in assisting either side in the war effort, during these strolls.

Frederick's home was in an apartment situated on the eastern side of Zurich. I realised when we climbed the narrow stairway to his first-floor apartment, just how lucky Marcel was to have a good-sized home with a reasonable back yard, sitting two streets back from the banks of the Lake. Fredrick's apartment was so tightly hemmed in there would be little privacy. I wondered why we would meet here to discuss confidential matters.

As soon as we entered, I saw Hilda standing beside a gramophone player. She smiled, then twisted the knob until the music blared. It was far too loud. I stepped back. Frederick shook his head smiling when he saw me do this. He then ushered us into the kitchen, where the noise did lesson – a little. His explanation for the loudness followed.

"The neighbours will not be able to hear our conversation." He chuckled. "Do not worry Louise, we do this all the time even if there are no guests. This puts the neighbours off being suspicious when we do have visitors." His craggy face creased deeper with a knowing smile.

"Surely it is a dead giveaway Frederick that you're trying to hide something," I said.

"No, no, not at all. I play the trombone in a band, this is my own music. The neighbours just think I'm mad and conceited and I need to hear my own recordings all the time." He laughed. I thought then that he may be just a little off-centre but in a very nice way.

Marcel sat next to Hilda on one side of the kitchen table and I sat next to Frederick on the other. Hilda seemed anxious, as if she was holding onto a secret which had begun to eat her up. She took my hand in hers and said:

"I know Louise that you needed to talk about Miss Millie this morning. I am sorry."

She then hung her head, which gave me a heart wrenching moment, I thought she was about to tell me Millie was dead.

"Please Hilda can you tell me all you know, even if it's bad news, please tell me." Hilda lifted her head. Her blue eyes danced, and her tone lightened.

"No. No it is not bad. It is just a little tricky that is all. You see Millie is in hiding. I am not supposed to know, nobody is. But Miss Millie trusted me, and I suppose if anything happened, nobody on the outside world would know where she was, would they?" She then smiled, her eyes glowing with conspiracy.

I was beginning to think she was also slightly off-centre. I needed to call on all my patience now. I felt if I rushed her, she may close up and not tell me where Millie was.

"Do you know where Millie is hiding Hilda?" I asked gently.

"Oh yes, she's in the ginger bread house." She giggled again. "That is what we call it." She looked lovingly towards her uncle. "Don't we Uncle?"

Frederick nodded.

I asked her where the ginger bread house was. She gazed upwards, her hand extended towards the ceiling.

"It is very, very high up, and over the other side of Mount Uetliberg. Mr Stromberg's grandmother lives there."

Hilda smiled briefly before taking on a serious frown, then leaning her body over the table she whispered:

"Now I'm going to tell you a secret. If anyone finds out I know they will kill me." she frowned toward Frederick. "But Uncle Frederick say's I must tell you anyway!" Hilda then nodded yes, as if agreeing with herself.

I sat on the edge of my chair waiting, until she sat bolt upright and said sternly.

"I do not know if I can trust you Louise, or you Marcel. You might tell somebody, and they might tell somebody else who is really bad. Somebody who is on the German side and they will kill me, I know they will!"

I let out a deep sigh of frustration and tried again to gather her trust.

"Hilda I'm not really interested in what you know or don't know about war secrets. I'm only interested in finding Millie and taking her home to her family in Australia, I'm her friend." Hilda almost screamed at me.

"But she does not want to go home, she loves Mr Stromberg!"

Hilda then cried, what looked like crocodile tears, but they triggered Frederick's compassion.

"There, there Hilda, it is alright, you do not have to say anymore if you do not want to. It is alright Hilda do not cry." Frederick looked at me then as if I were the wicked witch of the west.

I tried hard to control my anger at her stupidity.

"Please, I don't want to upset you Hilda or you Frederick, but you must understand, Millie has her whole family in Australia worried about her. I need to at least talk to her."

Marcel then stepped in – thank heavens. He tried to sort out exactly what the secret was which Hilda held so close to her chest. He asked in French was it anything to do with Millie being placed in hiding away from the Stromberg Chalet. Frederick then translated in Swiss-German to Hilda. I was unable to fathom what they were saying, but after a very long conversation, Frederick stood up from his seat and went to find a pen and paper. He then handed it to Hilda.

I watched her hand shaking as she wrote down the words. *You must burn this note as soon as you read it. Mr Stromberg and some of his friends are planning to kill Hitler at the chalet in five night's time.*

Apparently, Hilda's reasoning for writing the note instead of telling us was that nobody could accuse her of speaking it out loud. I thanked the Lord she'd finally told us this incredible piece of information, even though it was in her own frustrating way. Marcel went on to ask Hilda how she knew these facts and was it the reason why she'd left the Stromberg's employ. Was this also the reason they had placed Millie in hiding? Frederick immediately placed his hand over Hilda's and gave Marcel a serious look.

"I will answer your questions Marcel. Hilda is a little delicate you see, she cannot handle violence or intrigue." He then went on to explain.

"This news, Hilda overheard when she was in the wine cellar and Klaus and his father came in. She hid away from them, as she was not supposed to be there. Hilda would have been in trouble if she were caught. You see Miss Millie had asked Hilda to go and fetch a bottle of champagne. Mr Stromberg did not like it when Miss Millie drank alone in her bedroom. Anyway, the men began to discuss plans for the night they would assassinate Hitler. Hilda was able to hear everything and so she told this information to Miss Millie." Frederick sighed, looked deeply into my eyes and said.

"And now we are the only ones outside of the chalet who know this plan."

Total bliss is the only way I'm able to describe how I felt. Marcel sat dumbfounded. A long silence ensued before he spoke.

"This changes everything Louise. We must inform our friends of the Stromberg's plan as soon as possible."

I'll say it again; it's hard to explain my utter relief and joy at that moment. At last, the idea of Millie being a traitor was resolved. Klaus Stromberg had been keeping her safe it seemed, hidden out of the way until the deed was done. Tears of joy welled up into my eyes.

"Do you know what this information means to me Marcel? It means that everything important in my life is still solid. I cannot tell you how happy I am." After I said that, Hilda threw her arms around me.

"I am happy because you are happy Miss Louise." She whispered in my ear, "Now we will burn the paper."

I could see the relief on her face, as we watched the flames engulf her words. Poor darling girl; at least her burden had been lifted.

Frederick went on to draw a map of how to reach the ginger bread chalet (the grandmother's chalet). Frederick then offered to guide me, as it was in an out-of-the-way part of Mount Uetliberg. I refused.

"This is my mission Frederick. If we strike trouble, I don't want to have to worry about you, only about myself. I've already put too many people in danger."

It had become even more urgent for me to see Millie now, especially now we knew for a fact that Klaus and his family were fighting from the inside against Hitler and the Third Reich. I believed now what Marcel had said about the Stromberg Family being good people and him not believing they would be sympathizers. I lingered for a moment on how Nina and others in the group, wanted to see the family burn in the Chalet. Wouldn't they be surprised to hear this information? My heart literally soared. I felt alive for the first time since Alain's disappearance. I asked Frederick if he had any alcohol to drink so we could celebrate.

116

"Of course, I have. Only the best champagne for you Louise!" Frederick said.

I laughed whole heartedly. "Is it from the Stromberg's cellar Frederick?" I asked still laughing. He gave a devilish grin and winked confirmation.

Before we left, Frederick informed me.

"When you are within a stone's throw from the grandmother's chalet Louise, please throw three stones at the door and wait until she comes outside, then wave a white flag."

I asked why as I giggled at these somewhat childish dramatics.

"Don't worry Louise, it is a long story, but if you do as I say you will be welcome."

I took him at his word, as it was getting late and we had unfinished business to attend to. Feeling happy from the effect of the alcohol, plus the good news, we bade Frederick and Hilda farewell, then walked two miles directly to our leader's home. When we walked inside, we were invited to have a glass of Snaps. Marcel then settled down to tell Juan, and hopefully convince him, of the Stromberg's plan. Juan said he would call an extra-ordinary meeting to be held the following evening.

Once I'd returned home, I sat beside PP's cot and quietly told him the good news.

"You will soon see your Aunty Millie and then we will go home to Australia to meet Poppa and Nanny." Of course, PP didn't wake with the news. He slept soundly in his cot which sat close to my bed.

Chapter 17

Assassination Plan

The string of arguments which had taken place during the underground meeting the following night would see me leave immediately for the grandmother's chalet. My urgency stemmed from the small group of members, who'd refused to believe Hilda's story.

Marcel and I were at risk of becoming the only supporters for the Stromberg's intentions. A vote was eventually taken, as to whether we should wait and see if the Stromberg's plan was successful, or if we should proceed with our own plan to blow up the chalet as soon as Hitler arrived. Our initial plan sounded easy, but in actual fact it would be extremely difficult. Even with the people we had on the inside working for the Stromberg's, setting up the bomb would be tricky. The massive security around the chalet would lessen the chance of us being successful. We thought it to be a fifty to one chance. However, if we'd let this rare opportunity pass there may never be another time to act on assassinating Hitler. The argument turned into a matter of trust, especially when Nina suggested we bring Hilda to the meeting to question her more closely. Marcel tried to explain how delicate Hilda was mentally to which Nina said:

"Okay, then we should bring Klaus Stromberg's mistress here. I have found out where she is. She is in the grandmother's chalet. She is an alcoholic you know. They have her there to dry out. We could bribe her with liquor. I am sure she will tell us all we need to know with a skin full of Champagne!"

This statement brought laughter from the entire group. It took all my strength to laugh along with them and not raise suspicions. It would have been relatively easy for them to find out my real name, although my true identity on my war correspondent's badge was well hidden. I'd purposely left my false passport lying about where anyone could easily find it. They all seemed to like and trust me and of course Marcel was their hero. His word was golden.

This immediate discussion about Millie made me feel sick and uncomfortable. I wished they would make up their minds as to what should be

118

done, then I could leave immediately to warn Millie. Finally, it was decided. A chosen group would wait at the ready to give us a signal. If Hitler and his hierarchy did in fact arrive at the Chalet as planned, Sven, the spy within the Chalet, would then relay a message. This would say if the Stromberg's were successful in killing Hitler. If nothing eventuated by midnight, the chalet would be blown to pieces. This was the best plan they could come up with. They said it would give the Stromberg's a chance to redeem themselves or die.

Before our meeting ended, I suggested that Sven might warn the Stromberg's about what may happen to them if their plan to rid the world of Hitler was not successful. This suggestion was met with loud disagreement by the majority. Nina spoke again:

"We are not certain of this news about the Stromberg's. If they're not with us, they may kill young Sven or torture him to find out about our group. They are very lucky we are giving them this chance to prove their loyalties!"

I had no further arguments to offer, so the majority agreed this would be the best plan of action. The group then gathered closely together and prayed, finishing the prayer with 'God is on our side, Amen.'

On our way home, Marcel tried to talk me out of leaving.

"It's too dangerous for you to go alone Sally. If you must go, there is a train leaving tomorrow that will take you almost all the way there. You would simply have to trek a few miles. If you insist on going tonight, I will have to go with you or ask a friend to take you."

"Thank you, but I must go alone Marcel. You have to stay and protect my son if anything should happen to me. I can't risk anybody we know seeing me on the train. Besides, you saw them tonight; they think Millie is one of the Stromberg's so she's a sympathizer until proven innocent. I think their plan is far from being a test for the family to prove their loyalty. We don't even know at what time the Stromberg's plan to kill Hitler. What if its five past midnight and we've already fused the bomb? It's all a fucking mess as far as I'm concerned!"

I then assured him, I would only be gone for forty-eight hours. He'd have to cover for me, say I was sick, had a contagious disease, then nobody would want to come near me. I'd be back the afternoon of the fateful night.

Marcel took hold of my arm.

"What's the problem now Marcel?"

He looked a little nervous.

"Sally I have never told you this and I do not know whether Millie knows, but Klaus Stromberg is married to a German woman. I thought you may have picked up on it when they called Millie his mistress."

119

I furrowed my brow; a bad habit I have whenever curious.

"What's that got to do with anything?" He shrugged his shoulders. Our body language it seemed was in sync.

"I do not know; except I do believe he has a young male cousin who is in the German S.S. and it is he who took off with Klaus's wife."

I must say, I was a little staggered with this information, Marcel I'm sure noticed.

"It was some time ago now Sally. Klaus and his cousin have always been competing with each other."

I looked around for a bench to sit on and digest what he'd just told me. After a moment I said, "I still don't know Marcel, what this has to do with Klaus and Millie?"

"I don't know either, except I have a feeling there is more than meets the eye with this family. I have bad vibes about you taking this trek Sally. I do not think it is wise. We know Millie is safe and she will not be involved in the bombing at the Chalet, please do not go."

I must admit, I too, was beginning to have reservations and voiced my frustrations aloud.

"Damn Millie! I'm sorry Marcel, but I have to make doubly sure Millie doesn't go near the Chalet and now I have to make sure she's not a bloody alcoholic!"

I then softened, noticing how the moon shadowed Marcel's gentle features, casting a soft haze over him. He shared the same loving nature as my Alain. I stood and kissed his cheek, then apologized.

"I'm sorry Marcel, you are a wonderful man and I appreciate your concern, but I have to go alone."

We then entered his homely kitchen where the aroma of hot bread greeted us. Marcel and I joined Jane and Bridgette at the kitchen table. I then explained what I needed to do. We spoke at length about my decision and the what if's should anything happen to me. Jane soon realised there would be no talking me out of my decision, so we packed food and water for my journey. I borrowed her snow coat and walking boots and went to my room to pack extras.

Memories flashed by, as I studied Suzan's floral dress. I pushed it in my back pack, along with the essential white handkerchief, which put a smile on my face. I thought of the meeting with Frederick and Hilda. It had been strange to say the least. A feeling of surrealism had enveloped me during the time I'd spent with them. But who was I to judge if Frederick was extending his offbeat humour into code for approaching the chalet, or if it was for real. I chose not to take any chances and packed a second white handkerchief in case I somehow lost the first. The last thing I did was to kiss my sleeping baby and whisper in his ear, "I love you PP, I'll be back soon my darling."

I stood entranced, looking down at my beautiful son who so resembled his father. My heart then shuddered with grief for the loss of Alain. It did every day.

Jane lent me her push bike with a torch attached to the front handle bars. This allowed me to avoid the train trip and possible recognition. I was soon on my way and rode easily the few miles to the entrance of the mountain track. On arrival, I noticed the rack where Jane had told me to leave the bike. It was three am and lucky for me, the moon was shining at its brightest. I smiled up with reverence.

"Whenever I need you, you're always there."

Part of me was a little concerned to be all alone and climbing an unknown mountain in the dark. But once again, my gung-ho ego helped me forge ahead.

Twenty minutes into my climb, I began to relax a little, mainly because I believed I'd taken the right path. I'd reached my first landmark and I knew there would be many more signs leading the way. The first three hours were relatively easy, and I was thankful for the exercise which kept me warm. If I stopped at any stage, the night chill would begin to take its toll. However, after four hours, I really needed to rest.

I wrapped Jane's snow coat around my shoulders and gave myself a moment to reflect on how far I'd come up the mountain and also in life. From the young woman who had aspired to be a journalist and to ride horses and surf every weekend – simple I know – and yet here I was sitting all alone in the Swiss Alps on my way to rescue my young hedonistic aunt. Reality then hit. I suddenly remembered how most of my life Millie had caused me grief. Was my effort in saving her going to be worth leaving my son behind and perhaps being captured? I shrugged off the thought. After all, how was this going to be any different from the past four years, where I'd rarely been out of danger? But now I had PP to think about. My heart mellowed at the thought. Yes, most gratefully, I had a son to live for. This revelation forced me to re-think attempting any future dangerous missions. After my meeting with Millie, I would re- join Bridgette and Jane and sit the rest of the war out. I'd then return to Australia.

I began to climb the well beaten trail and continued for another half hour until I came to a sign, 'Chalet-Stromberg'. Its entrance took a turn to the right and it was the last chalet which could be reached by four-wheel drive. The rest of the chalets were only approachable by foot. The grandmother's lodging was well over the summit. I gazed up at the daunting climb wondering why on earth an elderly lady would choose to live this far away from neighbours and food sources. After standing still for a moment, I shivered with the cold. Funny how, when the sun begins to rise, the air actually becomes chillier, or was it because I was so high up? I continued to climb quickly. Well past the turn off to the Stromberg's chalet I found a secluded spot off the trail, so I sat to rest a while. It was time for sustenance. Jane had packed a block of cheese, a loaf of bread, apples and homemade biscuits. I fossicked around in the bag trying to find a knife to cut the cheese; instead I found a small stainless-steel flask full of brandy. I studied the flask with a smile. I'd keep this for a celebration drink with Millie. I'd never thought for a minute she'd turned into an alcoholic when I discussed it with others, but the truth is, I did think it. I mustn't lie in this journal.

I relaxed, taking time to eat and admire the pretty little mountain birds hovering about, ready to dive for crumbs. Their happy twitter was the only sound filling the silence. I sat in awe of the perfect sunrise spreading out into a glorious morning. How lucky was I to be alive on such a day? I could have sat there for hours embracing the silken mist drifting across Zurich's valleys as the sun's beams formed dancing shadows. I needed to shake myself. If I hurried, I should make the chalet by mid-morning.

Another reason for me beginning this mission through the night, was that I didn't need to have the company of strangers on the trail. Even in war time, the Swiss Alps accommodated dedicated climbers and determined sight seers. I hadn't the time or the energy to waste my breath chatting with passers-by. With my head down and my walking stick plunging hard into the ground, I took huge strides. After some time feeling the strain on my legs and lungs, I stopped and lifted my head to take a breather. Whilst wiping the sweat from my brow, I stood transfixed. Directly in front, and walking toward me, were a group of German soldiers. *Where in the fuck did they come from*, I asked myself. I hadn't packed my passport, and then I remembered I was in a neutral country, I didn't need to show these soldiers anything, but how was I going to approach them?

Without a second thought, I smiled, waved and took a sharp turn left. My blonde hair and blue eyes seemed a blessing. With my hiking clothes on, I simply looked like any other Swiss mountain climber. They stopped to look after me. I could make out a few of the German words I heard.

"She's beautiful, let's have her."

The other older looking guy with a kind face said:

"No, we must keep going. General would not be pleased if he found out."

I was only ten metres from them, before I found a small track and turned left. I hoped they wouldn't follow and thank God they left me alone. My heart had literally jumped into my mouth at the thought of being alone with five horny Germans. I wondered where they'd been. The only place left, once over the summit, was the grandmother's chalet.

I dared not look back again until I figured it was safe. I'd walked very slowly in the opposite direction to where I should have gone due to this encounter. They were out of sight, so I turned back. That's when I jumped up onto a large bolder to have a better look and be sure they'd gone. Lodged below that bolder was a smaller one which shifted under my weight. I fell forward and as I landed; I twisted my ankle. The smaller bolder began to roll. I tried to stand, to avoid it but the pain in my ankle prevented me. I couldn't move. Within seconds a larger rock dislodged and crashed down onto me. For a moment I thought I was going to be pinned under it, but it kept rolling, crushing my lower leg as it did. I screamed with pain as I watched the bolder gather speed and hurtle towards the soldiers below. As it crashed along on its journey, it dislodged more rocks.

"Oh my God," I said as I leaned forward and watched the men cringing and ducking as they were showered by rock's. *Shit, I thought. If I'd wanted to do that I couldn't have. Hell, I think I've killed some Germans with the slip of my foot!* "My god, but you're a dangerous woman Sally Laurent," I said out loud, then grimaced. If I weren't in so much pain, I would have laughed.

My leg and ankle were possibly broken. What in the hell was I going to do now? The thought of crawling another four hundred feet over the summit and on to the grandmother's chalet, dragging my broken leg, was out. To go back down without help was impossible. The pain was excruciating. Realistically, all I could do was pray for help. My body began to shake with shock and pain. I struggled to reach behind and pull my snow coat out of the back pack. It would probably save my life, along with the brandy. I had to stay calm and wait. Yes, wait for one of those fanatical Swiss climbers to come along and help me up to the chalet.

After finishing the brandy, and feeling warmed by the coat, I managed to fall asleep. When I woke the sun was high and a German Officer with a kind face stood over me. With the help of three civilians, he was about to lift me onto a stretcher. When noticing my eyes open, he sat down beside me. I studied his tanned face, which close up didn't look quite so old. His choir boy features and blue eyes held a sad reflective look.

"So, Frauline, you are awake. Now, can you tell us what has happened? He spoke English. I didn't answer, so he continued.

"Do you know we think you must have started a rock fall which has unfortunately killed one of my men?"

I merely blinked and remained silent. I was not fully conscious, and the pain was overwhelming. The second reason I remained silent was I didn't know who I should be. Should I be me, Sally Darcy an Australian war correspondent, or Louise Du Pont? This officer might be involved with the Stromberg family and my Australian identity would surely blow my cover with the Swiss underground, not to mention the Stromberg's.

I had to be Louise DuPont I decided, although I looked nothing like her at the moment.

The only thing I could do was to fake passing out. It was obvious they would take me back down the mountain to the hospital in Zurich. I could then handle the questioning. This German officer appeared compassionate and didn't seem to think I created the rock fall on purpose, and I didn't. I lay still and silent all the way down the mountain, although my heart raced a little as we neared the Stromberg's home. A German army jeep had been parked at the turn off to the chalet; supposedly in the ready to transport me the rest of the way to the hospital. Thank God they didn't take me inside.

After being admitted, and my leg plastered, I was taken to a bed where I was questioned further by the Swiss Police. Marcel had been informed by Sven of my accident. Sven had been one of the civilians who had stretchered me down the mountain, not that I knew it then as I had never met him before. Marcel immediately came to the hospital to vouch for me, telling the Police I was an Australian- French woman, who was staying with him and his wife Jane. I was their friend and I'd simply come to do some hiking in the Alps. They then asked for my visa pass, which of course I could not produce. There again Marcel came to the rescue and said he would bring it to the hospital the next day. We were relieved when finally, the Police left. Now we could talk. Once again, I put myself through the guilt trip.

"I'm so sorry Marcel, I always try to do the right thing but inevitably I stuff things up, which puts others in danger."

I had a sniffle while Marcel smiled and held my hand.

"Please don't worry Louise. You have done us a great favour. Because of your distraction, it was easy to set up the bomb in readiness for tomorrow night."

"Well what do you know! I've killed one German and provided the

124

perfect decoy for execution of our plan. I've done well after all!" We both laughed.

Marcel left, and I consoled myself again with the facts. Although the thought of Millie, in a drunken stupor, making her way down to the Stromberg chalet on the fateful night haunted me, I had to hope she didn't do that.

I managed to sleep until early the next morning, when Marcel brought in my Swiss Visa, it was counterfeit but believable. I was grateful that he also thought to bring me my glasses and passport. I'd kept the same glasses I'd worn in the passport photo and smartly put them on. My blonde hair could be explained easily.

Later in the morning, the police officer from the day before returned.

"Unfortunately, Officer, I chose to die my hair dark just before I had my photo taken." I studied the doubt on his face, as he looked back and forth from me to the passport. "My father was French and my mother Australian. I often dye my hair dark." I then apologised and I've no idea why. "I'm sorry; it's not for any other reason than to make my life a little more interesting," I said this with a smile and a shrug of the shoulders. He seemed to accept my explanations and left after wishing me well.

That afternoon, our dippy-sweet Hilda paid me a visit. Thankfully it was some time after the Police had left. She handed me the most amazing bunch of wild flowers. I thanked her and then explained how I was on my way to see Millie when I fell and broke my leg.

"Oh, don't worry Louise, my uncle Frederick has gone there, he will tell her to stay where she is until you get better." Hilda smiled, more to herself than at me. Then she said as an afterthought, "Or Miss Millie can come to the Hospital and visit you." Excitedly she clapped her hands at her own suggestion.

I asked Hilda if she thought Mr Stromberg was angry with Millie because she drank too much champagne. Hilda tilted her head to one side, obviously contemplating her answer.

"Well I have never heard him talk angrily with Miss Millie. So, I do not think he is upset with her. But sometimes I have seen Miss Millie a little tipsy," Hilda giggled. "You know, when you have a little too much alcohol to drink. She does drink a lot of champagne. I used to get it out of the cellar for her."

"Just how much does she drink Hilda?"

"Oh, about three or four bottles a day." She furrowed her brow and placed her hand under her chin. "That is a lot of champagne for one person, is it not?"

"Yes, it is Hilda. Do you think Mr Stromberg has taken Miss Millie to his grandmother's chalet, so she can't drink too much champagne?"

"Um, I could not say. But I do not know why Miss Millie would want to go and stay with the grandmother. The old lady is a bit … well, you know … she is a bit strange. She has a herd of goats. She loves them and will not leave them. Nobody can make her leave – all have tried. I have heard them say; they will go up there one day and find her dead. She is really odd, she does not talk to strangers and she has a shot gun and fires it at anyone she does not know!"

I suddenly thought of Frederick.

"What about your uncle, I hope she won't shoot him."

Hilda laughed.

"No, she will not. She knows him, silly. That is why he told you about the stones and the white flag. When he was a little boy, he would hike up the mountain and help her milk her goats. He took the milk down the mountain to Mr Stromberg's chalet and then he was allowed to take the rest of the milk home. That is how I got the job as a house maid, because they knew my uncle Frederick."

I was a bit miffed and asked. "Well why didn't he tell me that the other night?"

"I do not know."

I let out a sigh. "What about her food Hilda, who takes grandma's supplies up to her?"

"When I was working there, Sven took it; he works for the Stromberg's. But when the war started, sometimes the soldiers who came to the chalet would go, if Mr Stromberg asked them to that is."

I'm sure it was where the German soldiers had been that passed me on the track. I noticed they had empty back packs.

"Just how big is her chalet Hilda?"

"Oh, it is really big, but not as big as Mr Stromberg's. His is a mansion. It has ten bedrooms!"

I smiled and said, "Well I do hope your uncle finds Miss Millie well. She may then come and visit me in the hospital."

Hilda's expression suddenly changed. She pulled her chair up close and whispered.

"Do you remember about tonight? You have not told anyone that I told you, have you Louise?"

I held her delicate hand and whispered. "No, I'm sworn to secrecy Hilda. I will never tell another living soul, I promise you."

She stood, smiled and said in a very loud voice, although nobody else was in my two-bed ward to hear her.

"I cannot stay any longer Louise. I have to go home and cook my uncle's dinner. We are staying home tonight; we are not going anywhere. Yes, nowhere outside of our home. My Uncle is at home waiting for me. He did not climb in the mountains today." She then whispered. "Do you understand? Goodbye Louise I hope your leg mends soon," and she left.

God bless her. How delightfully innocent and charming she was. With Hilda's information I was able to conclude that Millie was definitely taken to the grandmother's chalet for two reasons. One was her alcohol intake and the other was to keep her safe. But then, why on earth would Klaus Stromberg send soldiers up to his grandmother's chalet with supplies? This would only show them where to collect Millie if things went wrong. My train of thought was broken by a nurse coming in to tell me.

"Doctor Hugo Stern will be visiting you shortly."

Once again, I felt useless and before I began to really feel sorry for myself, Doctor Stern, a short, dumpy, unattractive man approached.

"Why the worried look Miss Du Pont. You are in the best place for your leg to heal, you have a wonderful view of Lake Zurich and excellent food?"

I managed a smile, "I miss my son, he's nearly ten months old, I hope my friends bring him in to visit me later." I was telling the truth. I was missing PP.

"Oh, you have a son, well I have a son too, he's ten years old. I have taught him all I know about skiing; he is a great skier. He will take part in the National skiing championships this winter and he will win!" An arrogant smile brushed his face before he inspected the plaster on my leg.

"It was an unfortunate accident Miss Du Pont. Things like this rarely happen, mostly only in winter when the snow avalanches form. They sometimes bring with them rocks and boulders. You were lucky you were not left up there to perish. But it was also very unfortunate that you killed a young German soldier."

He hung his head for a moment to look once again at my plastered leg. My instincts decided I didn't like this pompous little man. When finally he lifted his head, he raised an eyebrow and said in an accusing manner.

"No matter what side you are on."

He paused then to see my reaction, there was none, so he continued.

"We try to keep all things neutral here Miss DuPont, but it is difficult. You must have been worried that the soldiers would take action against you, especially being French-Australian." I looked at him defiantly: with venom to be exact.

"What can they do in a neutral country Doctor, shoot me? It was an accident after all." He smirked.

"Ah yes, but some would question the real reason you are here Miss Du Pont. It seems strange that you would come to Switzerland hiking alone in the middle of a war."

I felt like saying, mind your own fucking business, but I gathered my composure and remained silent. He smiled: I even hated his smile.

"I am sorry. I do not mean to pry Miss Du Pont. It is just that I am Swiss-German, if you get my meaning."

He then stood smartly back from the bed. I thought he was going to do the Nazi salute. I turned my head and gritted my teeth.

"Thank you, Doctor. No doubt I'll see you again."

"No doubt at all Miss DuPont. Please, just relax now. You won't be going anywhere for quite a while."

The tone of his voice and his innuendo struck me as threatening. Fucking hell I thought, why was my life getting more complicated by the minute? Here I was laid up in hospital, with nothing to do but twiddle my thumbs and now to top it off, I'd have to contend with a Nazi-loving doctor.

"I'll go crazy in here," I said aloud.

I then remembered Marcel had brought in some supposedly good novels. One was written by Earnest Hemingway. I reached for it. Uppermost on the pile of three by my beside table, it was the easiest to reach. Holding the well-worn book in my hands, I opened the cover and smoothed back the first page which held coffee stains. This story tugged at my heart. It took me back to my days in Ireland, the time Colleen excused herself from going on the walk with Michael and me. She'd said, 'No thank you I want to finish my Earnest Hemingway story.' Well this was the same novel, *The Sun Also Rises*. I'd never read it. As I opened it further, I prayed the story would transport me to another time, another place. And if the story didn't interest me, I would amuse myself imagining all the people who had read this book before me, then guess what they may have been eating or drinking while they turned the pages. Anything to defeat this boredom.

Chapter 18

Doctor Hugo Stern

The novel definitely held my attention. However, after reading twenty or so pages an overwhelming tiredness drew me into deep sleep. In that sleep, I dreamt the same vision of Alain and his mother looking at me through pitiful eyes and skeletal bodies, begging for help. I woke in a cold sweat. I could hardly breathe due to the reality of the dream. At the same time, my bladder was uncomfortably full. I rang the bell for the nurse to come. Instead, Doctor Stern appeared. I sat up a little shocked. He noticed my surprise and I'm sure he also noticed the beads of perspiration on my brow, not to mention my hyperventilating.

"Bad dream Miss Du Pont?" he asked, smiling with that smart-arse smirk. He went to wipe my brow with his handkerchief. I pushed it away.

"I'm alright Doctor, I just need a bed pan, where's the nurse?" I looked over his head not wanting to meet his beady little eyes.

"I shall go and fetch her for you. Remember, I will be close by at all times if you need me."

I could have thrown my book at him. "Little Nazi bastard," I said in a whisper after he'd turned to leave. He faltered for a moment, shook his head and left the room.

The nurse with her charming smile (I'm being facetious), more a scowl that highlighted her ugly face, couldn't speak English, or French. So I acted out a charade of needing a bed pan. Dr Hugo Stern had obviously told her to come, but never explained why. My message was understood soon enough.

I reprimanded myself, I'd been in Switzerland long enough to have learnt their basic language. I spoke a little German, fluent French of course and could speak with the proverbial plumb in the mouth when having to mix with the aristocracy in Britain. But this nurse seemed to speak only Swiss. I realised this after I'd tried a few badly pronounced German words. I thought this was unusual, as most of the Swiss I'd met so far, either spoke German, French or English as well as their own Swiss language.

The curtain was then drawn around me and I could hear Dear Doctor S.S. Stern speaking in what I presumed was Swiss to the nurse.

"Lillian is going to be your personal nurse," the doctor informed me before the curtain was drawn open again.

"That's nice, but we don't speak the same language. How am I going to explain my needs to her Doctor?"

"The same way you just did. We are very short of nurses who speak English or French."

"Why doesn't she speak German if she lives in Zurich?" I asked.

"Oh, so you speak German Miss Du Pont?" His tone lifted.

"I do speak a little yes, it gets me by when needed, but Nurse Lillian did not appear to understand my German."

"Well then that changes everything. Thank you for telling me Miss DuPont. Nurse Lillian will now converse with you in German. She will teach you how to pronounce the language properly and then she will be able to understand you."

Strange but they then had a lengthy conversation in what appeared to be a very different language. It resembled something between Swiss and German. Maybe it was dialect or even coded. I'd have to ask Marcel.

The only visitor I'd had was Hilda. I assumed all my friends, including Bridgette and Jane would be lying low and staying safe at home with PP. I hoped so. I knew I wouldn't hear anything until tomorrow morning about what had taken place this night, which was the night of the big event. I tried to calm my mind by reading the novel, however I was soon interrupted by Nurse Lillian bringing me dinner. This was crumbed veal steak, carrots, beans and potatoes. I was well fed and comfortable, but this was overridden by my anxiety to see Marcel. I had so many things to discuss with him, plus I needed to find out if everything had gone to plan so far, regarding tonight's bombing. Then I realised it would be near impossible to talk to Marcel about the underground movement while Stern and Lillian kept me on a round-the-clock visual. Doctor Stern was obviously suspicious, and he'd stationed Lillian as a spy.

There was one way to find out if Nurse Lillian spoke English, I'd trick her. When Marcel came in, I'd ask her to leave the room, then I'd ask Marcel after a few minutes to find her. He would speak in English and tell her, he thought I'd stopped breathing. If she ran in straight away, bingo we'd got her! This would confirm that they'd been waiting for me to say something which may incriminate me. Was I being delusional?

I thought Marcel, through his network, would be able to find out about this little Nazi sympathising doctor. It seemed nothing was impossible within the underground. It had struck me again and again; just how important these people were. They were every bit as important as the soldiers on the front line. Just as well the underground trusted Marcel and took his word about my identity. So far it seemed no one really suspected, or had taken the trouble to find out, if there was any connection between Millie and me.

I ate my dinner which was delicious, then became jittery with the thought of
what would or should take place tonight. Should I ask for a sleeping tablet? No, I thought, I'll just read it usually puts me to sleep. Just as well Hemingway writes more or less, soothingly. Thirty pages I'd read, before I drifted off and that was despite that last page holding the bloody and exciting description of a bull fight.

I was disturbed several times throughout the night by Nurse Lillian feeling my pulse and taking my temperature. By early morning light, I realised she'd actually stayed in my room. She sat sleeping in the armchair beside my bed. Bloody hell, she was probably waiting to hear me give away secret information in my sleep or wait to see if some underground members entered to take me away. After all, I only had a broken leg I wasn't dying. I just couldn't contain myself when I realised this.

"Wake up Frauline!"

She coughed and spluttered, before jumping to her feet. Once again, I expected the Nazi salute. I was wrong. She straightened her uniform and apologised in German.

"I must have fallen to sleep," she said.

"Never mind love, a little kip never hurt anyone, where's my breakfast?" That caught her unaware. Still groggy, she replied:

"I shall get it." She spoke in German of course but understood the English. Mmm, that was interesting!

This game was beginning to amuse me rather than annoy me. For a doctor, Hugo Stern was not very bright. He should have gained my trust and sent me an English-speaking nurse who would become my friend.

"Bloody idiots," I said out loud. This play of Hugo's was so amateurish, and what did he think he would accomplish?

As I lay in bed waiting for Lillian to bring breakfast, plus the newspaper which I hoped would accompany it, I became a little nervous imagining the headlines. '*Hitler Assassinated in Switzerland!* Or, '*The Stromberg Chalet, blown to pieces!*'

Before too long, Nurse Lillian came in with a tray of food and a bed pan tucked under one arm but no newspaper. I tried again to speak understandable German.

"Bed pan first please Nurse."

She placed the food tray on my trolley table, struggled for a moment to remove the bedpan from under her arm, and pushed it under my bottom.

"Thank you." I said.

I didn't want to appear anxious to read a paper, so I went through the routine of using the bedpan. I then ate and settled back with a cup of tea before I asked for, or rather did charades to try and obtain, a newspaper. She smiled and left.

I must have waited ten minutes before Lillian returned with a tub of warm water and all the trimmings needed to wash me.

"No paper?" I asked again, trying to use my best German, "Nurse Lillian, would you please bring me the newspaper."

She simply went about washing my back. I played her game until she'd finished, then asked again for the paper. She smiled and left while carrying the dirty water. I waited (what else could I do?) until Lillian returned with the newspaper. I flicked open the doubled-up paper and saw the headlines, they read. '*Another allied plane drops bombs on Schaffhausen.*' The date was yesterday, so I asked again.

"I would like today's newspaper thank you Nurse." Lillian responded arrogantly in German.

"What for Miss DuPont is there something you want to know?"

Oh fuckin' hell, I was going to have to kick her in the arse with my plastered leg. Frustrated, I tried to be tactful.

"When do you take a break Frauline?"

She simply shrugged her shoulders. What was that supposed to mean? Was it that she didn't know, or was it she didn't understand?

It had become obvious to me that she was testing me, so once again I played along. I took a very deep breath and sighed, opened my novel and pretended to read and not worry about the paper, when all the while I fumed. The not knowing what had happened the previous night was almost more than I could bare and to make matters worse, she simply sat in her armchair staring at me like a bloody hypnotist.

Ok, let us begin the German lessons. I slammed the book shut and stared back at her until she had to look away. Ah yes, I'd got her again; I smiled and said in faulty German.

"Okay, let us begin to learn German shall we?"

132

She yawned and said, "Not now, I'm tired."

I could make out that much German. My patience was just about finished! If she couldn't understand English like the Doctor had said, then I'd give her a lesson.

"Alright then Nurse, I'll give you an English lesson instead." I yelled. "Get off your bloody arse and piss off out of here. Do you hear me, go away and find somewhere else to sleep?" With that, she smiled and curled up in the chair.

I was in no position to win this argument – more like torment. I waited until she seemed to be asleep and then slowly and carefully proceeded to make my escape. I managed to get out of bed and quietly enter the corridor. While using the hand rail, which ran the length of the wall, I slid my plastered left leg behind my leading right leg. I was making good progress until a nurse spotted me.

"What are you doing out of bed Miss? You should have your leg up at all times!"

She grabbed my arm and proceeded to turn me around towards my room. I pulled my arm away and demanded she go and get me the morning newspaper. She almost laughed.

"Is that all you want; well why didn't you ask your nurse to bring it?"

"She doesn't want to. Do you know Nurse Lillian?" Her voice lowered, and she answered somewhat despondently.

"Yes, I know her."

"Well she's antagonizing me. Do you know what that means?"

"Of course I do, she is the same with everyone, well everyone except Doctor Hugo."

Ah, a confidant, so I asked her name.

"My name is Frieda."

"Well, Frieda, what is it between those two? I feel like I'm under surveillance all the time. It's like they suspect me of something. It's driving me mad. Can you tell me where to find another doctor, or the matron?" Frieda looked sympathetic but shook her head.

"I am sorry," she lifted my name bracelet, "Miss Du Pont. Doctor Stern is the chief doctor here; I cannot go above his head. Nobody can. But I can get you today's newspaper if you go back." She smiled and supported me while I shuffled back to my room.

As I slipped back into bed, Nurse Lillian remained huddled up sleeping in her chair. Nurse Frieda shushed me with her finger and then left the room. Two minutes later she returned with the day's newspaper.

133

What a fizzer. Disappointment swallowed me up. I only read about the bombings that were here, there, and everywhere. No mention was made of the Stromberg Chalet. I thought maybe they'd killed Hitler, and nobody knew. Oh, how stupid. Of course, they'd know. What a bloody disappointment! It brought to mind the biggest and best firecracker we'd longed to let off as children, when after lighting the wick and waiting in anticipation the dam thing fizzled out. It was a dud – same feeling now.

Nurse Frieda had taken it upon herself, to do my observations and write on my chart while Lillian slept. I took the opportunity.

"Would you come and see me from time to time like two or three times a day, Frieda? I shall go mad in here under their surveillance if you don't."

She smiled and puffed up my pillow.

"Yes I will, when I can. You know Miss Du Pont, I would like to go to Australia one day. It is a country that has always intrigued me."

"Please call me Sa— I mean Louise. I would be honoured to show you around Australia one day Frieda and let's hope it's sooner rather than later!"

"That would be very nice. Thank you, Louise."

And with that Frieda left slamming the door behind her. She then peeked to see if Lillian had jumped with the noise. Frieda obviously had the same wicked sense of humour. I laughed as Lillian nearly hit the ceiling

Marcel walked into my room at nine am that morning, looking very smart in his work suit. His face held the same disappointment that I felt when reading the morning's newspaper. Nurse Lillian sat close by, so not a word could be discussed. We spoke about PP, the weather and then Jane, until I asked Lillian to fetch me a bed pan. She seemed reluctant to leave. We had two minutes once the coast was clear, to discuss what had happened. The news was obvious: Hitler had never turned up. Whether it was all hype and never true, we would probably never know.

The good news was our Resistance group as a whole now believed the Stromberg's were definitely allies. Sven had since relayed further information about favourable conversations he'd overheard in the chalet. I asked Marcel if Frederick had gone to see Millie.

He let out a sigh before he said. "No," he was about to elaborate, when Doctor Hugo Stern walked through the door. It was impossible to speak further.

"I have to go to work now Louise. I will return this evening. Heal well," and Marcel turned and left, pushing past Dr Stern.

Later that morning Jane and Bridgette brought PP to see me. I hadn't realised just how much I'd missed him until he cuddled into my chest, especially when he said, 'Mum - Mum'.

My pent-up emotions took over, and I sobbed, rocking PP in my arms until Nurse Lillian tried to pry him from me. This reminded me of Alain's leaving. Thank heavens for Jane who spoke fluent German. She spoke to Lillian and within a few moments Lillian softened. I cried my tears dry, while holding PP in my arms. After my outburst, came the awareness that PP had not cried when I'd cried. I'm sure he felt my heart breaking and seemed to know instinctively how to calm me with his soft cuddles. Was I imagining this? Probably.

Before too long, Doctor Hugo paid another visit. He fired more questions at Bridgette and Jane than in a game of trivia. Jane soon became tired of his interrogation and asked in a demanding tone.

"Would you please leave us to enjoy some privacy Doctor? After all, it is Louise we have come to visit. She finished by saying, "and we won't need the nurse here either thank you!"

We remained silent until Doctor Hugo and Nurse Lillian left the room. I then whispered.

"Please don't speak of anything that may incriminate us. They're Nazi sympathisers. Just get me out of here Jane! I don't have to be here any longer. There's not much pain in my leg. I just need crutches and a car to transport me home."

My release from Hospital certainly took some doing. It became a real battle with the arguments for and against my leaving so soon. This bickering raged for days. Finally, after nearly a week, we convinced Doctor Stern that I had two nurses at home to look after me twenty-four hours a day. Finally, he signed the release papers and I was out of there.

A 'welcome home' sign hung in the entrance hall. Just how special that made me feel, took me back to when I was eleven years old.

"I made this especially for you Louise," Nina said.

I was speechless, but after a minute I managed to thank her with a promise to share it with everyone right then and there. We celebrated not only my home coming, but the many victories which the group had shared while fighting together. The clock struck midnight before we sculled our last schnapps. I slept like a brick that night with my darling son beside me in his cot.

Chapter 19

Alain's Alive

My leg had healed a lot quicker than expected. It was five weeks to the day when the plaster was removed, and x-rays were taken to confirm how well the bones had knitted. I thanked God for all the Swiss cheese I'd eaten. I felt sure it had something to do with my healing. Normally, they said, it would have taken another two weeks in plaster, but I still needed crutches to get around. I became rather nimble on them as the days went by.

In those six weeks I heard disturbing news about Millie's situation. Klaus was apparently under investigation by the German S.S. Word had leaked that Klaus Stromberg was the mastermind in an attempt to assassinate Hitler. Klaus had argued that it was all hearsay, and absolute rubbish; nobody could prove a thing. Our confidants thought Klaus had not been taken into custody due to his friendliness towards Hitler, as Hitler had been overheard to comment on how he admired Klaus's looks and aristocratic breeding. Maybe Hitler thought Klaus to be the perfect sire for the Aryan race, hence he'd dismissed the allegations against him. These ideas had been discussed over and over within our underground movement. Notwithstanding, Klaus had not been let off entirely. We'd heard he was now under close surveillance by the SS.

This news must have caused Millie to drink even more. For after her return to the Stromberg family chalet, she was discovered by Sven swigging champagne in their wine cellar, straight from the bottle. Sven said she'd cried to him about being an alcoholic and that she was pregnant. She had refused Sven's help, so he reported this news to Klaus's housekeeper.

"I have called for the doctor to come and visit Millie. Do not to worry about her Sven. I will personally help her back to her room," said the old housekeeper.

Sven later told Marcel: "I think it was Millie's erratic behaviour that had been too much for the grandmother to handle in the past. The grandmother asked Sven to come and collect her, but Klaus went personally to bring her back.

That's when he told Millie what had happened, about him being questioned by the SS. I overheard it all. I was in the garden." Suddenly Sven blushed.

When I heard this from Marcel, I felt helpless. It seemed Millie had been overwhelmed by the tension of the intrigue and was now too much an alcoholic to cope. I promptly consoled myself with the fact that none of this had been my fault. Millie had refused to be saved, when she could have been. However, I did feel guilty that perhaps I should have given my true identity to the underground members and sent word to Millie that I was in Zurich. Even though Hilda later told Millie that I was the one who'd guided the French resistance men to her, Hilda had believed me to be Louise DuPont and not Sally Darcy, so how would Millie know who Louise Du Pont was? Oh what a tangle our lies create.

I felt so sorry for Granddad Jonathon and Margi, how would I ever be able to explain what had happened to their beautiful talented daughter, and all of it on my watch. I gave myself time to re-think this predicament. But the pendulum of guilt swung straight back at me. I knew in my heart I had to try and turn things around for Millie. Do something, anything to help.

We'd now concluded, the Stromberg's were definitely allies – no ambivalence. That's when I decided to go to the chalet and own up to who I was. I truly felt for Millie and knew in my heart she needed me more now than ever. When Millie saw me face to face, surely, she'd realise she needed to get out of Switzerland and return home to her family in Australia. I believed it could be done. I would take her home, broken or whole. I was determined to return the package to where it belonged. Yes, PP and I would go home to Australia with Aunty Millie and the person I needed to speak to about this plan was of course Marcel. He was my other Alain, not in a romantic sense of course, but he had the same attitude and understanding towards life. I was sure he would agree with me. And at last, I would be free to discuss Millie's problems with her as only a sister-cum-niece can.

After confiding my idea to Jane and Bridgette, I felt totally relieved, as if a great burden had been lifted from me. Of course, I would have to wait until Marcel came home from work even though we three women had already worked out the whole business of going to see Millie; this would be through Sven's introduction. We'd also discussed the best way of leaving Switzerland, but of course all plans had to go through Marcel and our underground contacts first. I hoped and prayed Millie was still there.

Although Bridgette and Jane would be deeply sorry to see PP and I leave, they had realised it would come to this one day. Through tears they admitted they'd hoped it would be later, rather than sooner. We hugged each other tight, until we heard PP cry upon waking from his afternoon nap. As usual, the three of us went to pick him up.

It became one of the happiest afternoons I'd ever spent in Jane's home. My spirits
were lifted with the thought of finally going home to Australia where I truly belonged. I felt satisfied that I'd contributed in every way I could in this war and now it was time to save myself and my son, and hopefully Millie. I sat watching my two beautiful friends playing games and feeding PP with sweet apple from Jane's strudel. Heavenly, is the only word I could use to explain that afternoon.

Evening approached, and the grandfather clock struck six pm, the usual time for Marcel to walk through the door and throw his hat on the hall stand, kiss Jane, say hello to Bridgette and me, then cuddle PP. I checked the time on my gold watch and remembered my mother Addy giving it to me on my twenty-first birthday. This was the watch given to my grandmother Bernadette by Jum her husband, hours before he was murdered. Mum told me that it was crafted by the finest watch maker in Switzerland and it would last many generations.

This information had been correct, it had never missed a beat and what was more intriguing, Marcel worked for the Le Brassus family who'd made this watch. They were respected as one of the finest watch makers in the world. I'd chosen to keep it hidden ever since I'd joined the Resistance. It would be the last thing I'd sacrifice if I had to for this war effort. But today, I chose to wear it as a reminder of where we'd be returning to soon – Australia.

I set the table for our punctual six o'clock dinner. The only exception for Marcel to be late was if the underground called him to a meeting. In that case he would phone earlier to say he'd been held up at work. Marcel had not phoned, and the clock had just struck half past six. We women had begun to worry and then the front door opened, and Marcel entered as if nothing was untoward. He went about his usual procedure of kissing and hugging, then took me by the arm and looked me in the eye.

"Sally, I don't want to get your hopes up too high, but we've received news about Alain." I gasped for breath and clutched my heart.

"Where is he Marcel? Please tell me everything, I need to know!"

"Apparently Alain came across an escapee from the Drancy prison camp which is near Paris. This happened when he was in the Alps and on his way back to my parent's chalet and to you Sally. Alain knew this young man named Oliver. They had stopped to rest and spoke of mutual friends and the people Oliver knew who'd been detained at Drancy and were on their way to Auschwitz. Alain's mother Suzan was one of them." Marcel dropped his head and went quiet for a moment, then continued.

"Alain immediately took it upon himself to try and save his mother. He gave Oliver his food and extra clothes, plus his radio, as it would only weigh him down. Alain did try to contact my mother Edith, before he handed over the radio to Oliver, but he could not reach her. Oliver had escaped from Drancy by hiding himself under the ambulance, hanging on to the chassis. Alain told Oliver to go straight away to my family's chalet, there he would be safe, and he was to tell you, Sally, what had happened. But Oliver it seems has simply disappeared. We think he must have met with his death in the Alps. He may have slipped and fallen into a ravine. The underground members are still looking for him."

"I remember Oliver. He was a boxer and one of the five men I'd met, when first I went to the cave with T-Jon, the tobacco man. But how did you find this out Marcel, has
somebody spoken with Alain?"

"It was your friend Berty. He wrangled himself an interview with the commandant at Drancy. The German's had been under attack for breaking the Universal law on how to treat prisoners. The Commandant intended to show Berty that this was false as long as he agreed to write exactly what he saw. Otherwise, the commandant said, there would be grave consequences! And so, for a week leading up to Berty's inspection the prisoners we suspect were fattened up and given showers and clean clothes to wear. Berty had free range and could question any prisoner he wished but only under the watchful eye of the Commandant.

Berty later told our French confidants, that the hardest thing he'd ever had to do, was to completely ignore Alain when he saw him. He had no idea Alain was there. Although Alain was still alive, Sally, he appeared only a skeleton of the man he once was. Thank God Alain was able to slip Berty a note that explained everything."

"Alain's alive. Alain's alive." I said these miraculous words over and over, twirling as I did. Marcel waited. Finally, he went on.

"Suzan has been taken to Breendonk in Belgium. At least there is still hope for her Sally. Breendonk does not hold quite the same certainty as Auschwitz – death. Now our plan is to get Alain out of Drancy. Berty stayed long enough in France to make sure the rescue plan was agreed to by the Resistance. However, things took a turn for the worse after Berty left France. As far as I know Alain has not yet escaped, nor has he been rescued. The news which has just come through to us from the French Resistance is not good. It seems that after Berty's visit, the screws were tightened within the camp. It has become almost impossible to get prisoners out for fear of reprisal. When one man goes missing, all of the prisoners will have to suffer. And anyone deemed to have assisted in the escape will be tortured."

I asked myself then, was one man's life worth so many? The other prisoners also had families waiting for them. Would it be fair to single one man out from the rest, especially knowing what the others would suffer?

An unnerving silence grew between Marcel and me. I'm sure we were having our own thoughts on the matter but finally I broke the interlude. With my heart ruling my head, I said:

"I am now going back to being Sally Darcy, War correspondent. I will go to Paris and make sure Alain is rescued. I won't allow him to die. We must also remember what he's done for his country. I have to save him!"

Nobody spoke, but I could read their looks, it wasn't that Alain didn't deserve being saved. It was simply that all the prisoners should be. I knew I'd spoken insensitively. But I adored this man who I'd thought to be dead, if only in my mind, never my heart. And to find out now he was alive: this was the most exhilarating feeling I could have imagined. Plus, I was determined that my son would not grow up without his father. No, he would not! I was more than determined that I would go to Paris alone and there, I'd help rescue Alain! I'd shake the world to do so.

Marcel knew me well. Yes, well enough to know there would be no stopping me, so he'd already pre-planned my trip. He'd told me of an underground agent, named Christen, whom I already knew. He would be travelling with me by train to Paris, but that was as far as he could assist. The train would be leaving first thing in the morning. Marcel made me promise, after telling me of his plans for my departure, that I should stick to my Louise Du Pont passport and under no circumstances should I give my true identity.

"When you arrive at the Paris railway station, Sally, I mean Louise, and after you have passed the checkpoint, you will then be met by a woman wearing a red hat and a grey dress. She will wave to you like you are her long-lost friend. Go with her. She will then introduce you to her division of the Resistance. You will get on very well with her, she's Australian."

I thought then I knew exactly who that was.

"Is she the little white mouse, Nancy Wake?"

Marcel smiled. "No, no Sally, but she is a close friend of Nancy's. I told her you would wear your floral dress, the one Jane unpacked from your bag when you were in hospital. You told me once it was your lucky dress, I pray it is. I'm sure with the help of the Resistance you will rescue Alain." Marcel's eyes filled with tears, before he said. "I think I should go with you Sally."

"No Marcel, you must stay and help look after PP, I'm holding you and Jane responsible for him while I'm gone."

I'm sure the reality of what I'd just insinuated reflected in their reluctance to let me do this alone. But they knew me well, so said nothing.

I tossed and turned that night, thinking of all the negatives. I hated being negative. It was definitely my unfortunate demeanour to be morose sometimes, but I'd never give in. My main concern was PP. If I found myself in danger and was possibly killed, what would happen to PP? I couldn't sleep with this dreaded thought, so I chose to write a letter to Marcel and Jane, just in case the worst happened.

Dear Jane and Marcel,

I have entrusted in you, on this evening of May the 29th 1944 to be God Parents to PP. In the event of Alain and I dying. It is my wish that you become adoptive parents to our son Peter Paul Laurent. I do know Bridgette and Pierre would have preference in adopting PP within the law. However, my wish is for you Jane and Marcel, to raise PP in our absence. You have already shown how much you love Peter-Paul, and of course you are much younger than Bridgette and Pierre. I only make one condition, and that is that you travel to Australia with PP when the war has ended, to spend time with PP's relatives there. And then every year after that, he is to visit Australia until he is sixteen years old. Then he will make up his mind in which country he wishes to live.

I cannot thank you enough my dear friends, for all you have done for us. I truly love and respect you both and I know you will make great parents for our son. Not to mention what a wonderful aunt and uncle he will have in Bridgette and Pierre.

Yours sincerely and with great love,

Sally Darcy.

At last my mind was settled and I was able to catch four hours sleep before Marcel woke me at six a.m. If I'd thought of anything after I woke, other than saving Alain's life, I would have held my baby tight, unable to let him go with the thought that I may never see him again. But I had to be strong: I had to do this for his sake. PP lay in his cot sleeping while I slithered into my lucky floral frock. I then stood admiring my baby's perfect profile, just like his fathers. I would keep this picture in my mind forever.

Farewells are always hard, and I don't really want to dwell on just how difficult it was to say goodbye to my dearest friends. However, I had no regrets about my decision. If I didn't try to save Alain it would haunt me forever.

Chapter 20

The Saviour

Before I left, Marcel became a little upset that I chose to leave my crutches behind. I told him they'd only get in the way; besides, I was doing just fine without them.

Luckily for me he was able to borrow a car and drive me to the Zurich Hauptbanhof railway station. Upon arrival, Marcel introduced me once again to this bright young man named Christen. I say *again*, as I'd met him at one or two of the meetings of the Swiss Underground. Although I'd never been on missions with him, I knew Christen to be a brave and intelligent fighter. I respected him and felt a hell of a lot safer in his company.

Once seated in our carriage, I relaxed and enjoyed chatting with him. He was a remarkable and entertaining young man. Of course, when we are young, I'm sure we all feel invincible no matter what life throws at us. Most times we believe in happy endings too. This is what Christen was able to do, convince me I would experience a happy ending.

To the other passengers who shared our carriage, perhaps we seemed like innocent friends travelling to Paris for the weekend: definitely not underground soldiers seeking to make a difference in this war. We laughed, told jokes and shared happy memories, speaking in French of course. I was confident the German Guards at the Paris Railway Station, would never suspect I was not French.

Bridgette had dyed my hair dark and cut it into a bob style. I appeared like the Louise Du Pont in the passport photo now. The reason I'd give to the German officials for coming in from Switzerland, was that I'd been visiting a sick friend. With my neat Du Pont looks, I was sure there would be no problem.

Later on, during the train journey, I remembered what none of us had. My passport
had not been stamped on the way into Switzerland as we'd made our way in over the Alps, virtually sneaking in the back door.

Every now and then, important information I needed, would hit me like a plank of wood. It seemed to me it came from above. Maybe it was my grandparents? Were they really watching out for me, just like my mother had always said? As I'd escaped death on numerous occasions with my dare devil antics and 'bull-at-a-gate' personality, perhaps Mum was right.

I'd been speaking with Christen until I thought of this new problem and that set my nerves scrambling. How in hell was I going to explain this to the German guards? I smiled at our fellow passengers while asking Christen to look at my passport.

"Tell me Christen, do you think I look any older from when this photo was taken?"

I pointed my finger to where the stamp should be – he caught on.

"No not at all Louise, you still look very young to me." He smiled. "Would you care for a cup of tea in the dining car?"

"Yes please."

We left the carriage immediately. Halfway to the dining car, Christen asked for my passport. He took it and disappeared into the men's toilet. I waited outside smiling at whoever passed by. Within a few minutes he'd re-joined me in the hallway, and we proceeded to the dining car. Once seated, Christen handed me a napkin with my passport hidden inside. I placed the napkin on my lap, drew out the passport and carefully put it in my purse. I'd have to look later, as it seemed we had many admiring onlookers.

I breathed a sigh of relief. I was lucky to travel with such an entertaining and resourceful companion, so I sat back and enjoyed the tea whilst I admired the scenery of the Alps flashing by. During that time, I remembered the paths and ascents in my journey to meet Millie in those magnificent Alps. I then pictured my future with Alain and PP where we were hiking in the Alps, climbing the same tracks. I willed it, knowing in my heart that one day my dream would become a reality, I would make it so.

Once the dining was finished it was back to our carriage where I looked at my passport. Christen had stamped it. I looked at him quizzically; he then folded his leg and tapped the heel of his shoe and made a fist sign of a stamping. This was where he'd hidden a replica of the stamp used by the border guards. I nodded with a wink as he changed legs and tapped the other heel of his shoe and then flicked imaginary cotton off his trousers, making it obvious that he had one stamp for leaving Switzerland and one for returning. I was duly impressed.

The clickety-clack of the wheels soon lulled me into sleep. But not long after that I woke gasping for air. I'd dreamt a German SS officer was trying to suffocate me. I began to blurt out the horror but Christen suddenly pushed my head into his shoulder. I'd begun to speak in Australian- accented English. After a moment, I caught my breath and sat up to see all eyes were looking at me. I stammered in French.

"I … I had a bad dream." The faces lost interest and the dull expressions returned.

I then looked down at my gold watch, it read two o'clock. No wonder I was hungry. I asked Christen did he want to join me for lunch in the dining car.

"Yes, I have been waiting for you to wake up Louise. We should go right away, as it won't be long before we arrive in Paris. And oh yes, the conductor has been in to inspect your ticket and your passport. I hope you don't mind, I showed them to him, as you were sound asleep."

"Of course not, after all we are good friends." I kissed him on the cheek. We left the sober people in our carriage and hurried out. While making our way to the food carriage again, I squeezed his hand.

"Darn close," I said.

For lunch we chose a salami sandwich and shared a pot of tea. Then, as usual, I needed to eat something sweet. I suppose it was the way I was brought up. 'Eat your dinner Sally and then you can have pudding' or sweets as we say in Australia. Yes, we're trained at a very young age to look forward to the rewards for being good. I chose a Swiss chocolate bar for my instant reward on this our final hour of what had been a pleasant journey back to France. Not long after, the train pulled in.

Christen and I stood, ready to leave, then he whispered in my ear.

"You are on your own now Louise. I will go to the men's toilet; you go straight ahead to the checkpoint. Your assistant will be waiting for you on the other side. You will see her in a red hat and a grey dress. She will be waving a white handkerchief."

I giggled, which took Christen off guard.

"Don't worry Christen, the white handkerchief brought back a memory." He gave a faint smile and continued to speak while the train grunted and groaned to a halt.

"It is good you laugh Louise; it takes away suspicion. Good luck."
I thought then, how could I not be happy? Alain was still alive, and I would save his life, just as my mother had saved my father. Of course, I would be jubilant.

Christen walked beside me until he'd spotted the men's toilet. With confidence, I walked briskly towards the Guards who were sitting at their table. About ten people had lined up in front of me. I looked over the gate to see if the woman wearing a red hat was there waving the handkerchief, but she wasn't. *Don't panic. People run late all the time, besides our train had arrived ten minutes early.*

I handed the German Guard my passport. He stamped it and was about to let me go through, when another guard, who I'd noticed talking into the telephone, walked over to him and snatched the passport. He then smiled that unmistakable 'got you now' smirk.

"Miss Du Pont, did you have a pleasant journey?" He spoke in French.

"Merci Monsieur"

My heart resembled a drum with no control, hammering out a warning: 'flee before it's too late'. I searched for an escape but saw groups of armed guards everywhere. If I made a run for it, they'd simply shoot me. Maybe that would be better than torture? Then the officer in charge said:

"We would like to ask you a few questions about your trip Miss DuPont. We may be able to improve the service on the train. Come this way please." I shrugged pretending not to understand English.

He came around from the other side of the table and took me by the arm. This could be genuine; yes, they may take random passengers aside to ask if they had any complaints. Who was I kidding! I guessed they'd been informed by some bastard that I'd arrive in Paris on that particular train.

I was taken out to the front of the station and pushed into the back seat of a Mercedes Benz. An SS Officer sat beside me. I was immediately handcuffed and blind folded. The driver took off with such force my body was flung back into the seat. *Why didn't I run when I had the chance? They would've shot me dead, or sent the dogs to bring me down, that's why. Oh fuck, this isn't what was supposed to happen. Why is my life like a bloody roller coaster?*

When we stopped, they dragged me from the car. I could hear Germans talking and laughing as we walked inside what seemed to be an enormous building, before they threw me into a small room like a prison cell. I ripped the blind fold off and sat there shivering for what seemed an eternity, even though it was almost the first day of summer. I looked at my watch, the time told me I'd been sitting there shaking for nearly two hours when they came. I was marched to a room where four SS officers waited to begin their interrogation. However, the first thing the officer in command did was admire my watch. I fought him as he pried it off my wrist.

"I'll hold onto this until you have told me what we want to know. And you do want it back don't you. I can see it has not only quality but sentimental value."

That afternoon dissolved into waves of pain as they applied different tortures. I prayed for the Lords mercy in those first few hours and every moment after that.

I'd become fairly good at shutting off my mind, as they broke my fingers and tried to break my spirit., But in my next interrogation, his first sentence jerked me from my self-imposed stupor.

"You'll never be able to write your war stories if we smash your hand to pulp, now will you?"

This evil worm hadn't used that threat before. What had they found out? Had I somehow leaked information unknowingly?

"You have one last chance to tell us your contacts in the Resistance!"

I looked up, staring into his lizard-like eyes. I saw a glimmer of hope in them as I opened my mouth to speak. He was so expectant; thought he'd broken me. Instead I spat at him. The baton sliced down with such force it took my breath away – then I found the scream. He swooped his baton down again. Suddenly, my face was pulled up by another guard; I shuddered with the pain. He wiped the spit from his mouth with his sleeve and removed a flick knife from his pocket. Arcing his arm up he slashed down. As my cheek divided, I felt my head explode with the force of another blow.

In a vague swirl I heard his words, 'take her...' before the glorious black of unconsciousness hid me. Sometime later I woke. Pain pumped through my body to the beat of my heart. I prayed for sleep, if only to dull my senses. I tried to dream. I found one. I'm hidden amidst a dense rain forest, swimming under an inland waterfall; it flows endlessly into a deep rock pool. Surely peace and serenity await me there. I long for if, for sanctuary – for release.

The dream quickly evaporates reality has found me again. I'm aware of pain and in the same dark cell. With the only part of me that doesn't agonize when I move, I feel with my left hand the fresh wound on my cheek. The blood has congealed; weather infection sets in or not is of no consequence. I don't expect to survive another bout of torture, especially the one where they force me naked into a tub of icy water with my legs and arms tied askew. A chain is then used to pull my head underwater. They do this at intervals until I'm almost drowned. Next time I'll breathe water in and try to end it.

The damp air in my tiny cell has penetrated my aching limbs, reminding me to beg again for them to finish me. But when I beg they only prolong the agony. So now I've chosen not to speak but even my silence annoys them. I pray silently to God for strength while they implement their barberry. That's when I feel the presence of my deceased grandparents and the pain seems to lessen, if

147

only a little.

Between interrogations, I forced my mind to travel back to my childhood. It's the only thing that has kept me sane. I cling to my memory of the happiest day of my life, the day Dad retired from the army. I wish he'd kept his promise. I guess he's out there somewhere now winning more medals or conducting decisive campaigns in this rotten war.

I'm pleased my brother Patrick Junior is too young to fight. He turned fifteen this past September 1943. Mum, at the same time as Dad supposedly retired from the army, also retired from the Adelaide Hospital. However, she too has now agreed to operate on severe cases needing plastic surgery. I guess she's back patching up soldiers again. I touch the wound on my face. If I survive, she'll fix it, but I won't let her: a scar to be proud of – perhaps.

My mind is now in the present. Despite the aches and stiffness from the bashings I need to pee. I manage to lean across and pull the bucket closer. The noise of my urine trickling into the empty bucket is drowned out by two men speaking German. They're standing just outside my door.

"Dear God, not now. Leave me alone, just a little longer please," I whisper.

To my surprise they move on and I finish peeing. When I stand I hear heavy boots forging down the corridor, they stop at my door – purposeful. I dread the sound of the door un-locking.

I haven't quite pulled up my underpants when the soldier enters. He grabs my left arm and hauls me out of my cell. I trip along trying to keep up with him. Pain is shooting everywhere, it's unbearable. It can't be long now, and I'll be free of it – surely. A young officer, who I've seen from time to time, appears from around a corner. His soulful eyes show a hint of compassion for my predicament. He speaks German.

"Wieso halst du nicht an und cast sie ihre hose anziehen?" (something …stop …pants …up)

I understand some of what he's saying, about letting me pull my pants up. It worked. I'm allowed to stop and with my workable left hand I hitch them up. My thin floral frock hangs over my figure, whereas before I was taken prisoner, it sat snug.

We walked on, in my case limped, to another part of the building. This is in the opposite direction from where they usually take me for questioning. I smell soap and hear water flushing before my captor pushes the door open to a large communal bathroom. The shower cubicles are open – no doors. A German officer is having a wee in the urinal. After shaking his penis, he turns to look at me with disdain. As he passes, he comments in English.

"You stink."

"Thank you, God," I say under my breath as I ignore him and focus on the showers. I then say another prayer that the water will be hot and not cold. I'm handed a plain grey dress by a female officer who appears from behind Schultz, as I call him. She walks, almost marches, and turns the water on in one of the cubicles.

"Zieh dich aus und wasche dien schmuteigen koiper!"

(Strip and shower your filthy body) she says in German.

I obey, thinking, *like it's my fault I'm filthy?* I'm having trouble undoing the buttons down the front of my dress, as my right hand can't help. Eventually I'm free of the clothes and when I look down, I see how swollen my knee is. *Stop feeling sorry for yourself,* I think. I limp across to the shower. Thank heavens it's hot. The water flows over me like warm satin, soothing and calming my pain. I start imagining I'm free and my body will soon heal from its trauma.

Smiling up into the warm luxurious flow, I delight in the water cleaning my teeth and mouth. After gargling I spit it out. This reminds me of the first and last time I spat a mouthful of watered-down toothpaste at Millie. She could annoy me like no other person I've ever met. But I still love her – oh, where is she?

Oh shit, Frauline just turned the water off and my memories too. I could have stood under the shower forever. Her robot blue eyes look into mine and she smiles through yellow teeth.

"My name is Frauline Evelyn, I am here to help you dress and make you look respectable. I will then take you to the Commandant." She uses English this time.

I detect a different tone in her voice from when she abruptly told me to wash my body. Was it because I was now clean, or was it because she was speaking out of earshot of the men? Why was Evelyn now drying me gently with a soft towel, helping me dress, brushing my hair and patting the wound on my cheek with antiseptic cream? I'd noticed she'd left the room while I showered, leaving a young officer to stand watch and that he did – intently. I had no modesty left, I didn't care, I was already dead just waiting for the ride to heaven. Perhaps Evelyn had been briefed on something that would go in my favour. Did she care? Was she a chameleon, a traitor to the Reich's cause deep down? How was I to tell?

I took a deep breath, if only to enjoy the scent of my clean body. My skin tingles with gratitude and I feel alive again, the feeling takes me back to riding the surf. They are living things waves and you're best to make friends with them. Maybe I will survive this ride, but I know very well, the power of nature and the power of evil are completely different. One you go with and become part of, the other you must fight until you win or lose. This is what I chose to do now, fight until the end. The shower, it appears, has cleansed me of despondency.

I'm back in the moment: my sense of smell seems to be heightened. I suppose all of my survival senses have kicked in, like an animal being hunted. I smell furniture polish mixed with the aroma of roast lamb. I'm shuffling along another part of the building, a building I cannot fathom. I've become a little confused; I thought I knew this place. But I'm at a loss now to know where I am. Frauline Evelyn walks slowly beside me, considerate, I think. Then she stops at an oversized door and knocks twice.

Chapter 21

Meet the Devil

"Come in, come in." A man's voice says in English.

The commandant is all smiles and charm, welcoming me like a long-lost friend, although his smile is cold below his sky-blue eyes. He comes from a refined German family I assume. His teeth are perfect, no doubt cost a fortune at the orthodontist. His face reveals intelligence and strength; a strong jaw line, fine bone structure, flawless skin; handsome in anyone's language. Although he can't fool me; he's a wolf in sheep's clothing my mother would say. What tack is he going to use? Obviously the charming one. He'll try to flatter me, but he doesn't know flattery plays little part in my life, another trait from Dad. My Dad, the hero that he is, would always make fun of his good looks and heroism.

I'll play his game. I'll smile sweetly when he flatters me, even with this wound on my face. Yes, I'll go along until he reveals his hand.

"So, Miss Darcy. It is a great pleasure to finally meet you."

He knows my real name and holds his hand out to shake mine. He sees my right hand is grossly swollen, deformed and covered in blue-pink shiny skin. He dismisses it and takes my left to his mouth. Oh, here we go, he's begun the charm. The look he gives me is pure unadulterated lust. Please, I think to myself and almost laugh at the thought. Now that's a good sign, laughing. I pray silently to God. *Please forgive me, I'm just playing his game. Is it wrong to enjoy a little mind pleasure before the pain?*

I choose not to speak, not in English. I ask in French who he thinks he's talking to. He doesn't answer. He walks away, ignoring me, intent on inspecting the label on a bottle of red wine. So, I repeat what I've been telling them the whole time I've been captured.

"Mon nom est Du Pont, je suis Francaise. Je m' occupe que de mes affaires." (My name is Louise Du Pont; I am a French citizen just minding my own business).

He smiles and says kindly. "You can stop the play-acting, Sally Darcy.

151

I have found out exactly who you are. Come, please take a seat. Lunch will be served directly. Would you care for some French wine? I believe this vintage will sell for over twenty thousand franks to those who have to pay for it." He smiles wickedly.

I ask myself why evil has to wear such a handsome mask. Well of course silly me, I momentarily forgot, it's a disguise to charm, thus soften me. He thinks he can trick me into telling all I know, give him anything he wants. Ah yes, the tantalizing and irresistible seduction of the devil himself.

I'm now seated at a round rose wood table. I admire the place mats showing English hunting dogs, gathered around their masters who are seated straight backed on fine horses. Their red coats and white breeches add brightness to the picture. Very English, I think. I wonder if they hunt foxes in Germany. But there's no tablecloth. One would assume white linen should have been added before the place mats.

The kitchen door swings open and a stout middle-aged woman hurries in, carrying a joint of roast lamb on a large silver tray. I wonder if she's German or French. She looks more German I've decided. She doesn't speak so there's no give-away, although she does show me a look of compassion. I smile and nod my silent thanks. She then places the tray next to the Commandant and throws him a venomous look. He's not aware of this. The perfectly cooked lamb, crusted with rosemary and thyme, is surrounded by crispy roast potatoes, pumpkin and parsnips. It all looks magnificent. I can't help but breathe in the welcome aroma. I gaze at the feast for a moment.

"You are daydreaming, Miss Darcy. I asked, would you like another slice of lamb? It has been cooked especially for you, knowing all Australians love lamb. Is this not correct?"

"Je ne comprend pas" (I do not understand.) I say in French.

He smiles and carves another piece of meat. I look at my plate filled to the edge with delicious food and my mouth waters. But I feel ill, caused perhaps by guilt at eating decent food when so many people, including children, were being starved to death by these degenerates. My first mouthful is forced down but then I greedily eat. It tastes so good. The commandant notices.

"I suppose this meal takes you back to your childhood in South Australia. Does it not?"

How the hell does he know that, where the bloody hell is he getting this information? I speak again.

"Je suis navree Monsieur je ne parle pas l' Anglais," (I'm sorry Monsieur, I do not speak English.

He grins through those perfect teeth.

"Well allow me to ask you in French, Miss Darcy. Does this meal remind you of being home in Australia?" He speaks fluent French, another sign of his upbringing.

I shrug my shoulders and tell him again in French, exactly what I have been saying ever since I was captured.

"My name is Louise DuPont. I am a French citizen minding my own business." The smile leaves his face.

"You are beginning to antagonize me, Miss Darcy. Would you prefer I send you back to the S.S. officers? They are waiting for you."

I hurry down my last mouthful, this just may be my last supper. I place my knife and fork neatly together, at twelve o'clock.

"Merci, c'etait delicieux," I say, and then realise placing the knife and fork together is an English custom which I'd been told to do all my life. Oh shit, it's a dead give-away. He looks me in the eye and smiles arrogantly. I try not to notice his smugness.

I smile and say. "Encore une fois merci."

"Oh no we are not finished yet, Miss Darcy", he says in English. "We have a famous apple pie recipe that the chef has followed meticulously. I would like your opinion as to whether it is as good as Mother Matilda's, or perhaps Mrs Thompson's."

My heart sinks. There was only one person that could have told him that – Millie.

Is this when I break down and cry? No, this is where I keep repeating my line. I shake my head and shrug my shoulders. He immediately stands and moves close, towering over me. For a moment I brace myself for the slap to my face. Instead, he holds my face firmly in his hand. I cringe.

"You are beautiful, Sally Darcy. It will be a shame to have to kill you."

Before I pull my head from his grip, he kisses me softly, passionately. I want to spit at him when he releases me, but part of me enjoyed his soft lips – so unexpected. I feel guilty and suddenly I can't help myself. In English I shout:

"Where's Millie you bastard, what have you done with her?" He laughs like the evil victor.

"I must be Prince charming; I have awoken sleeping beauty with a kiss." He keeps laughing as he paces the room.

I watch, drenched in self-loathing, until instinct kicks in. I grabbed the carving knife and with all the strength left in me I ran at him yelling.

"You fucking bastard, where's Millie?"

153

I'd taken him by surprise. I thrust the blade hard up against his throat. Then out of the corner of my eye, I saw the main door open. I could just make out a woman dressed in fine clothes and a German officer. Was I imagining it? Had my senses become blurred with rage? Then a female voice spoke calmly.

"Let him go Sally I want to kill him."

I turned to see Millie holding a pistol.

"Millie!" I gasped. At the sight of her I lost concentration and the Commandant grabbed my hand, we fought for control of the knife before he threw me to the floor. Millie took aim and shot him six times. Each bullet jerking him forward until he fell dead. I struggled to stand, feeling relieved, shocked and numb all at the same time. Then I realised the German Officer who stood beside Millie, was the same Officer who'd taken me down the mountain on the day I'd broken my leg. He'd locked the main door, then looked shocked when the kitchen door swung open. The cook and her two male helpers stood over the dead body before spitting on it.

This scenario had become too much for me to comprehend. I began to stagger before this involved German Officer found me a seat. Millie stood on the same spot, staring down at the lifeless Commandant. I asked her gently, seeing how rigid and mentally fragile she suddenly seemed.

"Millie who was he?" She said nothing.

Herman, Millie's German officer friend then introduced himself properly before explaining.

"He is Klaus Stromberg's first cousin, Bjorn. Millie has killed him because he had convinced Hitler that Klaus had planned to assassinate him. Hitler finally believed Bjorn and so Klaus faced a firing squad. We found out about you Sally, because your Doctor Hugo Stern kept a tab on your whereabouts. He suspected you were a spy for the allies. Marcel then informed us about you're travelling companion Christen and he told Marcel about you being taken away at the train station. I must tell you Sally, I was lucky to have escaped the firing squad myself." Herman hung his head for a moment obviously emotional with his next statement.

"Klaus withheld all the information he had on his companions and connections, even while being brutally tortured. He was almost dead when they finally shot him. If he'd given information to the SS, I would have also been shot dead. And then you Sally would have been killed if it weren't for Millie."

The corridors became alive with the sound of men running in all directions. I expected the obvious; they were coming to take us into custody or shoot us on the spot. The cook witnessed my concern.

154

"Do not worry, we 'ave just 'eard on the radio the allied forces 'ave invaded France. Germans Soldiers from all over France are needed to 'elp defend the Reich against the allied invasion. Yes, it is true. Nearly all of the German soldiers 'ave been called away from Paris. Viva La France!"

"Vive la France." I repeated sombrely.

I felt great concern for Millie, who still hadn't moved. She was in a daze; frozen to the spot, I gathered my composure.

"Millie, can you hear me, it's all right now, he's dead, he can't hurt you anymore." She turned to look at me.

"He killed my beautiful Klaus. He killed my only true love Sally." She then cried uncontrollably. I comforted her as best I could, before offering her a brandy from the Commandant's supplies.

"I will never drink again! I could have helped Klaus if I weren't so drunk all the time. I hate myself. I'm only staying alive to have Klaus's baby."

I'd almost forgotten Millie was pregnant; I didn't know exactly what to say. However, I did try to convince her, it was not her fault that Klaus had been killed and reminded her that she was brave enough to kill the man responsible.

"You have so much to live for Millie. The entire world needs to heal from this war. We are all injured in some way. And you can help, by one day soon singing the bad memories away and lifting the spirits of the wounded. It will take time, but you will heal, and your baby will help, I promise." I studied her sad eyes, then held her tight.

"I have a son too Millie, his name is Peter Paul Laurent. We call him PP."

She gave a wry smile. "I know Sally I've seen him, but that's a silly name, you can't call him PP. We used to say that when we were little and needed to go to the toilet."

I laughed a little and held her more tightly.

I suppose one cannot express the sublime happiness which comes from looking death in the face and realising you have survived. That feeling can never be surpassed.

Herman left us and went to find his confidants within the building. When he returned, he was wearing civilian clothes. The plan was to drive us to a safe house, which sat about fifty miles outside Paris. We left through the kitchen door with the help of the cook and her friends. Bending so low we almost crawled, we made our way through a secret tunnel, which eventually led us outside to where a car waited. The driver, who also wore civilian clothes, sat with his hands upon the wheel, engine running and foot ready for the accelerator pedal.

On our way out of Paris, Herman told me the story of how he'd been Klaus's close friend. Their friendship began at boarding school in Germany and continued in Switzerland where they attended the same university. They'd shared the same beliefs, 'freedom for all mankind,' so they had planned together. Their belief was that the best way to fight for what they believed in, was from inside the fox's den, hence they began their strategies.

Herman was aware, through Marcel, that Alain was still being held prisoner at Drancy. This was Herman's next mission; he would try to free Alain. I knew after speaking with Herman that he held grave fears for Alain. He suspected when the soldiers at Drancy learnt of the invasion, they might mass murder the prisoners as revenge. The same thought had also passed through my mind, if only fleetingly.

Millie and I were to be kept safe until the coast was clear. Herman and his driver would then meet with the Resistance and try to secure Alain's escape. While doing this, Herman may learn more about Alain's mother, Suzan. There are no expressions of gratitude strong enough to describe the way I felt when Herman gave his word that he would rescue Alain – no matter what. Just thinking about holding Alain in my arms once again set my heart hammering.

The four of us drove for quite some time before reaching a charming farmhouse surrounded by fields of golden sorghum. This was a familiar sight in the countryside of France, if it hadn't been destroyed by the war. I was more than willing to stay anywhere we'd be safe, be it a cave, a barn or a cellar. However, this place looked so heavenly it was almost too good to be true.

After meeting with the owner, Mrs Ruby Chevalier, we were shown a secret room within the attic. A false door lay hidden behind a bookcase. Once Ruby had removed the bookcase, the timber slatting which made up the pattern on the walls, cleverly disguised an entry and when you pushed, it opened into a tiny room. Two mattresses lay on the floor, with a pillow and a blanket on each. There were no windows, just a small crack in the wall which allowed sunbeams to penetrate. A basin and a jug full of water sat on a wooden dresser. Hand towels and soap were provided and a tin bucket, I assumed for ablutions. This sat beside the dresser.

I turned to kiss our hostess on her ruby- red cheeks, thinking this may be the reason for naming her Ruby. She spoke only French, which Millie wasn't able to understand.

"I am happy to help such beautiful young women," she said, then looked at Millie's stomach. "I will cook you special food to keep your baby healthy."

Ruby seemed amused by the look of horror on Millie's face as she viewed the room.

"No, no, this room is only for emergencies. It has been used to hide many Jewish people, until we find them a safe way out. You are not expected to sleep here. Not unless the Germans come, which will be unlikely now the Allies have arrived." Ruby's face brightened. "I have a lovely room for you two to share."

I then translated all this to Millie, who, relieved thanked Ruby, by kissing her cheeks. "Merci, merci," she said.

The first week at the farm, I spent almost completely alone with Millie. It gave us time to bond on a level we'd never been able to before. The twists of fate that brought us to where we were right now, were shared through tears and laughter. For the first time in my life I began to really like Millie. It seemed to me it was the chain of events that had led Millie to become an alcoholic. When Klaus was killed, and Millie discovered she was pregnant, she broke away from her hedonistic approach to life. Suddenly, she'd become connected to what was happening around her. Her previous alcoholism had obviously kept her in a pleasant state of denial. Now her strong character and decent up-bringing had helped her rise from the ashes.

I was well aware she'd had a very unpleasant awakening to her true nature. I believed she'd been living in fairyland most of her life. Her ego now was tempered. However, I was confident the fun-loving magnificent opera star would find her way back to an inflated ego sooner or later. For now, we looked forward to our future together being much brighter, especially with the allies forging a path to end the war.

I chose not to ask too many questions of Millie, especially about why she didn't do this, or why she didn't do that. I felt she was still quite fragile, yet in another way strong. When she said 'I will never regret killing Bjorn I knew then how strong she'd become.

Millie told me how, even from childhood, Bjorn had been an evil little bastard and forever jealous of Klaus. Klaus had been a champion skier, an honour student, a perfect son and so on. It didn't matter what Klaus did, he was the best at what he tried. This had been the reason why Bjorn took a sadistic pleasure in romancing Klaus's wife away from him. Bjorn later shunned her completely and she ended up a nervous wreck.

"Would Klaus not take her back?" I asked.

"No Sally, he believed in loyalty first, although he forgave her and

Bjorn too, even though I thought they weren't worth forgiving. I think his forgiveness infuriated Bjorn even more. He wanted to really hurt Klaus, but Klaus could never pretend he still loved his first wife. He did feel sorry for her though and we offered her friendship. I wasn't jealous. She was a sweetie really, just weak when it came to false flattery." (I hoped Millie would take a good look in the mirror after that statement).

"That's the main reason I stayed with Klaus. I wanted to prove my loyalty. I told him I would never leave him, not under any circumstances. I hope you understand Sally. Plus, I loved him with all my heart. He was such a good man. I would have married him and stayed happily with him for the rest of my life." Millie then looked at me straight on and said, "I'm so sorry Sally, I could not possibly confide in you, or anyone. I knew too much about Klaus and what he was planning. He was fighting for our side. I just had to stay put and wait until the war ended. I had to appear as if I were on the German side, I couldn't risk even the wrong word in a letter to anyone. Do you understand? Can you forgive me?"

Even Millie's melodramatics had gone now. A sincerity that I'd never seen had surfaced in her. Of course, I forgave her. Millie hugged me and began sobbing into my chest. At last I completely understood her predicament and her sorrow.

Chapter 22

Not Over Yet

Day after day we waited to hear news of Alain's rescue. Hearing no news at all, especially from Herman, was more than I could stand. I was consumed with worry. Perhaps Herman had been killed before he could free Alain. I was unable to sleep at night and often paced the kitchen floor. After three weeks of going through agony, I decided I'd go to Drancy myself, or at least I'd go and see my confidant, who lived not far from Drancy. This would be dangerous, as the battle for Paris was still in earnest, but I would go, nonetheless. When I told Millie, she begged me not to go. Her excuse was, she could not possibly go with me, not while she was six months pregnant and she didn't want to be left alone. I understood. It appeared that either Alain was dead, or Herman had struck trouble. Whichever it was, I had to stay put.

"Don't worry," was the last thing Herman said to us before he left, but I did.

After my escape from the Commandant, along with the cook and her helpers, we would surely be hunted down. We would all be main suspects. I couldn't help but feel now that Herman had been captured or killed.

The same news came over the public radio every day. 'Paris remains under German rule. They are refusing to relinquish power to the Allies'. That meant Drancy was still being held too. My hopes were diminishing fast. Millie sensed my worry, although I'd tried very
hard to hide it from her.

I reminded myself that she had to come first, nothing was to happen to her baby. I knew exactly how Millie felt; it was her only living connection to Klaus. Reluctantly, I gave up my dash to save my love, or was it to become a hero once again? I remained safe in our domesticity with Millie and our hostess. This did give me the chance to teach Millie some French, so even more re-connection came from the time we spent together.

Ruby received only a few visitors while we were there and for anyone who did come, her dog MiMi would bark. We'd then hurry to our hiding place. Ruby didn't trust a soul, plus we were still not entirely safe even though the allies had almost surrounded us.

One day, after we'd been staying with her for nearly seven weeks, she finally had the courage and I suppose, she felt close enough to tell us that her husband had died of a heart attack on the very day the Germans took control of France. And two weeks later, her only son, Anton, had joined the French Resistance. With tears glistening in her blue eyes and her voice wavering, she said:

"Anton has gone missing and I pray every minute that he is still alive."

I gathered her in my arms as she cried and cried.

"I only wished I had a daughter like you Ma Cherie...."

Before Ruby could finish her sentence, MiMi began barking madly. Quickly we made haste to the attic. Ruby followed, placing the bookcase back against the wall once we'd gone behind.

We waited nervously until the familiar sound of the bookcase slid open and we stepped out. That's when we saw two Aussie Soldiers standing alongside Ruby. One took off his slouch hat, scratched his head and said:

"Christ it's her!"

I thought they meant Millie, but no, it was me they were referring to. I was shown a photo of myself.

"Your Aunty Colleen, the Matron, passed around your photo in the London hospital. She hoped a soldier or civilian returning to France may see you."

"Well I'll be buggered. It worked!" the other one said.

Millie and I laughed so much we cried. Their Australian drawl was like heaven to my ears. After pulling ourselves together, we made our way to the kitchen. We sat and heard the whole story, over a cup of tea, about what had been happening outside the farm. Hundreds of ships carrying soldiers from Canada and other allied countries had stormed ashore, all along the French coastline. They moved like soldier ants freeing the villagers all over France and now they were heading towards Paris.

We introduced ourselves by our Christian names to these intrepid Aussies, Hunter and Digby. I felt no formalities were needed. I then told them we could hear the continuous blasts from the cannon's surrounding us and sometimes, when two or more went off together, the ground shook.

"It unnerved Millie, but Ruby and I have been close to action, so we weren't that concerned. Anyway, we knew it was only you guys coming to save

160

us," I said. Digby was quick to answer.

"That's right, but actually, we've just come to get some water for the billy."

We laughed at his laid-back attitude. It was something I missed hearing so much. Even Ruby laughed, and she could only understand a few words of English. Digby went on to say:

"We're with the Yanks, or Canadians really. They don't like us call'n 'em Yanks. There's only us two Aussies and our Sarg. We were left over from the first campaign. We was havin' a holiday in London after bein' patched up in the Hospital you see. But we jumped on the ship with the Yanks we did. Soon as we knew it was goin' to more action. We's wanna be there at the end. It won't be long now, and we'll be right outside Paris and then we'll get rid of those bloody Crouts once and for all!"

Hunter nodded in agreement and then added: "We've camped up the road a bit. That's why we need the water."

"Yeah. And we're not leavin' Paris till we see some of them beautiful can- can dancers."

I noticed whenever they stopped talking, they looked at Millie, obviously trying to work out where they'd seen her before. I put them out of their misery.

"You may have heard of, Millie Darcy the famous opera singer?" They nodded yes.

"Well then gentlemen, may I introduce THE Millie Darcy." Digby it seemed had a habit of scratching his head when surprised. He did it again before he said:

"God stone the bloody crows. We got the double act here mate!"

"Please excuse Digby's manners ladies, he's a real bushy, comes from far north Queensland." Hunter reached his hand across the table, "I'm pleased to meet you Miss Darcy, I mean Millie. My mum just loves to hear you sing, I can't wait to tell her about this. Fancy hey, just fancy meetin' you in the middle of a bloody war. Oops – pardon me French."

After the laughter subsided, we spoke about our respective homes in Australia. I then went on to tell them about my problem in attempting to free my French husband, Alain, from Drancy. They showed compassion for my situation and also respect for Alain, after I told them of his amazing work within the Resistance. They then said that if they had the opportunity to go to Drancy, once they'd freed Paris of course, they would bring him here to me. I went on to tell them the whole story, of how I was captured and taken prisoner, then

161

tortured and interrogated. I looked to Millie, for her approval to tell them how I was rescued. She nodded yes. After I'd explained, they sat gob smacked. Millie then asked could they keep an eye out for Herman. If it weren't for Herman, we wouldn't be sitting opposite them today. Enthusiastic nods were given.

Time was moving on and they had to leave, but not before Hunter asked once more:

"Could we please fill our water bags. We've got to get going or the Serg'll have us on a charge for AWOL!"

"Hang on a minute, we'll probably be stationed here for a day or two, how about a song for the boys Miss Darcy?" asked Digby.

For the first time in my life, I noticed Millie actually blush.

"I suppose if it can be done safely, I could sing one or two songs. Ask your Sergeant gentlemen," Millie said with a broad smile.

"Geez thanks a lot Miss Darcy, I mean Millie. I'll tell Sarg!"

We watched, as they ran to fill their water bags from the well. But I was only half paying attention. I had my eye on Millie's body language and how she'd plumped out her peacock feathers with their flattery.

"Well, well, Miss Darcy. Maybe this will be the beginning of your return to the stage and your baby's introduction, to what's in store for her." Millie looked surprised. For a moment I thought I'd offended her.

"So, you think it's a girl, Sally?"

"I don't know. I just said 'her' because it was the first thing that came to mind."

Millie's brown eyes looked wistfully into space.

"I feel it's a girl. Klaus told me he would love a baby girl, just as beautiful as me."

She became suddenly sombre and nursed her stomach, then turned and walked inside.

The next morning our Aussie mates returned with the news, they were about to move out. Digby spoke first.

"The Sarg say's to thank you very much Miss Darcy." He blushed a little, "Millie, I mean and 'e hopes you could sing for all the Allied soldiers when we conquer Paris."

Hunter then asked:

"Would you mind signing a few autographs for the boys?"

"A few!" I said as Digby then handed her a stack of tiny bits of paper, anything which would hold a signature. It took Millie nearly half an hour to write her thanks to all the soldiers. I have to say, it made her happy to know she was not forgotten and still admired. I just hoped her alter ego would not raise its ugly head too soon. But then again, maybe that side of dear Millie, had matured into something now deep and beautiful. Time would tell.

All we could do then was wait. Wait for news, whatever that may be. We spent our time mainly writing letters to Colleen in London and our family back home. This brought about many tears of joy plus tears of regret for the both of us.

It was what I'd call happy tension, waiting for Paris to be returned to the Allies. I was a little deflated whenever I thought about Alain still in Drancy. I didn't dare raise my hopes too high, thinking he'd survived, when he most probably hadn't. So, I prepared myself for the worst and prayed for the best.

The rest and recuperation I had in those two and a half months, had almost healed my body, so I practiced walking without a limp. It was difficult at first, as pain had prevented correct foot placement. Then, as if heaven sent, I rose one morning in August to walk absolutely pain free. It's not that I'm vain, but I began admiring my reflection in the mirror. To try and envisage what Alain would come back to. I felt happy with the flush of colour returning to my face, although the scar was still prominent on my cheek. I knew it had healed quite well. My skin glowed with its usual autumn tone and my blonde hair shone. Millie had cut the dark remains off the ends making it shorter than it had ever been. After she'd finished, I stood for a while, too long in fact, in front of the mirror enjoying the transformation. It prompted me to give thanks to the Lord for his mercy. I also felt happy thinking about the day when I'd travel safely back to Switzerland to collect PP. I chose not to include Alain in the vision, hoping the pain of the inevitable would lessen if I did.

The next day, on the eighteenth of August 1944, Millie and I were helping Ruby bottle some of her freshly cooked green tomato pickles. It had been a mild summer, and this was the final harvest of her large tomato crop. She'd preserve and make pickles with the first flourish of un-ripened tomatoes. Then she'd enjoy the ripest selection to eat and also make the most sensational tomato sauce I've ever tasted. The last of the smaller tomatoes, she would turn into tomato relish. This is what we were doing when the radio blared.

"The battle for Paris had begun in earnest!"

The 'French Resistance Soldiers, along with backup from allied soldiers, were making headway and it would not be long now before the beloved city of Paris would be returned to the French people'. We cried tears of joy, hugged each other and danced around the kitchen table. The dog began barking. We laughed thinking it was from our silly behaviour, but then we noticed MiMi

163

scratching at the door.

Today, for the first time, we chose not to run to our hideaway, instead we hurriedly walked to the window to see a Canadian Army Jeep driving slowly up to the house. As it came closer, I could see from the Slouch hats, it was our two Aussies. They appeared to be the only ones in the jeep and so I braced myself for the news. Alain was dead.

We stood together at the window, transfixed. Ruby began rubbing my back gently before she went to boil the kettle. I smiled at her kind gesture. I'd already prepared myself for the worst. However, there came an element of surprise when I saw the two Aussies jump from the front of the jeep and then open the back door. Digby stooped over and lifted a tall thin man to his feet. My eyes strained to see who it was, I then realised – it was Alain. I screamed, raced out the door, tears streaming from my eyes, and helped them bring him inside.

Being close and looking fleetingly into Alain's hollow eyes, brought back the haunting dream I had of Alain and his mother grey-faced and pleading to be helped. After I'd held his frail body against mine, I stood apart to study his lifeless face. I was unable to speak. I simply cried tears of anguish and happiness. Once again, I say no one ever knows true happiness, until the grim reaper shows himself and then turns away. Though I felt with my first embrace, our personal journey had only just begun. I could see my emaciated husband would need the very best of loving care to survive, not only his physical pain but his mental torture. Once inside and seated, I hovered over Alain, not knowing what to do first.

"Sally stop fussing. It was only the thought of you which has kept me alive. I'm not
about to die now. I'm with you." As he said this his voice rasped with the effort.

He caressed my hand and kissed it before holding it up to his cheek. His grip was weak but frantic, as if he were hanging on for life itself.

Millie placed her hand on his back, before she spoke.

"Alain I'm so sorry. I seem to have been the cause of all your problems. Please forgive me." She then kissed him on his forehead.

He forced a smile.

"No, no, Millie. It is I who should thank you. If it weren't for you, I would not 'ave met my beautiful Sally. So thank you. There is no forgiveness needed."

Rubies kitchen had become our meeting place and it seemed nothing could be discussed without a cup of tea. I was unable to contain my happiness and it soon became contagious, especially with Ruby delighting in our reunion.

But every now and then I noticed waves of sadness brush her face. I assumed it was the memory of her son still missing and the memory of her deceased husband. My heart ached when thinking she'd be left completely alone after we'd gone. I'd asked her before this day, did she have any close family and she told me.

"No, my family have all been killed in both wars. But Herman's mother is a good friend of mine, she is French. We grew up together, until she went to Switzerland as a young woman. There she met and married Herman's father."

This was of some consolation I suppose. Even though Herman appeared to be missing and feared dead, the two women friends may be able to console each other. Amidst my own elation, I was able to feel ruby's suffering and so I made her a promise.

"I will take every avenue possible to find Anton for you Ruby. I will search Paris and use every contact I know to help." I witnessed in her eyes the hope and joy, my promise gave. "I must also reimburse you Ruby for your kindness and the cost of our food." She laughed, waving her hands about.

"No-no, you are more than welcome, we are friends now. Maybe one day I can come to Australia for an 'oliday and you can look after me."

"I would love you to come. And, Ruby, I will make it possible, the very day I return home to Australia."

The joy of returning home with my family intact flowed out of my mouth like a prayer to the Lord.

"I can't tell you how much I long to return home," I said then looked at Alain.

My smile met his cold stare; how could I be so thoughtless? I knew he had ahead of him, the shocking business of trying to find his mother. I scolded myself. I should not be showing so much happiness and definitely not be in a rush to get home. He needed my total love and support. Therefore, I should be the one to go to Breendonk and as soon as possible.

"I am so sorry Alain; I know we must find your mother before we discuss going home to Australia. I will go personally." Alain's expression remained lifeless.

His blank stare I felt was not intended for me, so I turned to Digby for an answer.

"I'm sorry Sally, we should have told you first. Alain's mother was taken to Auschwitz, not Breendonk. She was deemed an undesirable. Only Jews and undesirables went to Auschwitz. Suzan, we fear is most certainly dead."

I wanted to scream – undesirable! Who invented this bloody tag? How dare they! But I had to quell my anger; it was not what Alain needed. I said nothing.

I then consoled myself with the fact that the worst was over and what was done, was done. Suzan was gone and now we had to take tiny steps before making plans for our future. Studying my frail, almost broken husband I was sure it would take months, if not years, for Alain to regain his passion for life. My heart went out to him and I vowed to myself, I would never give up on him. I could only hope and pray the zeal we'd once shared would eventually return and last. I rocked Alain in my arms, before Hunter coaxed him into bed with the promise we'd wake him when lunch was served. I appreciated how kind these diggers were; especially when they laid Alain down and gently covered him with a blanket. It touched me.

I was more than pleased they didn't have to rush off and could stay for lunch. It gave them time to fill us in on all that had happened, between the time they left and when they found Alain. It was so complicated and such a long story, I cannot possibly repeat how many battles had to be fought, before the seventeenth of August, when Drancy prisoners were freed. The entire garrison had helped Digby search for Alain and they almost missed him. Unlike most other prisoners, who'd rushed from the place, Alain lay on the floor curled in a foetal position. This fact sent me reeling with indescribable pain.

"I'm sorry but I need to hold my husband. Thank you again for what you've done." I had to excuse myself.

"It was our pleasure to be able to help two heroes; or should I say one hero and one heroine." I turned to Hunter.

"I'm no heroine. I'm no braver than you or any other soldier. God bless you both, and I thank you again for finding my love."

I slipped my body into bed close to Alain's. He murmured, "Is that you Sally?"

"Yes, my love, please go back to sleep, I will never leave you again, we're free."

Alain's thin body felt strange and fragile against mine. I smiled then with the thought of fattening him up. I realised it would take some time before I'd see the magnificent man he'd once been, but for now I felt whole again. I worried then, could Alain ever feel complete again? I chose not to fret anymore, not then. In that moment of sublime peace, I drifted into sleep.

Chapter 23

Alain's Recovery

Under Ruby's insistence we stayed until the battle for France had been well and truly won. She seemed more than delighted to have us there. Alain, I knew was trying hard to be happy, however, every now and then he'd slip away into another world. One I was not part of, one I couldn't reach.

In those first weeks together, we enjoyed long walks. I hoped in this time alone we'd be able to make plans for our future. However, to my frustration, he seemed hell bent on going over his horror at Drancy. I never needed to know every detail of his terrible ordeal, or the reason why he'd survived when others hadn't. I hated to hear of his pain, but I showed empathy and listened. I sensed there was still worse to come. Then it came. Alain began to talk about his darkest hour. I had to stop him and perhaps I shouldn't have. *Please God forgive me*, I said silently. I was simply not ready for this final ghastliness. A weak excuse I know, but I felt it wasn't fair. I shouldn't have to feel his agony over and over again, not when I'd never told him of my torture when captured, all be it for a very short time before rescue. Alain's internment had been nearly twelve months – totally different. But just before he divulged his worst experience, I said:

"Alain, I don't want to appear heartless, but unless you really need to tell me of these dreadful truths, could we just accept the past is the past and now is the beginning of our new life together."

The expression on his face gave me the answer. A look of surprise, almost shock I suppose, in realising what he'd been actually telling me. He seemed to consciously shake himself.

"You are right Ma Cherie, looking back does me no good. I must not go over and over my pain. We need to begin again. I am sorry." With effort he then said in a forced but happier tone. "Please tell me more about PP, I want to know all about him, I can't wait to see 'im."

This was the glimmer of hope I'd been looking for.

"You will know him soon my darling. In two weeks' time we'll go to

Paris and stay two nights and then by train to Switzerland. Paris will be one big party, we'll have some fun, what do you say Alain?" He held me tight.

"Yes, we will Ma Cherie."

I then told him of my other plan, as gently as I could.

"You know Alain; I must keep my promise to Ruby. I have to at least try and find her son, Anton. I will be going to Paris tomorrow, alone." After seeing the expression on his face, I explained quickly. "We couldn't possibly leave Ruby without her knowing if Anton were dead or alive."

He froze on the spot, then stated.

"You are not leaving me Sally. You promised you would never leave me again. Our war 'as ended, let the Aussies find im!"

I stepped back, shocked at his anger.

"The Aussies have done enough for us Alain; besides they're going back to England tomorrow. I'll be safe, the war's finished in Paris. I just need to find my contacts and put the search in place for Anton."

"Aven't you 'eard of the telephone Sally," he said with sarcasm.

"Yes of course. But I have to show Anton's photo around and ask if anyone has seen him." I noticed the little-boy-lost expression on Alain's face and kissed him gently on the cheek. "Alain, there's nothing to worry about, I'll be back in three days' time. I just need to get the word around about Anton and of course his photo."

I could see moisture cloud his beautiful eyes. I kissed him on the lips, taking in his salty tears. I would then refuse to speak any further of my plan, as I knew it would only upset him. However, I did give him one last reason why he was best to stay behind.

"You know I have to go alone Alain. I'll move quicker alone and you're not yet strong enough to go with me." He had no argument and remained silent for the rest of our walk.

I'd given Alain my assurance that I'd be safe, although I knew there were still Third Reich fanatics, mad men if you like, out there trying to hang onto something they fought for and lost. I likened it to a bully kid fighting over a new bicycle which didn't belong to him and then the parent of the boy he took it from came to retrieve it. A funny analogy I know, but none the less simplistically true. I was not stupidly naive anymore, so I would stay alert. I was also informed there remained around France, a number of German troops which had dug in like cancer. They sat north south and east of Paris, holding on to small posts of German influence. In my opinion, it would take some time before France was totally free. There were still elements of danger no doubt, but before the Aussies

168

had left, Digby gave me a hand pistol and a flick knife. If I struck trouble, I would certainly use them!

The next morning brought with it a foggy mist which matched my mood. I experienced the last-minute jitters and seriously questioned myself, why I needed to do this. Of course, Alain had been right; there were telephones to reach the right people in charge of finding missing relatives. Nevertheless, I did as I'd always done; I went forward with my conviction.

I walked down the driveway to the road. I was to wait outside the front gate for a lift to Paris. Ruby had phoned a neighbour who took his produce to the Paris market every Tuesday, leaving before dawn. This was perfect. I'd get an early start. I was also lucky that I'd escaped without waking Alain. If he'd begged me to stay one more time, I would have. Maybe it was the reason I'd walked slowly, hoping he would come running after me.

My driver, Henry, seemed either painfully shy, or didn't want to talk, so I spent my time in the old truck reminiscing on happy times. It always helps to think of the positives. We'd recently heard from Colleen, she'd become very friendly with Michael, my old boyfriend. Just how friendly, she never let on. I owed her big time though, as I'd asked her to tell Michael about Alain and PP. This news, I knew, wouldn't be easy for anyone other than Colleen to explain. She held compassion alongside truth and could tell things as they truly were. In this department, she was above and beyond anyone I'd ever met. I loved her dearly.

My parents had been in contact with Colleen and so she was able to pass on their news in a letter. All things remained as they were at home, although Dad had been a genius in organizing a major offensive in Syria. He of course was the obvious choice as he held such extensive knowledge on the Middle East and its people. Dad would have been of great benefit to the Allies. His job had been mainly planning, or strategy as Dad would prefer to call it. It added to my happy memories, knowing they were all safe and well. Colleen had written, *the family are beside themselves with excitement to have you, Alain and Peter-Paul coming home*, I had to giggle. She was like Millie, refusing to call our son PP.

As always, my mind drifted back to Alain. I'd never told him; it was the memory of my childhood that saved my sanity while being tortured. The pain of thinking of him and PP would have weakened me. And yet for him, it was the thought of returning to us that saved his life. I thought about the final confession that Alain seemed desperate to tell and scolded myself for not hearing him out. I mustn't let anything come between us now, this included dark secrets. One day soon, I would muster the strength of mind and heart to listen to his full story.

Chapter 24

A Final Twist

When we arrived, it almost seemed to be the same Paris I'd known and loved, pre-war.

"Vive la France!" I said before I turned and kissed Henry on the cheek.

Hundreds of allied Soldiers embraced French mademoiselle's who in turn flaunted appreciation to their saviours. Sidewalk café's bustled with patrons and shop windows were adorned with the latest fashion. Arm in arm, men and women walked happily about. Yes, this was the Paris of old, even better. This is what we'd fought for.

Henry dropped me off on the footpath leading to the Eiffel Tower. Then, before I had time to thank him and shut the truck door, he said:

"Now remember Sally, if you need a lift back to Ruby's, I will be 'ere at the same spot next Tuesday at three pm, okay. You got that young lady?"

"Yes, thank you Henry. I'll be here or, I'll get word to you if I don't need a lift. Thank you again!"

From then on, I was on a mission. I began contacting my fellow underground members. Then I searched the telephone book for Julia Noir's mother's address. It was partly for Bridgett's sake that I'd like to meet her, and tell her of our coincidental connection, although it would be good to talk about Julia too. I'd been told by Colleen that Julia had survived the London bombings and she'd asked about me all the time. I wondered if maybe she would return to Paris now it was free. Julia and Colleen had become good friends when sharing the same underground shelter during the London bombing raids. I missed Julia and so hoped her mother would have news of when Julia would return to Paris.

The euphoria of Paris was seductive. It allowed me no thought of why I was actually there. I had to shake myself occasionally to keep on track with my plans. Yes, I would go next to my friend who was a specialist in photography. He'd taken Julia's modelling photos which began her career. After he'd made copies of Anton's picture, I went to my next friend who would pass them around to all his contacts. The police of course had already been informed of Anton's disappearance, as had the army missing person's bureau. However, they held no photo of Anton and because he was a member of a small branch of a somewhat informal French Resistance movement, he would be harder to track down. All of the above I'd accomplished in a great hurry within the first day.

As twilight bathed the Parisian evening in soft tones, I decided I would take the chance that Julia's mother was at home. The need to enjoy a glass of wine with a friend became paramount. If she were anything like her daughter, there was sure to be a wine or two in the offering. Ms Noir lived in an apartment in the centre of Paris. Thankfully, I was able to walk there easily from where I stood outside the police station.

I rang the doorbell and was surprised when she answered so quickly. She looked like a slightly older version of Julia. I introduced myself.

"I'm Sally Darcy, Julia's Australian friend." Immediately, her hands flew to her cheeks.

"Oh, my dear girl, I know all about you, you are a great 'ero, yes a Great War 'ero!"

I was taken aback for a moment, where on earth did that story come from.

"No mademoiselle, I am not a hero. But may I come in?"

"Please, yes come in Sally. Julia is coming 'ome tomorrow, I cannot believe this. She will be so 'appy to see you. Julia said in many letters she feared you 'ad been killed, as nobody 'ad 'eard from you."

Ms Noir, or Jacqueline, she introduced herself as, sat me down in a most comfortable armchair in her delightful lounge room. Photos of Julia posing in the most glamorous gowns covered the walls. In other photos, she appeared casually draping her near naked body beside forest trees or amongst wild flowers. I stood admiring them while Jacqueline, who'd obviously read my mind, left to bring back a bottle of red wine. She filled my glass with God's nectar. I almost gulped it down.

"Thank you, Jacqueline, I needed that. I'm all tuckered out, as an old friend of mine would say. It's been a long day and my suitcase feels like a ton of stones."

"Oh, you poor girl. You must stay 'ere. I would love your company."

I was more than happy to take up her offer and I think after my third glass of wine, I began to slur my words. Jacqueline took the cue and went quickly to the kitchen. She returned with freshly baked bread and cheese, how very perceptive she was.

171

The wine relaxed me enough to speak for what seemed like hours, about my travels and ordeals. Jacqueline listened before telling me her story of the French people's struggle with the German invaders. I decided I liked her very much. She was so like her daughter. Perhaps raising Julia on her own had attuned them to the same mystical qualities, along with undeniable strength of character. But at the same time, this was mixed with a light-hearted attitude towards life.

The clock covering the only space left on the wall, read midnight. From memory, we'd shared by then three bottles of red wine before I admitted happily to being very drunk. At that point, I asked Jacqueline if she could play some music that we could dance to. It would be our own personal celebration of freedom.

"Of course, Ma Cherie. Vive la France!"

I remember dancing to the tune of 'Mademoiselle from Armentieres,' until the room spun and I became oblivious to everything.

The next morning, I woke up and realised I was lying on the couch, covered with a feather doona. I attempted to sit up but my head refused to lift off the cushion. I could hear Jacqueline singing in the kitchen and smelt the familiar aroma of a cheese omelette cooking. I asked my stomach, 'are you up to eating'? No, it answered, so I lay my head down again and began admiring the photos of Julia once more. Jacqueline then entered, carrying a tray with a pot of coffee, freshly baked bread, and of course a cheese omelette. I'd have to eat this. I'm sure the dear sweet lady had given up her only two eggs for me and probably her last piece of cheese. I was about to force down my first mouthful, when my stomach convulsed. I quickly handed her the tray and ran to the bathroom.

With my insistence, Jacqueline ate the breakfast. It appeared she'd escaped with no harm from the enormous amount of wine we'd consumed the previous night. This confirmed what I believed: all French people were raised on wine as if it were mother's milk.

After having a shower and an aspirin, I began to feel human again. I asked Jacqueline if I might stay with her for a couple of days.

"Of course you will Ma Cherie! Julia will be so 'appy. You must stay with us for as long as you can. We will celebrate tonight."

The chance to spend some time with Julia would be like old times. Although I felt a little guilty for having such a good time, while Alain and Millie remained in states of sad reflection. At the same time, I felt to celebrate something as profound as reclaiming one's freedom was the very essence of life. Selfish, if you like, but I would enjoy now all the celebrating I could. I

172

convinced myself I deserved it, but then we all did.

I took the opportunity of using Jacqueline's telephone to ring Ruby and tell her of my advancement so far, in particular, getting the word out about Anton. Plus, excitedly I told her all about my friend Julia Nior coming from England to visit her mother in Paris and I would stay with them. I filled her in on all the details.

"In view of this Ruby I'll stay in Paris, until next Tuesday when I'll come home with Henry."

She seemed happy for me, but at the same time, Ruby begged.

"Please do not forget the reason why you have gone to Paris Sally."

I felt her concern and assured her I would stay on the job, with just a few celebrations in between. I then asked if she would break this news to Alain, as it would be impossible for me to speak with him while I was so happy.

Later I phoned my three main contacts and informed them where they could find me if any news came through of Anton. They told me they had no news as yet, so I decided to visit the Police Station again and then the Missing Person's Bureau. This would see me through the rest of the day, including time for a coffee and shopping. I wanted to buy a dress for this evening. Julia was expected at one pm, which would give her time to catch up with her mother before I returned to the apartment. Then we'd celebrate, well maybe not as hard as the night before, but celebrate none the less. It would be like our time together in London, when Julia and I would party all night. I kissed Jacqueline goodbye, after telling her my plan for the day and saying how it was my treat tonight. We would go out to paint the town red!

"Ooh la, la, I will wear my best party dress," she said with animation.

The happiness of feeling totally free in Paris that morning struck me again as being selfish. Quite often on my journey to be the best person I could, I had to admit that sometimes my intrepid adventures (trying to turn wrong into right), came from the selfish ego I pretended not to have, or at least I wouldn't acknowledge. On the other hand, this expression of freedom before I had to return to probably the most heartbreaking duty I'd ever have to perform (bringing Alain back to his true self), meant I just had to let my emotions fly.

All morning, I trudged around Paris, only taking cabs when my feet refused to accept any more agony. I followed my plan to the letter: firstly, I showed everyone I met the photo of Anton. I stuck the information poster on lamp posts, and walls. After taking the long walk to the Police Station again, I was disappointed because it was impossible to be heard over the crowd. The station was literally overrun with the frantic pleading of relatives, missing their sons, daughters and husbands. It was the same at the Bureau of Missing Persons. However, I waited my turn to hear if there was any news of Anton. I had to do my utmost to find him. I needed a clear conscience when I returned to Ruby.

Heartbreakingly, my gold watch had been confiscated when I was first captured by the SS so I had to ask a young Frenchman for the time as he came walking toward me.

"*We Ma Cherie*, I 'ave the time and I 'ave the place, so let us go there right now," he answered cheekily.

I laughed, "Thank you Sir, but I'm happily married to a Frenchman."

"Oh, then it is my 'onour to give you the time of day. It is a quarter to four. Au revoir mademoiselle," He tipped his hat, smiled, kissed my hand and walked backwards blowing me kisses. I just love Frenchmen.

I was only two blocks from Jacqueline's apartment so I walked. My feet ached like hell and the mere thought of dancing was unthinkable.

Extremely tired, I dragged myself up the flight of steps to Jacqueline's first floor apartment. Then my heart raced – I heard Julia's voice. I rang the doorbell and within a minute Julia stood before me; the Goddess she'd always been. Not a hair on her head had changed. Her slim figure was still the same and not one wrinkle creased her flawless skin. We embraced forever it seemed. Tears flowed freely before we were able to speak. So much to catch up on and of course I would have to go through my entire story with her, as I had with Jacqueline. I suggested that we simply party tonight and leave the gory details until tomorrow. They agreed. After I'd bathed my tired feet, and had something to eat, we took time dressing in our finest for our night on the town.

One thing I'd managed to do for myself during the day, I'd bought a simple black dress and a string of cultured pearls. Black suited me, plus I adored pearls. Anything derived from the ocean I loved. The evening shoes I'd bought would probably be far too big, once the swelling in my feet went down, but for tonight they were fine. I'd always thought, no matter how good I looked, I scrubbed up second best to Julia. When she walked into the lounge room, I knew tonight would be no exception. She simply looked stunning in a figure-hugging satin frock. Jacqueline also looked amazing in her red sleeveless crepe dress which clung to her hips. It belled out at the bottom as she twirled around to show the effect.

Our friendship was the kindred spirit type, along with the physical attraction of opposites. I appeared the sporty Nordic blonde and she the exotic dark temptress. Tonight however, it appeared I won the beauty pageant, as both Julia and Jacqueline could not throw enough compliments my way. I must say, when looking once again in the mirror I had to agree, I did look lovely. My womanhood it seemed was returning. I'd evolved from the gun-slinging jillaroo from Australia, to the sexy blonde. However, for some reason I placed the pistol that Digby had given me in my purse. Instinct or premonition I suppose.

After sharing a bottle of champagne to inspire our partying mood, we strode out arm in arm along the pavement into the romance of the Parisian night. How magnificent the world appeared. Music filled the air and lovers kissed openly beneath the stars. The scene sent me a flood of longing for Alain's soft kisses.

To begin our night of decadence, we chose to enjoy a cocktail in a small wine bar opposite the Moulin Rouge. Julia ordered three martinis, which I insisted on paying for. I'd been cashed up with the money Colleen had wired through from England to the main Post Office in Paris. I wisely kept the larger amount within a safety deposit box at the post office. Tonight, I'd kept only what I thought we needed to have a good time. Forever the girl guide Dad would say, as it didn't matter what situation we were in, I'd always think to bring something along which might come in handy. A piece of string, a box of matches a couple of nails, you name it, I always seemed to have something helpful on me at the right time. I hadn't changed. With that long-ago memory of preparedness, a shiver of fear went down my spine. I dismissed it as silly.

Our first cocktail we drank like thirsty lizards and the next we savoured in a more lady like manor. I gazed around the room in a relaxed and happy demeanour. It seemed Paris's freedom was being celebrated by all.

Three Canadian Officers sat opposite and it wasn't long before their admiring glances became admiring words. Julia was all about the look, she spoke very few words. Her eyes did the talking. I was always amused at her body language. She beckoned men to drool over what they thought they could have, when I knew the opposite. She was a haughty Fem Fatal. I'd seen it many times before in London. Actually, I'd never known her to have a lover for very long or even a male friend that stayed the course. Oh well, that was just Julia. Some women, especially famous models and actresses don't like to be tied down. However, there was a cold aloofness about her that even I occasionally found off-putting. Eventually, things became a little too hot to handle so I suggested, rather loudly.

"We have to leave ladies, or else we'll miss the dinner show at the Moulin Rouge and of course our rendezvous later with Major General Patton."

This statement was delivered in time for our Soldiers to be drunk enough to salute at the mere mention of Patton's name. With that, we ran out of

175

the bar and into the night, laughing like school girls.

The Moulin Rouge was the most popular night spot in Paris. I'm sure without Julia's charm and fame we wouldn't have been given the best seats in the house, let alone seats at all. Apparently, this caused an almighty ruckus with the true purchaser of the seats. The manager simply explained to the gentleman.

"We have the famous and beautiful Julia Nior here this evening and I'm afraid the table was doubled booked. I am sorry Monsieur. But Miss Nior was the first to arrive."

To calm the irate patron down, the manager refunded his money and gave him free tickets to the next show. I felt a little guilty, but Julia was used to things like that happening all the time. She expected to have her own way with everything.

I shrugged off the guilt and sat back to enjoy the show. The curtain drew back to reveal a line of breathtakingly beautiful women, flaunting their elegance and perfect half-naked bodies under the seductive lighting. I noticed how Julia, swooned at the vision. I remember her telling me once how she'd love to be a Moulin Rouge girl. I wondered during the recital why she hadn't become the star of the show. I thought she ticked all the boxes.

Halfway through the evening performance, the lights dimmed and a waif like silhouette stood silent at centre stage. Then her heart-wrenching voice stilled the crowd. Edith Piaf sang with more feeling in her voice than any singer I'd ever heard. If I were to ever write a biography of anyone, I would love it to be hers, but then listening to Edith, I realised she'd told her own story and struggles through her songs. It was already there for all to hear. I just adored her.

Our delicious dinner, we seemed to consume unconsciously. It became a distant third to the all-consuming vision. 'Truly spectacular,' is the only phrase I could summon.

Later, after the show, the manager joined us for a drink, telling us we were very lucky this night to see the first return performance of Edith Piaf.

"Before the liberation of Paris, the Moulin Rouge was only a shadow of itself during the occupation. The performers would only half-heartedly go through their routines. They detested being forced to perform and act happy. And so tonight, our entertainers gave a superb performance. It was their celebration of freedom."

We left the funny little red building with the windmill on top and began to walk while singing the famous Edith Piaf song, 'Un coin Tout Bleu'. Julia suddenly stopped and spun around gracefully, I thought especially so, for someone who'd had quite a skin full of alcohol. She then declared for all to hear.

"I am going to be a star at the Moulin Rouge: yes, a star!"

Jacqueline, who definitely looked more like her sister this evening, laughed before whispering.

"She 'as always wanted to be a star at the Moulin Rouge, but they said she was too tall and should become a model, so she did. A very famous one."

I understood this concern, for Julia stood well over six feet tall. However, I disagreed. I thought she would make a perfect Venus on stage.

Chapter 25

Hugo's Demise

Julia became the leader for our next foray. Her grace and elegance flowed before us as she danced around lamp posts and kissed any man who lingered a moment to admire her. She left them dumfounded. Flitting off like a butterfly into the night, we ran to keep up. Gracefully she came to rest in a smoke-filled café-cum- restaurant, which I didn't notice the name of. I was too intent on catching up with our lovely butterfly.

The people inside seemed solemn, unlike the crowd outside. They looked serious, perhaps because they were clouded in smoke and listening to sombre music. Suddenly I shuddered, I didn't like the place. I felt the need to get out quickly, so I took Julia by the arm.

"Could we leave and find another place to have a night cap?"

"No, no Ma Cherie, I know the owner, 'e will give us free champagne."

She continued to throw her inebriated charm around, slowly working her way to the bar where she asked to see the owner.

"Sebastian, where is Sebastian, I want to see my old friend Sebby. I am 'ere Sebby. Your beautiful friend Julia is 'ere!"

While calling his name, Julia spun around so fast she faltered and fell against a man sitting opposite to an overly made up, very unattractive woman. He had this back to us but the woman smirked at Julia. While I steadied her so she didn't completely fall over this man, the woman brought her gloved hand up to drag on a cigarette. She looked directly at me.

"Get your drunken friend away from my man."

I took no notice of her threatening tone; instead I strained for a better glimpse of the gold watch on her wrist. Not sure whether to grab her arm and take a closer look at what I thought was *my gold watch*, or help Julia regain her feet, I chose to help Julia first. She then waddled off to find her friend Sebby. I courteously apologised to the woman for my friend's behaviour and asked.

"May I look at your lovely watch?"

She gave a wry smile and placed her arm out. I asked her where she'd bought such a lovely piece. By this time, I knew exactly who the man sitting with her had to be. I kept admiring the watch, while surreptitiously taking the pistol from my purse.

I can't explain how much pleasure it gave me to push the barrel of my gun into Doctor Hugo Stern's back and then quietly ask him to leave the cafe with me. But before he moved, I told Hugo in clear terms.

"Ask your woman friend to remove the watch and give it to me. Tell her to not to move. Inform her you will return in a moment."

He duly told the woman and with a concerned expression on her face, she did what he said. He went to speak again, but I pushed the pistol harder into his back. Hugo rose slowly and turned to walk out the door. I was right behind him, not sure whether this woman was a prostitute or a lover who Hugo wanted to impress with my watch. I didn't know if she cared enough for him to cause trouble, or if being a prostitute she'd simply find another man who'd pay her in cash for her sexual talents. Hopefully she'd shrug the incident off.

Meanwhile, Julia and Jacqueline had found Sebastian, along with a few other friends, and they sat in a corner laughing. They hadn't suspected a thing, I was sure. I kept Hugo walking in front of me until we came to a dark alley. I looked occasionally to see if the woman had followed but she hadn't. The streets remained noisy with revellers who took no notice of Hugo and me.

I pushed him deep into the alley by giving him a hell of a shove which caused him to trip and fall to the ground.

"Now I've got you, you fuckin' little weasel. You must have thought I was dead. Or do you know everything that's going on around this whole fucking world."

I watched him cringe and curl into the foetal position, then I shot him in the leg. He screamed with agony. I wasn't worried about the sound, I knew we were too far up the alley to be heard, plus the clamour of people celebrating and cars continuously blowing their horns would drown out any screams. Whilst I had him where I wanted him, I remembered what I'd just said. He must know everything. Maybe he knew something about Herman's disappearance. My guess was, he did. One bullet remained in the gun and I wasn't going to waste it. I cocked the trigger and pushed the gun into his bald scalp.

"Tell me where Herman is. You've got ten seconds. One, two, three…"

"Please, please don't shoot me. I only think I know where he is, I'm not sure anymore. Everything has changed."

"Just tell me where you think he is!"

Through his pain he whimpered.

"There is a detention camp, a work camp in Belgium, Breendonk they call it. They took him there, but I don't know if he is still alive. Please don't kill me, please don't."

"Why in the hell would they take him there, why didn't they just shoot him dead?"

"They wanted him to suffer, they needed more workers, I don't know!"

"Do you want me to put you out of your suffering now Hugo?"

"No please don't kill me. I can see if he's still alive and then maybe I can get him out."

I had to think about his offer. Could I trust Hugo, or would he double deal me? My first instincts told me no, stick with your own contacts. But then, if there was an ounce of hope that Hugo would stay true to his word, shouldn't I take it? I glared at this little worm and asked the Lord to give me a sign – there was none. I put the gun away.

"No thank you Hugo. I'll find my own way to Breendonk. You see I'm an Australian journalist, I'm a war correspondent and I'm so pleased you're in agony. Oh, and by the way, I know of a very good hospital. It's a shame though; it's a long way away, Zurich in fact."

I left him crying, it was far better than killing him. I may need the bullet later and I must admit that his son came to mind, the boy would be heartbroken. Although he'd obviously not held the same concern for my son when he'd set up my capture.

I needed to think quickly, about whether I should try to explain to the Military Police, the whole complicated story of how Hugo had suspected me of being a spy, which in essence I had been, and the story about what had unfolded since then. This I knew would take forever. Also, it would be Hugo's word against mine. I simply didn't have the time or the patience to deal with it. Before moving away, I reached into my purse and held the gold watch. I gave thanks to my grandmother.

"God Bless You Saint Bernadette."

I closed my purse and looked down at Hugo still grovelling.

"Don't move for a while Hugo and don't tell anyone who did this to you, or I'll kill you next time." I then walked away without looking back.

Moving quickly once I'd turned the corner of the lane, I made my way back to the café where I'd left Julia and her mother. When I walked inside, they were exactly where I'd left them. I looked around for Hugo's woman but she'd gone.

My trying to talk sense to the incoherent Julia was impossible, Jacqueline was no different.

"Oh no, do not leave so soon Ma Cherie. 'Ave some champagne!" Jacqueline slurred.

I kept tugging at Julia's arm to come away but when she flatly refused, I went alone much to Jacqueline's disapproval. I did manage to calm her down by saying I'd stay at a hotel for the night. Jacqueline only stopped pleading with me, when a good-looking man asked her if she would like to dance.

After walking two blocks, I found a hotel with a vacancy. I was extremely lucky, as they'd just received the cancellation. All hotels in Paris it seemed were booked out to Allied Officers. It was a miracle I slept that night, considering the events which had led me there. I woke at ten am, showered, dressed and had coffee before I walked to Julia's. I'd tell them I was sorry but I had to leave. Although confidant there would be no further trouble with Hugo, I had unfinished business to complete and I didn't need the worry of them becoming involved. I would have to make phone calls at Jacqueline's to set the wheels in motion and try to get Herman out of Breendonk. The chances of him still being alive were almost nil but I chose to live in hope. With the money Colleen had sent me, I'd buy a car and travel back to Rubies farm. I had it all worked out by the time I stood at Jacqueline's front door.

Chapter 26

Time to Let Go

I rang the doorbell three times before a weary, hung over Julia came and opened it.

"Sally, my friend, where did you go last night?" she giggled, her voice croaky. "Did you find yourself a man?"

I really wasn't in the mood for her insulting or silly talk this morning; I had too much on my mind and too much to do.

"I'm sorry Julia, I wasn't feeling well and I didn't want to spoil your fun."

"Ah, no, no, no. I know you Sally; you love to make love. You found a man!"

"Julia believe me I love my husband. I've had his son for Christ's sake. I wasn't well. Now please can I come in? I need to go back to Alain, but before I do, I have to make some important phone calls, may I use the telephone. I'll pay for my calls."

My anger took the smile from her face. She kissed me on both cheeks and held me tight.

"Please come in Sally, phone whoever you like, I am sorry. I will make us some coffee and Mama does not need your money." She then put her forefinger up to her mouth. "Shoosh, we must not wake her; she 'as a gentleman friend."

I raised my eyebrows. I didn't know why I did that. I shouldn't have been surprised, after all, she was still relatively young. I remember Bridgette telling me Jacqueline was only sixteen when she had Julia and so they were more like sisters.

While Julia made the coffee, I was able to phone a well informed and trustworthy friend. He would be able to tell me if there was any hope of saving Herman from Breendonk. He answered my question emphatically.

"No, it is not possible Sally. They have a wide mote filled with water; it surrounds the whole perimeter of the prison. I'm afraid you will just 'ave to pray like you always do. I am sorry."

I sat on the couch with my head buried in my hands. I hated to feel this helpless. I became angry that Herman had to suffer after he'd saved Millie and me. I was angry that Rubies young son could simply disappear from the face of the earth, but then so many had. The agony of not knowing where Anton was would probably put Ruby in her grave. The thought then crossed my mind, maybe I should go and find Doctor Hugo, he would most likely be in hospital somewhere near where I shot him. It appeared then he was my only chance to find Herman. But I hated the thought, dreaded the confrontation with that evil bastard, I'd had enough of not being able to trust people. My concerns erupted into a tsunami of hopelessness.

Julia brought in the coffee in a large mug; she sat it on the table next to me and asked:

"What is the matter Sally, you look like it's the end of the earth, and we should be 'appy!"

She wrapped her arms around me and rocked me back and forth. My tears flowed.

"There, there Sally, please tell me what is the matter. You know I love you and I will 'elp you. Please tell me."

I sobbed even harder. It took some time, before I could tell my story from the very beginning to the end. Julia of course knew about me going to France and then Switzerland to try and find Millie. However, she knew nothing of the in-betweens.

Well over an hour into my confessions, I was aware that Jacqueline had walked past with her lover, escorting him out. They chose not to validate the fact that I was there. It must have seemed to them I was in too much distress to be spoken to in a polite manner and for some reason, this thought brought me out of my misery. I actually laughed hysterically when Jacqueline came to sit beside me. Although, I did manage to say:

"It's funny how life and love keeps going on and on, no matter what happens."

I sniffed back my tears and wiped the rest on my sleeve. It was difficult because they were bracelet length. Julia jumped up to bring me a handkerchief. I laughed again while looking tearfully into her beautiful brown eyes.

"You could have given me the hanky half an hour ago you know!"

I managed then to finish my story and tell them exactly what had happened to me the night before. When I'd finished, I showed them my gold wrist watch, which Julia and Jacqueline knew had been confiscated. They didn't flinch when I told them how I'd shot Hugo in the leg.

"Why didn't you finish 'im?" Julia asked.

"Sally, I now know a lot about your life story, because Julia's told me. Now that I 'ave met you and 'eard what you 'ave been through, I can see why she admires you so much." Jacqueline then hugged me tight.

"I am now going to tell you something that I am very proud of. Something that may seem very small compared to your experiences, but I think it is what life is all about. When I was very young, only fifteen years old, I was raped by a friend of my fathers. I was too frightened to tell my parents because 'e was a very good friend to them, they loved him. When I finally 'ad to tell them that I was pregnant, I 'ad to also work up the courage to tell them who it was. They refused to believe me, and they blamed every boy in the village. I was a virgin before I was raped. They would not believe that either. But to make this story a little shorter for you, my parents forced me to leave 'ome. I came to Paris, where I found work in a factory. I made some friends and they 'elped me when I needed it, but they all said I should give Julia up for adoption. The only one who did not was Bridgette, your Alain's aunty. She said she could never give up her own baby. I agreed with her. I said no to everyone, I told them this is my baby and I will take care of 'er and I will believe in 'er. I will never put anything or anybody above the care and love of my own child. Do you understand what I'm saying Sally? This is your time now, to take care of your son. You 'ave done all you can in this war, you don't owe anything to anyone else only to your son. Yes, only 'im. I promise it will be your greatest pleasure to raise 'im and believe in 'im. Don't let anyone else take your son from you. I know you don't think you 'ave suffered when your parents left you to go to war. But for any child who 'as any sort of abandonment from their parents, it shows, sometimes not until later in life. I still don't trust anyone only my beautiful daughter." Jacqueline stroked Julia's face, smiling into her eyes. Then she turned to me.

"You don't 'ave to prove a thing to anyone, only to your children and to God. You must always show them you love them and will always be there for them. It is all that matters in life."

Julia then hugged me. "I am so sorry Sally I' 'aven't met your 'usband or your son. I was forgetting about them, I wanted to pretend it was the good old days in London. Please forgive me, my dear friend."
"Of course I do," and hugged her back: how could I not.

For the rest of the morning, and after Jacqueline's confessions, I felt relieved, somehow clear in mind and heart. I knew what I needed to do.

Jacqueline phoned a friend, who'd give me a lift to the farm that afternoon. Alain and I would then leave for Switzerland, sooner than planned. There we would wait for the war to end and hopefully, if Alain agreed, we would go home to live in Australia for the rest of our lives.

My idea to try and find Herman, via Dr Hugo Stern, was cried down by Julia and her mother.

"No, no, you must not become involved with that Doctor again, 'e will only drag you back to the place you 'ave escaped from. You cannot trust 'im!" This was voiced by both women, so I placed all thoughts of the wretched Hugo out of my mind. My heart told me they were right. I then centred once more on my two loves, Alain and PP.

We decided to have one last get together before I travelled back to Rubies farm. We'd have lunch at the delightful 'café Les Duex Magot' by the river Sein. I changed my clothes while Jacqueline and Julia showered and promised to be ready in half an hour. This gave me time to consider how right they were. I'd certainly done enough for the war effort and now it was time to be a good mother and the best wife I could to my wounded husband.

On our way to the river, we came upon a magazine stand, the newspaper headlines read. 'Man found murdered in alleyway'. I gave the money to the stand owner and read the rest of the story as we walked. Julia and Jacqueline were anxious to know what the story held.

"I'll tell you in a minute. You can read it for yourself later."

It seemed to take forever, before we reached the river bank where the water taxis moored. I folded the paper and smiled.

"I'll tell you later when we're out of ear shot."

We asked to be seated at a secluded table that had full view out over the Sein. I then read the headline.

"An unknown man was shot and then stabbed to death last night, if anyone is able to identify this man, please come to Police Head Quarters."

It showed a photo of Dr Hugo Stern, although it didn't look like him as his face was so swollen and bruised. It appeared Hugo had met with further foal play. The story told how Hugo had tried to fight off his attackers before being robbed of his wallet. They'd then stabbed him to death.

I was more than a little concerned that somebody may have seen me with Hugo, apart from the prostitute that was. Julia suggested we leave the restaurant and that I should leave Paris straight away. I laughed at her concern. But deep down I thought, maybe I was on a roller coaster ride again. I took a deep breath and decided I would enjoy my last meal in Paris, accompanied by a bottle of French champagne of course. And so under my insistence, we stayed to enjoy our lunch together and spoke only of happy times when Julia and I lived in London. Jacqueline was enthralled with our stories and admitted later she was a little regretful she hadn't taken up Julia's offer for her to go and live in London.

"But you know Sally, I felt it was time for me to cut the umbilical cord. Julia needed to find 'erself, without me forever watching and caring for her like a clucky old 'en." Jacqueline paused, then reached for my hand. "I will tell you what takes the greatest love Sally; you 'ave to know when to let the one's you love go." Mother and daughter hugged and kissed, which brought me to tears.

I lowered my head to hide them but smiled at my gold watch. I then felt most grateful I'd found it. However, it showed me it was time to leave. I walked over to the front counter and paid the bill, then just as I was about to turn and join my friends, directly in front of me stood Dr Hugo's prostitute. I gasped. She saw my reaction and quickly walked up to me.

"Oh it is so good to see you again Madam." She then kissed me on both cheeks before whispering in my ear. "It is all right. We finished the job for you. Go in peace my friend."

She kissed me again and I walked away, trying very hard to act as if I'd just met a long-lost friend. I turned and waved.

"I'm sorry I haven't time to chat, maybe tomorrow," I called over my shoulder.

"No", she answered, "I am leaving Paris for Switzerland, maybe next time, friend."

I never found out who she was, and I must say she didn't look at all ugly that day; I'd say she looked beautiful. She was on our side and that's all that mattered.

My lift back to the farm was graciously given by one of Jacqueline's male admirers. She had many, including diplomats, doctors and high-class clientele, some of whom I was to hear about on our journey home. My driver Lewis was happy to inform me, what many in Paris already knew. Jacqueline was a much admired and a highly respected call girl. I must say it didn't surprise or bother me in the least, especially after being told her story.

"Does Julia know of this?" I asked.

"Maybe she suspects it, but maybe she doesn't want to know."

I thought of what Jacqueline had said about all that matters in the world is your child. I sat back, thinking about PP, and in that moment, I decided to be his loving mother before and above anything else.

On our arrival at the farm, I was greeted with laughter and kisses from

Ruby and then Alain and Millie, who'd literally run outside when seeing the car drive up. I felt like the prodigal daughter, even though I'd only been away for four days. After many hugs and more kisses, I thanked Lewis and offered him a cup of tea or a glass of wine.

"No thank you Sally. It 'as been my pleasure, but I must be on my way. I have business to attend to in Paris tonight."

One of the hardest things I had to do was to tell Ruby there'd been no news of Anton from my contacts, or anyone else for that matter. Her eyes saddened before offering a half smile. She then thanked me again for what I'd tried to do.

Millie sat across from me at the kitchen table sipping her tea. I could feel her anticipation; I knew she was waiting for the sad news to pass before she dared ask me about Paris. She would be eager to know about the fashion, the night life, the buzz etc. I truly felt for her at that moment. I didn't think it was the time to add too much excitement to the current scene. I smiled.

"I brought you a present Millie. I'll show it to you later, it's the latest fashion."

She knew what I meant. I could tell by her quiet acceptance of the situation that she was beginning to think of others before herself. I was becoming very proud of our Miss Millie.

Alain had not left my side; he seemed to need my warmth and my touch more than anything. I can't explain how amazing this made me feel. I needed him to want me; make love to me impulsively as he'd always done. If only I could have been the bearer of good news for Ruby, it would have been the perfect scenario.

We stayed another week before it was time to leave. No news had come of Anton in that time and Rubies hopes were fading. I think the only thing holding her together was the fact we were still there. We'd become her new family. I for one would struggle to make the break.

Millie had changed her mind about going back to England. Instead, she would go back to Switzerland with us. She was due to give birth in three weeks' time and it was still not safe in London, plus Millie needed to discuss with Klaus's family about where she should raise their only grandchild. There hadn't been the time to discuss the matter before she and Herman made their dash to Paris. I'm sure she also needed to be validated by the Stromberg family, before making up her mind about which country she would live in.

On our final evening spent with Ruby, twilight radiated into a magical sunset. This image burned into my psyche. We were all survivors of a cruel war;

one I prayed would never be repeated. It was becoming evident that the Reich would crumble now and surrender. America's big guns were exploding far away beyond the beautiful sunset which blessed us that evening. We'd also heard Russia was on the forward march into German captured territory. Winning the war now seemed certain. We took the opportunity, while sitting under the stars watching the red sky drift into darkness, to share our last bottle of champagne – a toast to the future.

Millie refused to drink.

"Pregnant women should not drink alcohol Sally!" I'm sure it was her awkward defence about being an alcoholic. I felt sorry for her. It was exceptionally fine champagne.

Chapter 27

Five Years Later: 1949

I'd placed my journal in my suitcase before we'd left Ruby's farm. I chose not to write when returning to Switzerland. I needed every moment to enjoy the days we spent as a family, simply waiting for the war to end. Those days melded peacefully into each other. They held no danger, no exciting missions and yet, they were the most important and significant days of my life. It was the time I needed to bond once again with my husband and son.

On our return to Switzerland most things had remained the same, except we chose not to stay with Jane and Marcel in Zurich. We needed to spend time alone, so we rented a chalet not far from Geneva and Alain spent his days labouring for a man who owned a wood supply business. The exercise soon sculptured his body back into the magnificent physic he'd once had.

Jane and Marcel visited us often in our Geneva chalet and one fine day, we shared a wonderful celebration in Church; where Jane and Marcel became PP's official God parents. They have since, adopted two orphaned Jewish children, a little girl aged two and her brother aged four.

I never did listen to Alain's final confession, about when he was in Drancy. I really didn't want to know. So instead, I simply kept telling him the quote my mother had passed onto me.

"All the water in the ocean cannot sink a ship-unless it gets inside. Has this sunk in yet my love?" I didn't like to make light of the situation by using that pun, but we both laughed about it, nonetheless.

After the war ended, Alain was excited about going to Australia. I knew this is where I truly belonged and this is where he now admits, he does too.

Alain's Aunty Bridgette and Pierre left Switzerland and returned to their farm, which luckily had escaped erasure by the enemy. Most Resistance fighters' houses were burnt to the ground. Alain's Uncle Pierre had survived the battle for Paris, so he and Bridgette were able to strengthen their relationship in the peace that finally came.

Colleen and Michael fell in love while I was in France. They were married the day after the war ended. I couldn't be happier for them. They are due here next week for their first visit to Australia as a couple, which reminds me. Colleen managed to keep the silver locket safe; the one given to me by the fallen Aussie soldier whom I'd promised I would give to his wife, Patricia. The day after I arrived home from Switzerland, I kept my promise. The moment we met, and I looked into Patricia's eyes, memories reflected there of heart break bitter – sweet. They were branded forever in our souls, we the survivors. It struck me again just how lucky I'd been, but Lest we forget.

Millie remained living in Switzerland. Her reason, apart from rising to operatic stardom once again, was that the Stromberg family deserved to have their only granddaughter live with them, especially after losing their beloved son. Millie then received a great reward for her loyalty. Three months after the war, Herman came knocking on her door. He'd escaped with the help of the resistance and was 'looking healthier than ever,' Millie said. This good news about Herman had also helped to console Ruby, who'd been informed that her son Anton had died a hero.

Millie has paid us many visits to our home, here in Australia. She delights in her daughter, Katie. And now, on the occasion of celebrating PP's sixth birthday, Herman and Ruby will also accompany Millie down under. With what Millie's written about Herman, I'm assuming there may be a romance blossoming.

At this very moment, I look out of my office window where I see Poppy Patrick, riding his horse alongside PP, who is sitting up proudly on his new white pony named Little Charlie. Dad recently bought the pony for PP's birthday and ever since then, PP and his horse have been inseparable. I know a part of Dad's heart still remains scarred over the loss of his beloved Light horse Charlie who died in the battle of Beersheba.

Grandad Jonathon remains Chief Magistrate in Adelaide, although mentally apt and physically fit, our dear Marjorie never leaves his side. Yes, she is still our angel of mercy. Marjorie kept her promise to Mrs. Murphy and sent her an airline ticket. She came and stayed with Marjorie and Jonathon. It gave me great joy to see the two get on the same as Marjorie did with our darling old departed Colleen. Miss. Murphy has vowed to make the pilgrimage to Australia at least every second year. We were amused when Marjorie took her to Ballarat to do a bit of gold panning and to everyone's surprise, she sprang the mother lode. Well not quite, but her find was valued at just over one thousand pounds. She refused to sell.

"I'm takin' it back to Ireland for a show and tell," she declared with that unmistakable twinkle in her eye.

Mother Matilda turned eighty-six last month, on the twenty ninth of April and now spends most of her time at 'Wildflowers' with Jonathon and Marjorie. The Catholic Bishop of Adelaide gave a wonderful celebration Mass on her birthday, which coincided with her stepping down from her duties. Hundreds of parishioners, plus the families she'd helped throughout the depression years, came to pay homage to this amazing woman who is still able to tell us a thing or two about world History. Matilda will share yet another birthday celebration with PP next week. We're preparing for a huge gathering of family and friends, including old Doctor Liu, Mother Betty and Lizzy along with her ten children! I'm sure Matilda will give PP a run for his money in being the life of the party.

Uncle Angus and Aunty Clare have just returned home from England, where Clare had to tidy up her father, Lord Harris's, deceased estate. Clare and Angus went for a time to the Middle East during World War Two, where they worked together on the hospital ships. They now travel extensively and own many fine thoroughbred race horses. Their son James is busy following in his Grandfather Jonathon's footsteps, he's now a lawyer.

Patrick Junior, my younger brother, is becoming a respected would-be horse trainer. Now at the age of twenty, when he's not at University in Adelaide studying Law, he's working in the racing stables at Morphetville. I don't think he knows yet which career he wants to pursue. However, by night he's a formidable Don Juan, so the young women of Adelaide tell me. I wonder who he gets that from?

My beautiful mother, well what can I say. I am her daughter, although she would have me believe, we are the product of Jum Watt, her father, my grandfather. I quite often think his spirit still lives within the walls of Bulkawa. I know PP believes he does, as I hear him sometimes talking and giggling with an invisible person.

Mum finally had her way and operated on my facial scar. She did a wonderful job and now it's barely noticeable.

As I sit writing the closing chapter to my journal, my two-year-old daughter Suzan Marjorie Laurent, has been playing at my feet with Mums old brown velvet horse, named Sailor. Suzy is the image of Alain who at the moment is discussing a business deal with a friend of Dad's, about trawling for Lobster around Victor Harbour. This would mean he'd be away for many months throughout the year. I dread the thought, but I know all too well, we must follow our heart to be truly happy.

I best sign off, as Alain is still trying to learn how to throw a boomerang and he's just broken the lounge room window with the damn thing.

www.ingramcontent.com/pod-product-compliance
Lightning Source LLC
Chambersburg PA
CBHW071515100726
47908CB00004B/1174